DEATH

13

GRAVE MAGIC BOUNTY

THE FORTY PROOF SERIES
BOOK ONE

SHANNON MAYER

Copyright
Grave Magic Bounty
Copyright © **Shannon Mayer 2020**
All rights reserved
Published by Hijinks Ink Publishing
www.shannonmayer.com

GRAVE MAGIC BOUNTY

THE FORTY PROOF SERIES
BOOK ONE

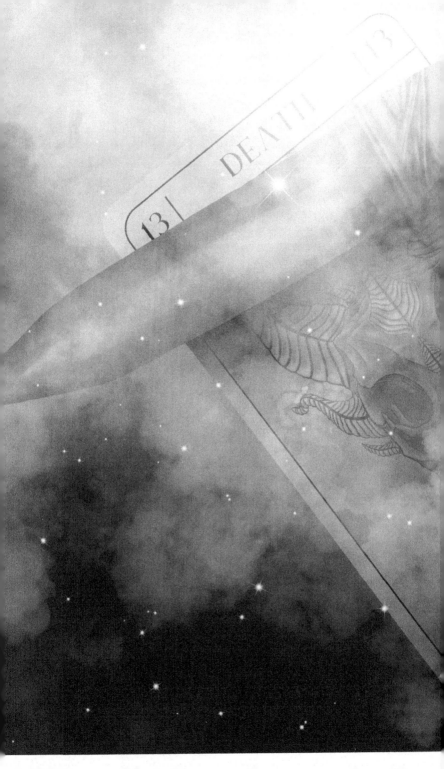

ACKNOWLEDGMENTS

Thanks as always go to my readers, my ARC team, editors and cover artist. This is truly a team effort to pull a book out and make it happen on a regular basis.

I also want to thank my author friends who have been with me on this journey. Denise Grove Swank, KF Breene, Christine Gael, Jana DeLeon, Robyn Peterman, Darynda Jones, Deanna Chase, Mandy M Roth, Eve Langlais, Michelle M Pillow, Elizabeth Hunter and Kristen Painter. Some of you I knew before this mind bending genre experiment, some I met along the way. All of you rock, I am proud to stand shoulder to shoulder with you and show the world that women over forty still have a lot to offer, in every sense of the words. Much love to you all!

1

The saying goes that doing the same thing over and over and expecting different results was the definition of insanity. I wasn't sure that was entirely true. I suspected that doing something completely out of the norm, something no sane person would ever consider doing, fell a bit closer to the mark.

I stood, résumé in hand, in front of a massive wrought iron gate that led into a decommissioned graveyard that was apparently so old, no one cared there were bodies in it. Of course, maybe that wasn't so unusual given there were bodies buried under every part of Savannah. Having grown up here, though, I had been surprised to see a graveyard I'd not known about.

A quick glance at the paper in my hand, my name in bold at the top—Breena O'Rylee—my grandmother's maiden name, thank you very much. The last thing I wanted right then was to be connected to Himself—also known as my a-hole of an ex-husband, may he rot in pieces after suffering through a case of testicular shrinkage that would take his voice into soprano octaves. See how he liked that when arguing a case in court.

"Hello?" I tapped the tip of my shoe on the gates, rattling them soundly. "Is this 696 Old Hollows Road?" I grimaced as my voice drifted over the early night air. Really, it was kind of a dumb question seeing as the address was hung clearly on the left gate. I was at the right place, but where were the interviewers?

Gawd almighty, this was...insane. *Insane.* I checked my watch. Eammon, the friend of a friend who'd invited me for the group interview, had said to be here at 6:00 p.m.

It was 6:15, and I'd shown up five minutes early. No other interviewees that I'd seen. So, either I'd gotten my time wrong, or I was the only one applying for the job. If I was the only one, maybe that would guarantee me the job. Not a bad thing if it paid as well as Eammon had hinted.

I sighed to myself. Here I was, being *crazy, impetuous,* and *unsafe,* or so Himself would say, but I'd still shown up early. At least I hadn't lost all grasp of my adult responsibilities.

Himself would probably disagree. He tended to disagree with anything I did. My mouth tipped downward into a tired grimace thinking of Himself.

Slick-as-snot divorce lawyer that he was, I should have seen it coming a mile and a half off. Well, that's not entirely true, I'd seen it coming. What I hadn't seen was how he'd hung me out to dry. But there you go, that's what I got for being trusting. A high-speed chase and some assorted hijinks later, here I was back in Savannah, a place I'd spent my childhood loving, a place my grandmother had lived her whole life. A place where bogeymen were real, ghosts could talk to you if you listened closely, and black magic could catch you if you weren't careful. Or so she'd always said.

I leaned my head against the wrought iron, the coolness of it offsetting the heat of the air, only a little. "Gran, I wish you were here."

She died six months ago, and the guilt of not being there for her threatened daily to undo me. I'd left at eighteen, told her that I didn't believe in a shadow world that didn't exist, and ran as far away as I could. Because that's what Himself had said, that it was crazy.

She'd told me I was welcome home whenever I needed a safe place to land. She'd loved me uncon- ditionally, and it had taken me years to grow up and realize that.

Because, fool that I was, I'd let Himself convince me that my life had been a lie, his love would save me, and the world was a place governed by unshake- able truths. The first of which was that magic was a lie, and if I believed in it, then I was nothing more than a child. Someone who needed protecting from herself.

Desperate to be normal, I'd...I shook my head at the memories. "I knew better," I whispered to myself.

I damn well knew better.

I'd followed Himself to Seattle and tried to forget it all, tried to forget everything Gran ever taught me. To pretend it wasn't real. But that's not how the shadow world worked.

There were shadows everywhere the light touched, and the creatures that hid in them—while not so numerous in Seattle—recognized that I could see them.

My jaw tightened over what he'd done when I'd woken screaming that there was a bogeyman standing over our bed. A bogeyman who laughed at me, chased me onto the street, and through early morning traffic.

Naked.

Screaming.

Someone had taken pictures and I'd made the paper.

Himself had not taken it lightly, his reputation being attached to me.

To be fair, I was startled, and the bogeyman was one of the worst monsters out there, creating fear in a way that not many others could. I'd not reacted the way I'd been taught, and for it, Himself had put me in a mental institute.

Gran had come to me, of course, even though Himself hadn't visited me once. I should have seen the light then, but I still believed he loved me.

I closed my eyes, the moment with Gran as poignant now as it had been then. The smell of her perfume whispered across my senses and I'd woken to see her leaning over me. Soft green eyes, a puff of white hair like cotton balls, pale skin with the hint of the freckles that had once been there, long before I arrived on her doorstep.

Her gnarled fingers brushed across my still-young cheeks. "Honey girl...what have they done to you? You are no crazier than I am. Seeing the shadows is more normal than not."

My arms and legs were strapped down as if I were a danger to myself. Bindings bit into my flesh, indenting it. I suppose seeing as I'd run into traffic, the doctors might think I was trying to kill myself, even if that hadn't been the case. "Take it away, Gran. I can't live a life and deal with the shadow world. I know you can take it away." My voice was sluggish from the sedation, but I remembered her face. "I don't want it anymore."

The tears that slid down her wrinkled cheeks cut into me, but I didn't draw back from what I wanted. From what I thought was best for me and Himself. Her hands cupped my face and she swept her thumbs over my eyes first, closing them. "Sight bind thee from the shadows," then her hands covered my ears, "ears whisper nothing," then slid to my hands, "touch be gone, let the shadows fall no more to thee."

The spell was simple, and then I was released from the institute.

Gran stayed only a few days; Himself didn't like her.

With that simple spell from Gran on her first visit to me in my new town, I'd finally stopped seeing the strange, dark things of my childhood. I'd almost stopped believing in them too.

"I was wrong, Gran. I was so wrong," I whispered now.

Erasing all of that hadn't been worth it. If I'd learned anything at the ripe old age of forty-one, it was that no dream could last forever, and no man can save you from yourself.

Despair is a funny thing, and it has the tendency to bring out the believer in anyone. The logical part of my head said I was being crazy, but that logical side sounded a lot like Himself. Anger snapped through me and I muttered under my breath.

If I'd been texting, the typo would have looked something like "Duck off."

Coming home to Savannah, I was ready to face the past. To see what I had to see.

And maybe, just maybe I could figure out who I was. Yeah, I know. You'd think I should've known that by my age.

Wrapping my fingers around the wrought iron, I whispered a prayer my gran taught me, oh so long ago. A prayer for help. Though maybe not the kind of prayer the normal populace would whisper at the edge of a graveyard.

"Sky above me, earth below me, fire within me, let my spirit see thee and the shadows that walk at my side." The metal under my hand trembled suddenly, and I lifted my head off the gate.

"That's lovely."

I spun around, my back against the gate, to see one of the tallest men I'd ever come across in my life. Well over seven feet tall, he was slim as a stick and moved carefully as if he knew he was a big guy who could scare people if he moved too fast. He wore big thick glasses that made his eyes seem larger than they probably were. Owl-like was my first thought.

He wore tan pants and a white button-down shirt with a dark green bow tie, of all things, which all only added to the look of a nutty professor. He touched the middle of his glasses, adjusting them on his face with fingers that looked way too long even for a big guy like him.

"I'm sorry, are you here for the interviews?" I arched a brow or made my best attempt at it. I couldn't raise them independently no matter how hard I tried.

He shook his head. "No, no, I'm here to hire Hollows Group. But they aren't answering my emails." He made a typing motion with both hands as if I wouldn't otherwise understand what an email was. "I thought I'd come and speak to them in person. They can be a bit difficult to track down."

"Sounds like a bad business practice to me," I said.

He clasped both hands in front of him and rocked on his heels. "I'm not high on their priority list."

Staring at him, I knew he wasn't quite human. There was a sense of *other* about him. I didn't have a better word for it, but it felt undeniable, and the realization that he was part of the shadow world did something funny to my heart.

Had the prayer worked that quickly? Was it so simple that just wanting to see would open my eyes? I wasn't sure. I'd been too long away from Savannah. I couldn't deny what I felt rolling off this tall fellow.

All those years away from here, and a part of me had started to believe Himself was right, that my childish mind had been influenced by my grandmother and her friends and their training.

I cleared my throat and pulled my purse around in front of me. "Why don't you write down your information, and I'll give it to them. I'm interviewing with them tonight."

His eyebrows climbed all the way up to his too-long bangs. "You? Aren't you…" He trailed off.

I paused in pulling out a scratch piece of paper. "You want them to get the message, or you want me to throw it in the first trash can I find, leggy?"

He took the paper, his skin flushing pink even in the dusky light, wrote on the scrap, folded it three times, and handed it back to me. "Thank you."

With a quick nod, I stuffed the note into my purse. Looked up, and he was gone. I peered down the road that led up to the gates, and there was no lanky figure walking along. Nothing.

Like a ghost.

I dug the paper out of my purse and flipped it open, half expecting it to be blank. But his name was there. Eric, with a phone number and a request to be called ASAP.

So maybe not a ghost?

But he'd disappeared like one, and I *had* muttered Gran's prayer of seeing.

It couldn't be that easy, could it?

I touched a hand to my head, wondering. She'd always said *part* of the reason so many people didn't see the shadow world was because they didn't believe in it. That lack of belief kept their minds and eyes closed. Gran had said even those who wanted to believe often didn't see because there was another part to the shadow world.

Well, I was embracing it now, even if it was about twenty years later than she'd hoped. I wished she could see me here and now; she'd be clapping her hands and cheering me on. A smile flitted across my lips. Gone a split second later.

I needed this job, and if I took it, I suspected I'd be plunging myself directly into the world I'd spent so many years denying. Although, Eammon had refused to tell me much about the company and the fact the business card had led me to this side of the river to an *unnamed, uncharted* cemetery across from Bonaventure Cemetery, had presented rather strong evidence.

I'd told myself it might be some gimmicky tour company, but I damn well knew the job was going to be related to the shadow world.

I put a hand on the gate and gave it a rattle, irritation flowing faster now. "Hello? I'm here for the interview. Hollows Group? Eammon gave me his card, said I'd be a good fit."

If this wasn't the weirdest interview I'd ever been to, I'd eat my purse and everything in it. Then again, if Eammon had been truthful, the pay was better than anything out there. He'd told me I could make upward of twenty thousand a month—more than enough to buy Gran's house. Himself had said he was going to sell it, and even though it was mine by rights, I didn't have a choice. I had to buy it back and do it in a way that he didn't know it was me, or no doubt he'd charge me double. Or not sell it at all. He'd manipulated the divorce paperwork in an outrageous manner, moving my signature from the papers I'd thought I'd signed to new divorce papers that gave him everything.

I frowned, something tugging at my mind like a word on the tip of your tongue. I couldn't quite pull the thought forward. Something to do with the paperwork. I shook my head. Nothing I could do about it right then. I had to keep my focus on point.

Which was why this opportunity sounded so tantalizing. Since arriving in Savannah, I'd had three phone calls from the debt collectors for a debt that was supposed to belong to Himself, and I'd been officially divorced less than a week. I was going to have to get a new number to avoid them.

I worried at my bottom lip a moment before I shook it off. Forget waiting around; I needed this job, and if that meant I needed to be a bit more aggressive, then so be it.

I took a look at the gate lock, gave it an experimental twist and then nodded to myself.

Gran's training had included some practical skills, useful in any world. Lock picking was one.

A quick rummage in my purse produced a couple bobby pins that had been in there for God only knew how long. I bent them at different angles and slid them into the lock. "A bit on the sticky side, but I'll get you," I muttered.

The pressure on the pins from the tumblers in the lock gave me a moment of fear that I'd snap them off. A sudden click and the lock popped open. Grinning, I unlatched the chains holding the gates shut.

Score one for the old broad.

There was always more than one way to skin a cat, or pick a lock, so you could get into an interview in a graveyard. Gran would be proud of me, watching over me from wherever she was. I did a mock salute to the stars, just in case.

The chains slithered across the wrought iron, clanging as they went. Not that I was trying to be quiet. I let myself in, then shut the gate and slid the chain back into place, dummy locking it, so I'd be able to get out. Adjusting my bag on my shoulder, I started down the hardpacked dirt path. There were stones here and there that said it had been cobble-stone at some point, but most of those rocks were gone.

Eammon hadn't said to bring a flashlight, but I'd snagged one from the entryway of the place I was staying until I could get a place of my own. My current living situation was not ideal, but at least I had a place to sleep and hadn't ended up on the street. A definite possibility after I'd been evicted from my home in Seattle.

Even if my temporary roommate was Himself's black sheep of a cousin, Corb. Again, a bit of a story how it all happened. This one involved an elevator, an airplane, and an unintentional friend request. Joke was on him, though—I'd taken him up on his offer of giving me a place to live while I got back on my feet. Through him I'd met Eammon.

I flicked the flashlight on and swept the beam around. There was no obvious person waiting for me. I tucked my résumé into my bag and pulled out the card Eammon had given me.

On one side was the name of the company "Hollows Group" and the address. On the other side was Eammon's scrawl.

Be bold. Show what you've got. We like brains.

Brains, I had those, and one of Himself's major complaints was that I was too loud and brassy. Bold was an easy step to the left of that, and surely my lock picking qualified. I lengthened my stride as the sun dropped and the evening cooled, scaling back the humidity that never quite died this far south. My mind whirred through the events of the last twenty minutes.

The locked gate, the absence of anyone waiting to greet me. Maybe this was some sort of test.

As soon as I thought the question, I knew I was right. Which meant I needed to figure out just what it was they wanted me to figure out.

How long had it been since I'd even thought about the shadow world? Too long, and I was going to be as rusty as that lock out front if I didn't pull myself together.

A slow circle with the flashlight and something danced off to my left, just out of sight, ducking behind one of the few gravestones that hadn't given in to gravity.

I froze, my gut clenching with that fear of the unknown that my grandmother had instilled in me. All the Irish in me reared its very superstitious head.

Bad enough that part of me thought Eammon was a leprechaun.

Not just think, you know he is.

I gritted my teeth and ignored that inner voice that sounded so much like my gran. Gran as she'd been in her prime, filled with love for the darker side of things, a love she'd instilled in me. It had all seemed so far away when I was on the West Coast. It had been easy to think Himself was right, that she was eccentric and maybe a little crazy.

"Crazy old lady, before you know it, she'll be over-run with cats and that house will be taken over by the city, ruining the value," he'd said more than once. The

value of the house always being the key point. What a ducking douche.

But here I was, stepping willingly into the same crazy waters that my gran had lived in. A part of me wondered if it wasn't a mid-life crisis kind of thing. You know, suddenly you start dancing under the moonlight and chanting together as you burn incense and eat mushrooms that make your head spin.

The other part of me knew I'd just opened the door I'd asked Gran to shut all those years ago with that simple prayer I'd whispered. Because seeing bogies in the dark of a graveyard wasn't something I'd experienced in a long, long time.

And that was exactly what I was seeing—a figure that wasn't human.

Maybe it had been, but it surely wasn't now.

What in the world was I getting myself into?

2

Yeah, I see your scrawny butt over there." I swallowed hard but kept my voice as steady as my flashlight. I'd come to this interview knowing in my heart that I'd be stepping into a world that would show its monsters to me if I asked. I'd asked, hell, I'd *prayed* for it.

Now the monsters were there, looking back at me.

Didn't mean I wasn't sweating like a pig in a hothouse.

"Come out. Right now." There it was, Gran's voice coming out of my mouth.

Sharp. Authoritative. I'd channeled her no-nonsense, kick-your-hind-end-if-you-don't-listen-to-me tone.

"No." The whisper-growled word sent a chill straight down my spine.

Be bold.

"Do not make me come over there, or you will be very, very sorry." I snapped the words. "I am here for an interview, and if you make me any later, so help me. God in heaven will not save you from me…"

The rustling behind the gravestone made every hair stand along the back of my neck and my bare arms. I kept the light unmoving as the person slid to the left. Head down, long hair covering his face and eyes, scraggly clothes that hung off a whip-thin frame that made the Eric fellow from earlier look fat.

"That's better," I said, even though the image was anything but better. He swayed side to side, rocking himself faster and faster. "Do you know where Eammon is?"

"Noooooo." Drawn out more this time, the voice was not…well damn, it was not human, but it wasn't aggressive either.

This was not just an actor dressed in a costume to freak me out. This was the real deal.

Holy crap.

"Fine. I don't know where anyone is either, so here's the deal: you're going to help me find them," I said.

The gate rattled behind me, and I did a half turn, seeing someone I knew stepping through, although he hadn't noticed me yet. Tall, broad across the shoulders, a very distinctive jaw I had thought about all last night as I lay in the room he'd let me have in his loft. Corb was Himself's black-sheep cousin, as previously mentioned, and about the only person who offered to help me get back on my feet. That being said, he hadn't wanted me to so much as *talk* to his buddy and co-worker, Eammon, when they'd had their visit the day before. Which was why Eammon had taken me out for tea unbeknownst to Corb.

I had a feeling my current roommate didn't know about the interview and wouldn't be thrilled to find out.

Which meant him catching me here, at said interview, was not good news.

Basically, this was about to turn into a turd tango.

"What is your name?" I didn't have a lot of time before Corb caught up to me, and then the yelling match would happen.

The creature that may or may not have started as human swayed faster. I snapped my fingers at him twice, once with each word. "Name. Now!" A trick Gran had used in front of me more than once to make people sit up and take notice.

His shoulders hunched a little. "Robert."

"Robert." He was probably lying but whatever. "You stay here until I get back." I pointed with the flashlight at the gravestone and he put his hand out… only it wasn't a hand. It was a skeleton with bones for fingers and not much else. And I just stared because I wasn't sure I could do anything else. My brain shut down a little, and I might have peed myself just a tiny bit.

Here's the thing. Believing is one thing; seeing is another, altogether. Don't believe me? The first time you see a ghost or a bogey, you and I can discuss the physiological effects. And while it was not my first time, it was the first time in a long time.

As it was, I just turned on my heel and strode toward the gate as if my body weren't totally freaking out. "Corb."

He startled as he lifted his head and saw me. "Bree, what are you doing here?" His blue eyes narrowed, and even in the dark, I thought I could see them glimmer. He said, "Damn it, Eammon gave you a card, didn't he? He asked you to come."

I nodded. "He did. He thinks I'd be a good fit, so I'm here for an interview." I tipped my chin up, daring him to challenge me.

He snorted. "You're too old. Our oldest trainees are in their early thirties, and even that is too old in my opinion for this job."

Oh, he did *not*. "Say that again? I think my hearing is going. Eh, sonny? What did you say to me old self?" Okay, so I'd slid into some form of pirate speak, but I figured there was no point in pretending to be normal now. "I can't be hearing you with my aged ears, not as good as they used to be." I bent forward for effect, touching my lower back as if I were a hundred and ten, not forty-one, thank you very much.

I looked up as he rolled his eyes. "This job isn't for...we don't hire women for the most part," Corb said, trying to take another tack that was almost equally insulting. "Go back to the loft."

Shannon Mayer

Sounded too much like telling the little woman to go home so the men could take care of things. I think not. I stood straight and gave him my best resting bitch face.

"No. If you'll recall, you have no say over me or my life. We aren't married. We aren't even," I made a rude gesture with the flashlight and my free hand. If he wanted old school, I'd give it to him. The light bobbed in and out of my cupped hand several times. "Not that us doing *that* would give you any say, either."

Would he get the *Seinfeld* reference? Probably not. Too young.

His jaw flexed and I flipped the flashlight up, so it pointed directly at his face, blinding him. "I've already picked the lock and made friends with one of your creepy skeleton people, so I'm doing just fine. Thank you very much for your lack of faith in me and my rickety old female body."

His eyes narrowed along with the line of his mouth. Pity, his mouth was lovely and full. "We are hiring because three of our recent hires were killed, Breena. On the job."

Oh. Well, I suppose that wasn't a shock. Eammon had mentioned it could be dangerous, and they didn't pay you twenty thousand a month to twiddle your thumbs at a desk job. Gran had always said the shadow world wasn't for the faint of heart or the slow of wit. I was neither.

I lowered the flashlight and shrugged. "And who would care if I was gone? Not Himself. My

19

parents and Gran are long gone. No kids, despite my *advanced age.*"

His very nice jaw flexed again, and he shook his head. "I'm one of the interviewers and I won't pass you. That would mean you'd need the other four to agree. And that's just to get to the training. It doesn't take into account the final test after all the training."

"Fine. If I fail, then I fail. You're acting like they might actually pass me, and you don't like that." My eyes widened. "Is that what you think? That they might hire me, and you don't want to work with me?"

"It's bad enough you showed up on my doorstep without any warning!" he snapped. "You're making my life miserable!"

"*That,*" I held up a finger, "was a funny night. I will hold on to that until the day I die." I laughed, remembering the shock on his face. The sheets wrapped around his waist and the very obvious arousal I was ruining as his girl of the night left in a hurry. It had been raining, my makeup had run down my face, and I'd had all of two bags and no money. He'd had to pay the cab driver for me. That part wasn't so funny, but the girl running out? Hilarious.

Maybe you had to be there. Or maybe you just had to be me with a terribly mean sense of humor.

"It was not funny! I'd been trying to get in her pants for months! You screwed me over!" he said, keeping his voice low and growly. Like he was going to intimidate me? I think not.

I burst out laughing. "It was funny, and *nobody* got screwed that night. If the worst thing that happens to you is that your plans for getting laid get sidetracked, you aren't doing too bad." I pointed the flashlight at him, right in his face again because he was irritating me. "And if you'll remember, you offered me a place to stay. I just took you up on it."

"I was drunk," he growled. "That's not the kind of offer you think your cousin's ex is going to take you up on! It's polite social etiquette to offer, but you were supposed to turn me down! And you didn't even call before you showed up." As if I'd broken social protocol by not phoning. Ha!

"Not my problem. I got it on video, remember?" I grinned up at him, and he glowered and made a reach for the flashlight which I dodged easily. "So. You go on to your place as one of the interviewers, and I will continue on with Robert as my guide."

Corb frowned. "Who the hell is Robert?"

"Robert. One of your people over there." I swung the flashlight over to the gravestone, where, of course, Robert was not. "Oh, you turd!"

"You...fine, go through with it. You'll see you aren't cut out for this job." Corb brushed past me, leaving a trail of that very fine cologne he wore. I couldn't quite pinpoint it, but I liked it. Part of me wanted to bury my nose in the crook of his neck and just breathe it in. Then again, I was single for the first time in twenty-plus years, and my hormones were off the chart.

Like, I'd never wanted to get laid so badly in my life, and I had nobody to jump. Sucked to be me.

"I like your cologne," I said. "What is it?"

He paused. "*Night.*"

I nodded because it figured. "You don't put too much on. Unlike the other young guys who seem to think they're going to waft out a circumference of smell that will draw the ladies in," I said as I turned.

Corb had disappeared just like that Eric guy earlier. I blinked and swept the flashlight around me, seeing nothing. "Going to be like that, is it?"

Fine. I swung back toward the gravestone, and there was Robert, his skeletal hand right where it had been before. "Really? Make me look like a loser, will you? Some friend you are." As I walked toward him, something my gran had told me bobbed toward the surface of my mind. I tapped at my head to encourage it. "What was it? Give a skeleton food or drink, and they'll stick around to help you?"

He leaned forward and his swaying picked up speed. I felt like there was something else I was forgetting, but I couldn't remember it. Damn it.

The food trick was worth trying, anyway. I dug in my purse and pulled out a nougat-filled chocolate bar, unwrapping it quickly, then holding it out to him. "You want a bite?"

His long-haired head swung my way as he rocked side to side, giving me a few glimpses of bone under the darkness. "Friend?" He reached out, took the bar with one hand and shoved it into his mouth, chewing noisily.

There was a thud and I looked down at the ground to see chunks of the chocolate bar sitting between his feet, chewed, but not digested. He gave a low moan like he could really taste it.

"You with me then?"

I think he said yes, but the chocolate and nougat were giving his teeth a bit of a hard time. The aroma of chocolate was strong, and I tried not to think about the smell it might be masking on the dead-who-knows-how-long skeleton.

"Come on then, let's go see what we can find, okay?" I flicked the flashlight forward, impressed that Robert could stay crouched at my side as he shuffled along.

Bones clacking.

I shook my head. This was crazy.

Crazy.

And I was embracing it like the nutter that Himself had accused me of being. I held my chin up a little higher, continually sweeping the area with the flashlight. I was not going to be surprised.

The tombstones I touched on with the light were broken and in complete disrepair. Terrible. That was going to make for a lot of pissed-off ghosts.

Fading in and out, shadows moved between the graves. My guess was on the ghosts that would be unhappy with how their graves were being treated. Let's be honest, that was a huge part of the draw for Savannah tourism, and it wasn't wrong.

Disturb the dead, and they will make sure you know about it.

I clenched my teeth.

A thick fog rolled in off the ocean, creeping around the remaining tombstones and masking the figures I'd seen. Hiding the path at my feet.

"You're kidding, right?" I muttered as my flashlight barely pushed through the thick ground cover. I adjusted my bag and glanced at Robert, who was still there despite the disappearing act earlier. "Any ideas?"

"Nooooo."

"Great."

Of course, that was when the interview took an unexpected turn.

3

As if I weren't already surrounded by ample evidence of the shadow world's existence—graveyard after dark in Savannah, Georgia, check; skeleton companion, check; fog creeping around my bare legs, check—a howl split the air, shattering the stillness.

I jumped; I'll admit it. Robert flattened himself to the ground in a way that was not natural and he... he freaking skittered away like a bug.

"Robert!" I snapped his name and he froze. "Don't you dare leave me! I gave you a chocolate bar!"

Robert trembled and said one word. "Wolf."

Wolf. Oh crap.

"Okay, go, go!" I yelled.

Wolves were just big dogs, right? And big dogs were something I knew. Dog groomer by day, part-time law clerk at night, helping Himself with his cases because he was too cheap to hire someone… never mind, that was beside the point.

I could do this. I dealt with bad dogs all day, every day.

Another howl cut through the fog and I blew out a breath. "Think, Bree, think!"

I needed something to use as…"A muzzle," I whispered. I yanked my bag off my back and dumped the contents onto the ground. The bag was mid-sized, leather, and had two long handles for carrying cross-body. You know, to keep the thugs from running off with it. We old ladies thought about things like that—muggers and thieves on every corner, if you'd asked my gran.

And, apparently, now me.

I shook it off. If I could catch the bag around the muzzle of one of the wolves, maybe…that would be enough.

"Crazy. You're crazy," I whispered to myself. And maybe I was a bit crazy. Maybe Himself had been right about me all along. Or maybe, just maybe, I was all out of ducks to give. My girlfriend, Mavis, had given me a happy divorce day card before I left Seattle. On it was a saying that had quickly become my mantra.

Behold, the field in which I grow my ducks. Lay thine eyes upon it and see that it is barren. Autocorrect might like it to be ducks, but we all know it wasn't a row of quacking fowl.

I started forward again, the purse hanging at my side in one hand, flashlight in the other.

I could almost see Corb's smug smile as he said I wasn't going to make it through the interview.

"Maybe he's right, maybe I'm too old for this shit."

A snarl to my right spun me around, bringing me face to face with a wolf that was no wolf. More like a damn bear. Its eyes were *level* with mine, and I stood a respectable five foot eight. The bright amber eyes narrowed as they took me in, dipping to look at the purse before settling back on my face. They shone with amusement, making it very clear that this wolf was *laughing* at me.

That was a solid no from me, thank you very much. "Robert, take him from behind!"

Now here's where things got weird. I mean, weirder, let's be honest, it was already as weird as Al Yankovic.

The wolf spun as if it knew what I was saying. Of course it did. It wasn't a wolf any more than Robert was a person.

This was my chance.

Be bold? How about jumping on the back of a big ol' wolf bold?

I scrambled up on a tombstone that crumbled under me as I used it as a launch pad, literally throwing myself across the back of the wolf. It stiffened under me and I clamped down with my legs. It had been a long time since I'd ridden a horse, but the theory was the same in my madly scrambling mind.

Get on, clamp your thighs for all you were worth and grab the reins. I swung the purse forward and, miracle of miracles, caught the opening over the nose of the wolf. Just like a muzzle.

Its body flexed under me as I squeezed for all I was worth and pulled the "reins" back hard enough to tuck its head tightly to its chest. "No eating the interviewees!" I yelled as the wolf twisted hard to the left, throwing me part way down its side, hanging there like a stunt rider. I still had the "reins" and I held them as taut as I could, keeping the wolf muzzled, and me barely still on its back. Its fur was black and mottled gray and smelled like a swamp of stagnant water and rotting something.

"Gawd in heaven, you stink! You need a groomer!" I yelped as it twisted again, that giant head swinging my way which threw me upright on top of its back once again. From behind it, I saw movement. A side-to-side, swaying shuffle moving in our direction.

"Robert! Grab him by the ear!" I yelled.

Ears were sensitive on dogs—they had to be sensitive on wolves too. The wolf didn't move this time. Maybe it thought I was bluffing.

But in a flash Robert was on its ear, tearing at it, the sound like a thick sheaf of wet paper being pulled in half.

Robert ripped the ear off as easy as if it were paper, and then *ate it.*

The wolf howled and swung its head hard toward Robert, which sent the skeleton flying through the air. My purse and the wolf disappeared into the fog, the sound of its whimpering fading into nothing after a few frantic heartbeats.

I grabbed for the edge of the gravestone closest to me, clinging to it as I stared at Robert pulling himself up from the ground. "You ate his ear." I mean, saying he ate it is relative, seeing as the tuft of ear was on the ground, having passed through his skeletal guts the way the chocolate bar had.

I could barely speak, my heart was racing, and sweat covered every part of me, down my spine and right into my butt crack where I was sure it was pooling. Legs shaking, I slid down the side of the tombstone. "Robert?"

"Help. Friend," he muttered and then did that weird swaying, if not quite as fast.

"Thanks," I whispered, only because I was still trying to breathe normally. I made myself push to my feet even though my limbs were full of strange tingling sensations that told me this was far more exertion than I was used to. I held a hand out, watched every single finger shake, and then shook my head. "A little adrenaline, right? Not a bad thing."

Robert just swayed where he stood in the slowly dispersing fog.

It took me a moment to realize my flashlight was gone. My purse was gone. I did a turn and could see in the distance the gate and the single light above it. I could leave. I could walk right down the path, take a cab back to the loft, and take the waitressing job at Pirates Restaurant, where I'd make good tips off the tourists. If I left, this would all just be a crazy moment.

Another crazy moment, for a crazy woman.

But then Corb would be right.

Himself would be right.

And I had a feeling that it would let Gran down if she was watching from somewhere.

My back straightened like I'd been hit in the ass with a paddle. I was finishing this, one way or another, even if it left me sore for a week, even if I had nightmares for months of a slavering amber-eyed wolf coming straight for me and being saved by a skeleton who liked candy bars.

Maybe the job would suck, and I'd turn it down even if they offered it to me, but I was finishing this interview.

I scrubbed my hands over my face in a quick motion. "Okay, Robert. You still with me?" I mean, at this point, he was my only option. Even if he did eat the wolf's ear. I frowned. "Wolves aren't common in Georgia, never mind Savannah."

Robert, of course, made no comment as I forced my jelly legs to start walking again. My mind shifted to my gran's book, a great big tome bound in red leather which she'd used to chronicle her spells and information about various creatures in the shadow world. Some had names, some didn't. I'd loved reading that book when I was younger.

The way the wolf had looked at me, the way it had reacted to me talking to Robert could only mean it wasn't really a wolf. It was…maybe a shifter of some sort? I gritted my teeth as my legs tried to shake again. Sure, I'd been raised with knowledge of the shadow world, but that was so, so different than being immersed in it. Gran had said it would take something big to bring me fully into the shadow world.

Maybe a divorce would do that?

The answer came to me then, and I said it out loud. "Gran dying." The wind stilled around us, the night noises fading as I realized that was exactly what had made the change. The night she'd died, I'd woken in a sweat, alone as I so often was with Himself working late.

I could feel the sensation of *something* sinking into my skin that night, and then the phone rang, and Gran's best friend Hattie sobbed out that she was gone. Gran was dead.

For a good minute, I stood there in the graveyard, letting the truth sink into me. I was not a child any longer, and I wasn't going to deny what was happening, what I was seeing with my own eyes and feeling under my skin.

"Into the darkness," I said softly, making my feet move. "And find the lights along the way."

Whatever Gran had done, she'd done it for a reason.

Which meant I wasn't slowing down.

The path took us under a long line of trees, the branches reaching low, tugging on my hair in places. Now that my eyes were adjusted to the darkness, there were other shapes darting around, ducking behind trees as they followed me and Robert. But none popped out the way he had.

"Any idea who is out there, Robert?" I figured it couldn't hurt to ask.

"Dead."

Well, maybe I was wrong about that.

"Not exactly the most comforting answer." I rubbed at my lower back, already feeling the jarring in my spine stiffening from riding the bucking, twisting wolf. I wasn't going to let the growing aches stop me. I'd go back to the loft after this, take a couple Advil chased with that whiskey Corb thought he was hiding in the top cupboard above the fridge, run a hot bath, and call it a night to remember.

"I won't forget this night, not if I live to be a hundred," I said.

Robert grunted.

"Don't you sass me," I said. No, I had no idea what the grunt meant, but let's be honest, men grunting usually means they're thinking something smart-assy.

Robert twisted his head to the side and shrugged.

The path came to a crossroads intersection, giving me three options. I paused and stared at the ground in the middle. As I crouched, the clouds shifted and the moon made an appearance, showing off the solid black stone in the middle of the juncture.

I dropped lower yet to get a better look with a grimace and the pulling of muscles that had only recently been activated after years of dormancy. A compass was set into the stone, its moveable parts made of bright, shining silver. I bent and pushed the little arrow and it swung around and around, finally pointing north. "What do you think, Robert?"

According to the compass, I'd come in from the east, so I could go north, south, or east.

His skeletal finger traced the compass and tapped the E.

"East it is." I stood and took a step, but Robert didn't come with me. I looked back at him. "Can't come any farther?"

He sat there, crouched over the compass, swaying faster and faster. Agitated, if I were to guess. "Dead."

"Yeah, you said that. Look, thanks. I'll try to bring you another chocolate bar, okay?" I tipped my head to one side. His skeletal fingers tapped over the compass again, sliding over to the S.

"Friend. Safe," he whispered and tapped the S again.

I smiled. "Friend. Thanks, Robert. You did good." I had a suspicion that my offer of a second candy bar had made him give me the better route. The safer path.

A quick turn on the heel, and I was walking down the path that would take me south. I made myself pat Robert on the head as I went by him.

Felt the scraggly hair.

The bone under it.

The lack of flesh.

I could see the words in Gran's old leather-bound book inside my head, as if I were actually looking at the page, the memory coming unbidden but still helpful.

Skeletons still guard the graves of those who are forgotten.

Robert reached up and took my hand in his skeletal one. "Friend."

Okay, the shakes I got then were nothing short of an earthquake. Because I wasn't...he wasn't...crap on toast, Robert really wasn't alive, and I just didn't know what to do with that. I'd been hanging out with him for the last hour. Talking to him. Asking him questions that he'd been reluctant to answer.

So, I said the only thing that came to mind.

"Well, I suppose I've been on worse dates with Himself than with someone who's legitimately dead."

4

I made myself give Robert's skeletal hand a squeeze even though my head felt like a balloon that would float off my shoulders. I found myself swaying a little, in time with him, wondering just how real he and this experience in the graveyard were. Yes I knew it was real, but that little part of me that had lived in Seattle for so long was struggling to keep up. "Gran, I had no idea just how much of what you'd taught me was really real."

Despite the indisputable fact that I was standing in the middle of a forgotten Savannah graveyard in the dark, holding hands with a skeleton, I couldn't get past the thought that none of this should be possible.

Which had to be part of the test.

They wanted to see how I'd deal with all the crazy of the shadow world. I hadn't told Eammon who my gran was, or that I'd been trained by her and her friends. And Corb likely didn't know much about me, black sheep that he was. He'd come to the wedding between Himself and me when he'd been a teenager, and I'd only seen him once or twice since then.

I let go of Robert's very real skeletal fingers and walked away down the south-leading path. "See ya 'round, Robert."

"Later."

I laughed. "Robert, be careful, I'll think you're flirting with me."

I twisted around, but he was gone, and I could barely see the intersection I'd just left. I paused and took a few steps back, and then a few more. The path didn't lead to any kind of crossroads.

"That's not possible." I shook my head. I counted the steps I took and covered easily twice the distance to where the crossroads should be.

A game, I had to remind myself this was a game, one that Corb thought I was going to fail. Himself would have bet against me too. Once more, my back straightened—if with a bit more difficulty, and a little groan when the muscles protested.

I had to keep going, that was all there was to it. The air cooled further as I walked, the path dipping closer toward the ocean, away from the graveyard, which was fine by me. The hard dirt and occasional cobblestone gradually shifted into sand that pulled at my shoes, filling them. I kicked them off, carrying them in one hand.

The sound of the surf tugged me farther south, and I let it carry me along, thinking a swim in the water would be refreshing, maybe just what I needed. Another sound wrapped around me, a lovely sort of singing. Yes, a night swim—I could go in, no one would know. I reached for my shirt to pull it off, and my fingers brushed against the pendant hanging off the chain around my neck that had been Gran's. She'd sent it to me in the mail right before she passed. My hand grew cold and my feet stilled. Night swimming? I hadn't done that since my twenties. What the heck was wrong with me? I smacked the side of my head as if I could knock the sound of the singing out of it. Singing? Why was there singing in an interview?

Confusion rippled through me, not unlike the waves that washed up over the beach, smoothing away the lines in the sand. Convincing me it would be fine, I should just…Get. In. The. Water.

"Yeah, no," I spat the words and shook my head again. Was this even part of the interview?

I frowned and looked down at my feet. Without realizing it, I'd strayed off the path that went through the old graveyard. I slipped my shoes back on, turned, and climbed up to the main path. From the top, I could barely hear the water, never mind any singing.

"Gran, what have I gotten into?"

The water didn't call to me anymore, and there was no singing, but I did see something in the waves, just a quick flash of silver, like the scales of a fish, but the shape was wrong. It almost looked like a person diving below the waves.

A person with scales.

Holy crap. I'd almost gone into the water with a nymph.

That was no sweet little mermaid waiting in the night waters. I'd read about nymphs in my grandmother's book. They were known to pull the unwary under the waves, drown them, and then take little bites out of the tenderest parts. The more tender the better.

I swallowed hard and, steeling myself, I started forward again. This was an interview. One I was going to get through intact with all of my tender parts, thank you very much.

The path underfoot grew rocky and started climbing upward. I wasn't even sure how that was possible. When I looked over my shoulder, the path behind me appeared flat. It was steep in front of me, and the more I looked at it, the steeper it seemed to become, until it was almost vertical. A mountain in the middle of the graveyard.

Not possible, but I would have said that about most of what I'd encountered in here.

"Great, this is a fitness test now," I muttered under my breath. I adjusted the waistband of my capris and started up the narrow track. There was open air to my right, and the mountain rock to my left. Which doesn't sound so bad, except that the farther up I went, the narrower the path got until I had to put my back against the wall of rock while the tips of my toes were hanging over the edge. I knew—logically—this outcropping was not possible. There were no rock mountains in Savannah. It was lowland, marshy and flat. Especially this area. Which meant this rock formation had to be man-made.

Or made with magic.

The flop sweat from earlier was nothing compared to the sweat that flowed from me now at the thought that this outcropping I stood on, high above the solid ground, could be made of magic. Magic could disappear, just like Robert had, and that would leave me in mid-air with nothing to catch me.

But that wasn't my biggest problem.

A howl cut through the air below me. I didn't bother to look down the path. I didn't need to check to know that my now one-eared friend was back.

"Crap, crap, crap!" I scrambled as fast as I could, sideways, up the rock path, my feet barely staying where I wanted them, my thin running shoes making it so I could feel every little pebble as I tried to hurry without falling. A fall now would mean bad things. Broken limbs. Lying helpless on the ground where the big wolf would no doubt gobble me up.

"Like little Red," I said and started to laugh because it was ridiculous. Why, oh why hadn't I listened to Gran? She'd told me that Little Red Riding Hood was based on a real story to keep children safe from, not wolves, but shifters. To keep children from becoming shifters.

Up and up I went as fast as I could, the howling and snarling of the wolf below sending my heart into overdrive. There was no Robert to help me this time, no bag to catch the wolf's mouth and hold it shut.

Sweat flowed down my body like dozens of little rivers, but I didn't slow. I was getting near the top, I was sure of it. It was less clear what I'd do once I got there.

As sudden as the thought hit me, I was there at the top, and my back no longer had anything to lean against. I fell backward with a screech that I couldn't catch. I hit the ground, knocked the wind out of myself, rolled, and ended up on my hands and knees, staring at four pairs of feet as I gasped and heaved for air.

Just a note, panting was not a good look on anyone, but especially not when you were on your hands and knees staring at a bunch of strangers' feet. Except they weren't all strangers.

One pair of shoes I recognized, and I glared at the well-worn cowboy boots that belonged to Corb. I reached out and rapped a knuckle on one, unable to help myself as I caught my breath. "One vote against."

A low laugh brought my head up, hair sticking to my sweat-slicked face. Eammon was on my left.

"Ah, lass, you made it. Quite the show you did put on for us." His dark hair was braided back from his head, just like the first time I'd met him only the day before. His beard was trimmed close to his

40

round face, and a healthy dose of good humor filled the bright green eyes that watched me.

Eammon's clothing was all done in a deep green worked with silver trim, a suit that reminded me of something from a bygone era, but with a modern touch. Like he was being proper but still holding to his roots. I liked it.

I sat back on my butt and gave him a wink. "Oh, that was nothing." Mind you, I didn't push to my feet. My legs were too jellified.

Eammon chuckled. "One vote for."

From my butt, I looked at the remaining two people. Both men. One was whip thin, his body all angles and points, but other than that, I could barely see his features given the way his long dark hair fell forward, hiding his eyes…

"Hey, you must be related to Robert!" I did push to my feet then, so I could get a better look at him. He slowly raised his chin until he was looking down his nose at me. His face was as angular as the rest of him. He wore black skinny jeans and a black T-shirt which made him seem thinner than he probably was.

"Who. Is. Robert?" His thick French accent was even snobbier than the whole look-down-his-nose move.

I looked at Eammon and then Corb for help, but they both shook their heads. Corb, of course, added a set of crossed arms that said it all. He was not helping me get through this.

"Robert," I repeated the name, "the skeleton you left near the gate. He's built similarly to you, but…

41

well, he's dead, so there is that." I wiped a hand across my face. Slick, I was totally slick with sweat and it wasn't just from the exertion.

French dude shook his head. "There is no one named Robert here; skeletons do not have names. They are dead."

Eammon thumbed at him. "He's a necro, so he has a bit of affinity with the dead."

Before I could respond, a scrabbling sound turned my head and the world seemed to go into slow motion as the big bad wolf burst onto the top of the hill, snarling, blood dripping from where his ear had been torn off by good old Robert.

The animal's huge head swung my way, amber eyes narrowed, and I found myself staring into the teeth of the thing. The men did nothing as the wolf advanced on me.

I didn't understand. I'd thought their test was over. But I didn't need to understand. I just needed to make it out of this alive.

"Bad dog!" I swung a right hook, not to punch the wolf in the nose, but to jam my fingers into the nostrils. The soft flesh was cold and wet, just like it would be with a dog, and I clenched my hand into a fist around it.

The wolf cried out, yelping, and fell back, which yanked me with him right to the edge of the mountain top we were on. I had to get control of this now, or we were both going over the lip.

"Bad dog!" I yelled at the wolf again. "Sit!"
Insanity. This. Was. Insanity.

Gran, you did not prep me for this!

Crazier yet, because the wolf sat. Whimpering. I let go immediately and stared it right in the eye. "Down."

The wolf flattened itself to the ground and coughed out a gunked-up chunk of paper. I bent and picked it up by a corner. What was left of my résumé, I presume? And what looked like Eric's card. I blew out a breath. I kept the wolf in my line of sight as I did a partial turn toward the interviewers and held out the résumé. "All my credentials are here." Take that, boys. Eammon carefully took my résumé, or what was left of it. "And a fellow named Eric wanted to hire you. His card is stuck to it with wolf spit by the looks of it."

Four sets of eyes rested on me, their perusal more interested than before. Even Corb's.

Eammon shook the paper. "Eric is nothing more than a paranoid pain in the ass. We have better jobs than his, jobs that pay more."

The French dude rolled his eyes and sighed. "He is an idiot."

That wasn't the impression I'd gotten off the lanky fellow at the front gate, but what did I know? Eric wasn't my concern.

"Did I pass the interview?" I put my hands on my hips and raised my chin just a little.

"I vote for her, reluctantly. I cannot deny she passed the tests," the Frenchman said.

"Already said I'd vote for her," Eammon drawled. "And I brought her, so she's mine to train."

Corb shook his head. "No. Even with this, it's still no."

The last man pursed his lips. I finally got a good look at him. Dark skin, dark eyes, salt-and-pepper hair shaved closed to his skull, and an unreadable face. He'd make an excellent gambler.

"I say yes." His voice was a baritone that cascaded down my spine. Like magic.

"That's only three yeses." Corb gave me a slow grin. "And I highly doubt that Sarge is going to say yes after you ripped his ear off and jammed your fingers in his nose."

The wolf at my feet grumbled something under his breath, something that sounded a lot like "agreed." But that wasn't possible. Was it?

Not usually one for hyperventilating, or freaking out, or passing out, I figured if there was any time that it would be warranted, this was it. I couldn't get enough air as the wolf curled its lips up.

"I agree," it repeated.

The wolf. Agreed.

I'd been right. He was something else, not just a wolf.

"Gawd in heaven." I spun on my heel and stared down at the wolf at my feet. Only his ear was back in place as if it had never been pulled off. I shook my head hard and held up both hands. "You can talk?"

"All werewolves can talk," he grumbled, his voice deep and gravelly, just the way Gmork sounded in *The Never Ending Story,* and damn it if it didn't do the same thing to my legs, turning them right back to jelly. I had to lock my knees to keep upright.

"See?" Corb strode around to stand beside the wolf sitting up now. "He agrees with me. You don't pass the interview. You're out. Get the whiskey for her."

There was movement behind me, and then a glass was pressed into my shaking and all-too-pale hand.

The dark-skinned man nodded to me. "Drink it down, girl. It will erase this night; you won't remember a thing."

The golden liquid beckoned to me to drown myself in it, to forget the adventures—yes, let's call them that. But I didn't want to forget again, no matter how much it shocked me that I was living in the shadow world. I moved to turn the drink upside down.

The wolf stood on his hind legs, and with one swift move knocked the drink from my hand. "I agree with the others, not with you, Corb. She stays."

5

All the way down the other side of the mountain that shouldn't exist, down to the graveyard I'd never heard of, Corb tried to convince his weird buddies I shouldn't get the job.

"...too old. And slow. You saw how slow she was coming up the mountain."

"...and she won't listen. She's unteachable because she's so set in her ways."

"...doesn't have what it takes."

Which was about all it took to keep me moving forward even though every damn part of me hurt like I'd been pulled through a knothole backward. A few strands of my strawberry blond hair fell forward, and when I went to brush them back, they came off on my fingers. I'd lost a chunk of hair somewhere along the line. So now I was old and balding? Awesome, that was what my already fragile ego needed.

"Rogaine," I muttered under my breath.

"She's too old! That alone should keep her from training!" Corb threw at Eammon, and I could feel him losing it as he lost his argument. "It's your fault she's here in the first place. Why the…why the fu…? Why did you give her the card?"

Part of me was totally gratified that he was so upset, because I'd proved him wrong just by finishing the "interview." Part of me was astounded and hurt that he was still pulling the "she's too old" card among other things.

"She's got the Irish in her blood, lad," Eammon said, brushing Corb off with a wave of his hand. "I saw it in her the second I met her. And it's about time we diversified. Experience and craftiness often outwit youth and vigor. We need more brains than brawn right now, and you know it. There is too much afoot to keep on doing as we have been and expecting different results."

Corb's jaw seemed to lock shut after that, and he didn't utter another word. Maybe Eammon outranked him in this company? That seemed plausible given not only their age difference—Corb was easily thirty years Eammon's junior—but the way that Eammon led the group along.

They took me to the east side of the graveyard where there were conspicuously fewer graves. The big trees hung heavy with Spanish moss that blew in the breeze, floating back and forth, adding to the overall creepy feeling of hanging out in a graveyard after dark.

We stopped in front of a fence surrounding a single oversized grave, and for a minute I thought maybe we were there to admire the elaborate gravestone. "Stunning" was the word that came to mind.

The tomb was made of marble, if the gray and white veining were legit, and it was easily over six feet tall and wide, a perfect square with a human-sized weeping angel perched on the very top. One wing of the angel spread wide, showing every beautifully carved feather, and the other wing looked like it had been broken off. I squinted up at the statue. No, that wasn't right, it had been made to look that way. The broken wing hung limply behind the angel, dragging past the back of the tomb.

In one hand, the angel held a spray of flowers, and in the other, a tiny flame curled up from the palm. I don't mean a carved flame either. I mean a literal flame burned in the angel's palm, flickering in the night, casting shadows across the angel.

The weather had dragged darkness down the lines of the eyes, streaking the face as though the angel were crying, and had been for a long time.

I found my feet taking me forward to read the name of the person buried here.

Lily. Carved lilies wrapped around her name and the scrolling words that said she'd died in 1879, at the age of eighteen, beloved daughter, may she find peace in death that she could not find in life.

I'd read the message softly to myself without realizing it.

The dark-skinned man held out his hand to me, palm up, pulling me out of my staring match with the stunning grave marker. "My name is Tomas; friends call me Tom."

I put my hand in his and gave it a shake. "Breena."

He didn't let go of me, but put his other hand on top of mine, holding me fast. "We can wipe your memory, but it only works with short-term memories. We're reaching the point of no return."

"No backsies, huh?" I patted the top of his hand and he let me go. "Look, Corb obviously isn't happy I'm here, but I've got nothing else. So why the hell not? Carry forth, good man, and let the chips fall where they may. I've a feeling I was born for this."

Tom smiled, a flash of white teeth. "Good. For the record, I think Eammon is right."

"For the record, I am on the fence," the Frenchman said, as snotty as ever. "But I am willing to give you a chance. I like sassy women with experience."

I looked him in the eye, ignoring the double entendre. "Well, Louis, I'll give you the same chance then."

He gasped and his mouth dropped open, a hand going over his chest. "How did you know my name?"

"You look and sound like a snotty Frenchman, so I took a guess." I gave him a wink. "Comes with age, the ability to read people, you know." That and I had a good track record with guessing. Made me hard to surprise, which was yet another thing that had come to irritate Himself. I'd figured out that he was going to divorce me before he could pull the plug. Hence the high-speed car chase and other hijinks as I mentioned earlier.

Eammon chuckled. "Yup, I do like the lass. More and more."

Corb growled, and the wolf, who I'd been deliberately ignoring, gave a woof. "Sassy. I like her too."

Tom put his hand on the gate around the grave, pushed it open, and went to the marble stone. His hands moved quickly across the carved lilies, touching them here and there. And the places he touched? They freaking lit up, glowing like Christmas lights. The colors stretched across the spectrum, and I found myself smiling.

Gran had a word for this kind of magic. "Recognition magic, cool."

The four men who had been leading me along all stopped where they were and looked straight at me. I smiled. "Might know a thing or two about the shadow world." More than a thing or two if I could dredge through my memories.

Louis gave me the slightest of nods, and Tom just grinned wider. Eammon, though, had that look cats had perfected. As if he'd just swallowed the canary whole and gotten away with it.

Himself would have pooped his pants had he seen the stone light up. I really wished I could show it to him.

A grinding of stone on stone growled through the air, and slowly the entire standing tombstone rotated, angel and all, onto its side. That opened a hole in the ground that was pitch black, to my *aged eyes*. I snorted at the thought as I peered into the dark. Cool air rushed up and out, curling around us, smelling of old graves. I thought maybe I heard a voice come with the air, but I couldn't be sure.

Corb brushed past me, going down first.

I smiled. "Agreed, Corb, ladies first."

His back stiffened for just a split second, and then he continued down the stairs. Tom let out a low laugh. "Oh, girl, you are going to be so much fun."

I shrugged and winked at him. "I don't have time to be bothered with fools. I mean, especially at my age. Gawd in heaven, what have I got left? Ten years at best? I'll be dead before you know it."

Tom waved for me to precede him. "Oh, only five, girl. Assuming the consumption don't take you, or you fall and break a hip."

I laughed. "Or yellow fever?"

Old-school banter, I could do that all night. Only they didn't laugh at that bit, none of them did. Crap. So much for my moment of levity. If anything, Tom's eyes went deadly serious.

"Yellow fever wasn't much what people thought it was. But you'll find out nearer the end of your training."

"Really?" I tipped my head to the side.

Louis went down the stairs next. He glanced over his shoulder. "Not yet, Tom. She doesn't need to know that until she gets through the training."

Intrigued, I leaned toward Tom. "I can keep a secret. And now I'm curious."

Gran had never mentioned the history of yellow fever being anything but what it was—a devastating disease that had terrified people.

"Ah, don't be getting me in trouble already." Tom sighed. "Maybe you can get Eammon to talk to you about it."

And that was that. All the men had gone down the stairs, leaving me at the top all by myself. Well, not quite. From the corner of my eye, I noticed a swaying body.

Robert tapped a finger bone on the wrought iron fence. "Friend."

"Robert." I gave him a little salute, somehow feeling better that he was there, watching over me. Silly, I know.

The space was so dark I couldn't see a single stair, but there was a good railing on the one side. I gripped hard, took a deep breath, and followed it down in a long curve that led to the right in two big loops. I found myself counting the steps. Eighteen, that was an unusual number. Like a flight and a half.

A glowing light beckoned to me from the bottom of the stairs, and I followed it into a room sunk down another five feet, which made the ceiling quite high. I blinked a few times at the things hanging from said high ceiling. Thick ropes. Chains. And a...I'd say fireman's pole, except that it didn't lead anywhere.

My eyebrows shot up as the implications hit me. "Eammon, tell me you aren't a stripper."

He barked a laugh. "Not anymore."

I threw my head back and laughed. "I want proof."

Eammon and Tom laughed with me, and even Louis gave a soft guffaw. The sound acoustics were amazing in the big room and our laughter rebounded nicely. Of course, no one else laughed (certainly not Corb), and then I realized that everyone was staring at me. Everyone included four people huddled in the middle of the room, who shared the same shell-shocked look of someone who'd just seen a ghost and peed their pants at the same time, and two men on the outer edges of the room, watching them. Like guards and prisoners.

Shoot, that couldn't be good.

Corb strode to the middle of the room, and I got to take him in. Yeah, he was nice to look at, probably lovely to hold, but strip it down, and he was a control freak, just like Himself. Bossy, trying to make me into someone or something I wasn't, trying to make me into a mold of what he thought I should be.

That was a very large nope in my book of Breena. Or, at least, it was now.

Forty-one and rocking it. I wasn't really sure what *it* was, but I'd figure it out. Maybe it would involve finally putting Gran's training to use. Maybe I'd show the shadow world a thing or two. Ha, I could only imagine trying to explain hot flashes and divorces to a bunch of men. Easier for them to believe in magic than the mysteries of a woman's body.

"You…five," Corb threw a sidelong look at me, "have passed the interview. If anyone wants out, this is your final opportunity to leave with no memory of this place or the horrors you have faced." He strode across in front of them, and I watched as the only other girl—God, was she even out of her teen years? —eyed him up like a prime piece of steak. I wanted to laugh but managed to choke it down by clearing my throat.

The three guys in the middle were shaken, not stirred, and I felt an immense amount of pity for them. They were young, early twenties at best, though they might have been even younger. I had a hard time telling now how old young people were. They all looked like babies to me with the lack of experience in their eyes, and the softness of their faces.

What I did notice was that they were all dressed in leathers, big boots, heavy jackets. I frowned when I saw that one of them had on what looked like a flak jacket. I did a slow turn to glance at Eammon. He grinned, winked, and shrugged. "I figured you wouldn't need all that stuff. Those lads did. Fear makes you more of a target in our graveyard of horrors."

That "stuff" he mentioned? Weapons of all sorts hung off their sides. Knives for the most part, but one of them had a gun! A gun?

A nose butted me in the middle of my back. I turned and looked at Sarge. "Yes?" He sat behind me. Was he…hiding? I tipped my head and frowned. "Really? Now you're a scaredy cat?"

Except when I turned back to face the group of what I'd dubbed kids, one of those guns was pointed right at me.

My eyebrows shot up. What was this crap now?

Corb was talking low and calm, his hands spread wide while the boy with the weapon continued to stare at Sarge behind me. The kid had the bluest eyes I'd ever seen, but maybe that was only because they were trying to bug out of his head. The gun was not really pointed at me, and I took note that his finger was resting on the guard, not the trigger. I could handle this.

"Hey!" I snapped my fingers while I snapped out the word, drawing his attention to me. The kid blinked hard a couple times as his eyes slid up to mine. I snapped my fingers in the air again. "You point that gun at me, and you are going to be very sorry, boy."

His throat bobbed and he lowered the gun. "But the…wolf…he attacked us."

"He's harmless. It's the skeletons you need to watch out for." I grinned and the kid's eyes impossibly widened farther.

"Skeletons?"

I shrugged. "Well, I can only vouch for Robert. He was pretty cool, but I'm guessing he was one of few good ones."

The kid's chest rose and fell rapidly, his eyes rolled back in his head and he fell backward, limp as a noodle. He hit the ground with a hard thud that made me grimace. "Ouch. That's going to hurt tomorrow."

Sarge leaned his head against my back, and I could tell from the shaking that he was laughing.

Tom stepped forward. "I was on the fence with this one. I don't think he'll make it through."

I found my feet taking me forward, right into the middle of the kids. "Move." I waved my hands at the remaining three and they parted around me. I crouched by the kid on the ground and patted his cheek. "You alive in there?"

A groan, and then his eyes slowly opened. "Mom?"

Corb snorted. "She's old enough to be your mom. You're right about that."

I threw a well-aimed glare over my shoulder. "Keep it up, chuckles. I'll teach you what a bad idea it is to fight with your elders." I turned back to the boy. "Gawd in heaven, what are you, a teenager?"

Big blue eyes looked straight up at me. "Turned twenty today."

"Well, happy birthday. Why are you here?" The thing was, I knew why *I* was here. The money that Eammon had talked about was way too good, and it would solve problems I needed solved. Gran's house among them.

"My mom is sick," he said. "We can't pay for the medical bills and..."

My throat tightened. Stupid hormones. To be fair, sometimes I got weepy with a well-placed kitten in a tissue commercial. I cleared my throat. "Then get up. Because they are about to oust your butt for being a pansy ass."

I helped him to his feet, and he swayed where he stood. Before he could lift the gun again, I took it from him, cleared the chamber, and popped the clip out. Corb let out a strangled noise.

I looked at him. "Didn't know I knew guns, did you?"

His look said it all. He didn't know much about me at all.

I shrugged. "I don't keep them around, and Himself is lucky I didn't." Because I would have shot the bastard the moment I found out he'd taken Gran's house from me. For good measure, I patted the birthday boy down and took the remainder of his weapons and ammo. "You don't need this, not with Sarge. He's a good boy. Well trained."

"Sarge." The kid couldn't take his eyes off the wolf who sat next to Tom. "That can't be Sarge. I talked to him. He's a person. Not a wolf."

"Sarge. That's the wolf. Didn't you talk to him at the top of the hill?" I was confused. Corb had said that everyone had to have at least four votes to get them through. Unless he was lying about that too.

I swung around to look at Corb. "Doesn't take four votes normally, does it?"

"Just in cases where one of us doesn't think the interviewee is capable." He stood his ground and I stood mine.

"Enough," Louis said with a wave of his hand. "You have all been invited here, one by each of us. The master who invited you will be your main trainer. You will, of course, train with all of us over the next twelve weeks as we decide where your skills lie."

My jaw dropped. "Twelve weeks?" I needed to be making the bucks like...yesterday. I had no idea when Gran's house would go up for sale, and I had to be ready. Though I supposed maybe Blue Eyes here was in the same boat. Hell, maybe we all were. Let's be honest, stepping into the shadow world was one of those things that took more than a little desperation if you weren't raised in it.

Louis placed his hands together and steepled his fingers. "Yes, twelve weeks."

The girl in the group piped up, her voice melodic in a way that reminded me of the songs at the water's edge. I frowned and tugged on my ear closest to her as she spoke. "Will we get paid for the training?"

Louis nodded. "You will all receive a training stipend of three hundred dollars a week."

A chorus of gasps slid from the others, but I was not surprised. Negotiations 101 were about to commence. They would lowball us; we would make a counteroffer.

I had, after all, worked for Himself as a law clerk for enough years to understand how these things worked. "No, that's not nearly high enough. An even grand a week will be just fine, thank you very much."

Louis's eyes narrowed. "You have no place to demand—"

"I have every right." I clasped my hands in front of my body. "That wolf over there? Totally not native to the area. The right authorities would have to be

58

brought in to remove him. They'd likely neuter him at the same time, what with his obvious poor breeding."

Sarge's jaw dropped open and his tongue lolled out. I did a slow turn taking in the room, making sure I locked eyes with each of the men running this place.

"That graveyard we just came through? Not on the maps. I would bet my bottom dollar that the tour companies would love to tell their ghost stories here. The sister graveyard to Bonaventure Cemetery, emerged from the shadows," I made a rainbow shape with one hand, as if seeing the name in lights. "None of us have signed NDAs that I know of. Any of you?"

I turned to the kids. Blue Eyes leaned forward. "What's an NDA?"

"A non-disclosure agreement. Employers have you sign them when they want sensitive information kept from the public, or competitors. Did you sign one?" I asked again.

They all shook their heads. I smiled and looked Louis in the eye. "So. A grand a week? Plus, expenses for all the equipment we will need to be trained properly. I wouldn't want to overlook that. So, an initial amount of…" I looked to Eammon. "Hey, boss, how much should initial setup be for each of us?"

Eammon's eyes glittered with humor. "Easily two thousand dollars for the higher end…equipment."

"Excellent. So, upon signing the NDA and our work contracts, we will receive not only our first week's wages, but the two thousand dollars needed for our equipment." I didn't move from my spot in the middle of the kids. Jesus, they would have been eaten alive without me. Maybe literally.

Louis pursed his already thin lips. "I'm not sure I like you anymore."

"We're going to work together," I said, not sure of that in the least, but I was bluffing all the way now. "Wouldn't you rather work with someone who has a shrewd brain? And remember that these negotiation skills will at some point work in your favor."

"Give them the money," Tom said with a shake of his head. "I'm tired and my bones are aching. A storm is coming in off the water."

Louis spluttered, snorted, and grumbled the whole way, but in the end, we signed the work contracts and NDAs that they apparently had ready, and were each handed three thousand dollars in cash.

Talk about a sweet way to end the weirdest night of my life.

Then again, the next morning wasn't a whole lot better in terms of weirdness.

6

The next morning, I rolled onto my side in a bed that was not really mine, in a home that belonged to Corb, to get a blast of dog breath in my face. When had Corb gotten a dog? Was I not at his house? Sleep confusion made my brain fuzzy and uncertain, except for one undeniable fact. That breath was rank.

"Get out of here," I grumbled and pushed blindly at the offending face, my hand going deep into a mouth full of tongue and teeth. I opened one eye and yelped, scrambling back from the wolf looking straight at me. The night before came rushing back, the night that I had partially thought I could chalk up to having eaten some sort of accidental hallucinogen.

Apparently not.

"Sarge," I croaked his name out through a dry mouth and probably nearly as bad breath. "What are you doing here?"

His wolf eyebrows rose, and he shook his head.

The thing was, Corb's place was in downtown Savannah, on east Perry, not far from the Colonial Park Cemetery. I mean, really there was no place in Savannah that was far from some sort of cemetery or graveyard, it was just a matter of knowing where you stood. And who you stood on. That wasn't the point, though, of my rambling.

The point was that there was a wolf. In a loft. In the middle of downtown super busy Savannah and I was struggling to understand how he'd gotten in unseen. "Did Corb let you in?"

Sarge grinned and his tongue lolled out, along with that rumbling voice that made me think of Gmork. "I was hoping for a better scream than that, but I'll take it."

He turned and trotted out of my room, the sound of four heavy feet shifting partway down the hall to a lighter tread, quiet, and fewer feet.

Fewer feet? Of course, he had a human form too. My gran would have had a field day with what had happened last night, and even more fun with this wolf that was not a wolf. What had she called them? Half-men.

I frowned, reached for the clock on the side table, and stared at the time. Noon.

Eammon had said training didn't start until six at night, which meant I had time to get some of my equipment.

"Shouldn't you be helping your trainee?" I yelled down the hall.

"He's still sleeping," Sarge yelled back, his voice clearer than before. Sharper, crisper. I tried to sit up and groaned.

Everything hurt. Whimpering, I rolled onto my belly, and my lower back reminded me I didn't flex that way anymore. More whimpering ensued, cursing of my body.

I surely did not bounce back like I had in my twenties. I wasn't the most fit I'd been in my life, I knew I had an extra twenty pounds or so on me—okay, maybe thirty. Probably would have been more if any of my pregnancies had gone past the twelve-week mark. I liked good food. My job as a dog groomer kept me moving every day, though, and while I didn't have time to go to the gym—or the inclination—I was active.

Apparently, that was not going to be enough for working at the Hollows, and I knew that it was time to get into better shape. My head filled slowly with the memories of training with Gran, of the things she'd tried to teach me.

A good deal of the time she'd spent with me, I'd been only half paying attention, especially through my teen years—typical child who thought I knew everything.

I'd met Himself when I was seventeen, and he'd pushed the idea that she was losing it even then. I ignored the things I did see, pretending I didn't see them at all. But Gran had kept trying.

Sighing, I lay there and cursed myself soundly for all the stupid mistakes I'd made. Some of them with my eyes wide open. Like Himself, one of my biggest mistakes. I closed my eyes, trying not to think about how I'd fought to keep the marriage together when I should have let it die. I kept thinking that a child was what we needed, but no pregnancy stayed with me. Not one. That had been the reason I'd stayed longer, because who else would want me? Nope, I was not going there.

"Won't be doing that again," I muttered.

"Doing what?" Sarge called out.

"Marriage," I mumbled, somehow knowing that he'd hear me.

"Cynical much?" he threw back.

I almost responded "Older and wiser" but figured I didn't want to reinforce the (true) perception that I was older than everyone else I was working with except the mentors.

Still, it took me longer than I wanted to admit to climb out of bed, scrounge through my meager clothes, find and put on a bra. No point in letting the girls dangle out the bottom of my shirt. A T-shirt and my capris from the night before followed. That much accomplished, I hobbled down the hall to the kitchen, feeling every step along the way in my calves, thighs, and rear end. At the entry into the kitchen, I leaned against the edge of the doorframe, the old brick wall digging into my bare arm.

A man with his back to me stood at the stove, cooking bacon and eggs by the smell of it. And when I say he had his back to me, I mean he had his bare back to me, just the barest hint of waistband showing that he wasn't completely naked. His *bare* back with a giant wolf tattooed across muscles that had no right to look so chiseled. Light from the big windows behind us played across those muscles, beckoning me to run my fingers over them, maybe take a bite and see if the muscles were as hard as they looked.

Have I mentioned that my hormones were in overdrive? Like, I'd never had a libido like this in my life, not even when I was young and stupidly wild for Himself. I blew out a slow breath, trying to calm the twisting in my belly that wanted so very badly to see if the front half of the man looked as good as the back half.

He glanced over his shoulder, and I got a glimmer of amber eyes that had been in a wolf's face just a moment before. "You eat meat, right?"

While I'd known what he was—a half-man, a type of shifter—I needed a minute to compute everything. And to remind myself that he was not flirting with me.

"Yes," I managed to croak out through the gutter that was my mind, then turned and walked—okay, limped—back into my tiny room that had been an office just a week before. I'd helped Corb clean it out enough that I could use the fold-out bed. That's what you get when your world is turned upside down. You end up in the office of someone who doesn't particularly even like you.

I shut the door and leaned back on it, tipping my head up. It felt like the wood floor under my bare feet was moving, as if the ground itself were trying to throw me off balance.

I swallowed hard and blew out a slow breath. Shifters or half-men, they weren't uncommon in Savannah, but Gran had kept me from them when I was younger. Her fear was that if I was bitten, I'd be taken from her.

I looked at my hand that I'd just unintentionally shoved into Sarge's mouth, then stood and went to wash my skin again. Just in case.

The desire to go home and lick your wounds was strong, a drive that my therapist had pointed out to me more than once when I'd been fighting to keep my marriage afloat. Every part of my head said this more than any other reason was why I'd come to Savannah, to where my gran was buried. I'd wanted to capture some of the magic of my childhood. To feel young again. To feel like I still had some magic inside of me somewhere. To remind myself I still had living left to do after forty. I could still hang with the big dogs.

I just really hadn't expected all of this to be so damn literal.

Everything that had happened the night before was real—I could feel it in my aching bones and my muscles reminding me I was not in shape in any sense of the word unless round-ish and slightly squishy counted as a shape.

But that didn't make me want to run, which I was pretty sure had been the crux of the test last night. The five men—Eammon, Sarge, Corb, Louis, and Tom—they wanted to throw us off balance to see how we handled change, to see what we did. To see which one of the interviewees would break under the pressure of having their world tipped upside down.

Joke was on them. I'd been living with a quasi-demon for years; last night was nothing.

I pressed fingers on either side of the bridge of my nose even as I smiled to myself.

A tap on the door. "You okay, Bree?" Sarge's voice was not a wolf's now. He was a man. A very handsome man with a back I wanted to run my fingers over.

Don't judge, you'd have wanted to touch too.

But he'd been a wolf ten minutes ago. I increased the pressure on the bridge of my nose.

"Just give me a minute," I said.

"You're freaking out."

"Maybe a little. I'll be fine. It's one thing to know something in your heart, another to have it make you breakfast."

He laughed and I focused on the sound of him walking away. "I'm banking on you being fine," he said.

Nope, I was not going to be that person who, when confronted with change, got her panties in a wad and couldn't deal. This was in my blood. Gran had always said that, and I could feel it now that I was back. Now that the spell was gone from me that kept me from seeing.

I blew the last of the nerves out and shook the tingles from my arms. I needed this job, and I was uniquely qualified, more so than any of the others who had been there last night. I was going to blow through the twelve weeks of training like it was nothing.

Sending Sarge to me, having him change from wolf to man…that had been a purposeful scare tactic, and I had no doubt it was Corb's doing.

I'd show him just how many ducks I had to give.

I headed back to the kitchen, but this time I pulled out a barstool and sat. Sarge was at the stove again, a pair of low-slung jogging pants hanging precariously off his slim hips. I fanned myself as my eyes traced the lines of his back, my face, chest and pretty much entire body heating up about ten degrees as I all but drooled watching him cook. Yup, he could give Corb a run for his money. Hell, with the way my libido was running, I'd give them both a run for their money.

I waited for him to speak first, not bothered by the silence one bit. Also trying to calm my hormones.

He cleared his throat after a solid minute of silence. "So. Tell me how Eammon convinced you to come to the interview." Sarge pulled a plate out of the cupboard and dished up a good amount of bacon, eggs, and a slice of toast slathered in butter. Not too dark. He pushed the plate across to me and leaned on his hands on the counter, that was how tall he was. Damn it, I was having a hard time looking at the food as my eyes traced his upper body, lingering on those very big arms. And he cooked. Himself had never cooked so much as a hot dog for me.

Did I mention I have a thing for well-muscled men's arms? Yup, I do.

I took a piece of bacon and bit through it, then used the remainder as if it were a pointer stick. "You know how it goes. Girl gets dumped by her husband, said ex dumps all the debt he's accrued onto her, and then the debt collectors come calling. The ex also took my gran's house, which is here in Savannah. I plan to get it back. Basically, I came here to get my life together."

"Right, but about Eammon, how did that happen?"

I took another bite and grabbed a fork. Cold eggs were a no-go for me, so I needed to get on them before they cooled.

"Eammon came by to talk to Corb. Eammon took an immediate interest in me. I thought he was just being an old flirt. Corb left the room to get some paperwork, and Eammon said he wanted to talk to me about a job, but that Corb wouldn't like it if I talked to him. He suggested we meet at Vic's Restaurant. Nice place that, good food, and I wasn't going to pass up a free meal."

I took another bite, swallowing the still-hot eggs quickly. "So, we met there, and we chatted a bit about the Irish down here. Our families.

Then he said he'd overheard me talking about a job that wasn't going to pay well, that I needed more money." I shoveled in a couple more bites, savoring the spices he'd put on the eggs. He was a good cook, even if it was simple fare. I wouldn't kick him out of the kitchen. Or bed.

"What did he tell you, though?" Sarge leaned forward.

"About the job?" I laid my utensils down. "That it was hard, possibly dangerous, and dealt a great deal with the mythology and superstitions of the area. I made an assumption that it was a new kind of tour, considering we were starting at the graveyard. Even if the money seemed stupidly high for a tourism job." Though, I'd put that aside quickly once I realized Robert was a real skeleton.

Sarge frowned, and even that looked nice on his face. "But why'd you take it all in stride? The others freaked out, just like people always freak out as they start seeing things that their minds say aren't supposed to be real. I think you might be the first person who didn't lose their marbles even a little."

That wasn't entirely true; I'd almost lost it with Robert at the beginning. And I hadn't much liked facing down a ravening wolf, although it didn't seem polite to say so to his face.

I picked up the toast and took a bite. "I grew up here, with my gran. My parents died when I was young." I felt like that should explain it all. I wasn't about to tell him how they'd died. That was not something I wanted to remember.

70

Sarge made a go-on gesture with one hand. I sighed. "When I was little, she'd take me around town and point things out. And…I could see them." I wasn't about to tell him that I'd ended up in a psych ward for "seeing the bogeyman" and Gran spelling me so I was unable to see the shadow world anymore.

"See them?" His eyebrows were high.

"Don't you get all judgy on me, man who is also a wolf. Half-man." I all but spat the words at him around a mouthful of toast. "Also, do you know where the ibuprofen is? I'm hurting after last night."

Sarge scrounged in a cupboard near the stove and came down with a handful of over-the-counter drugs. I searched through until I found some Advil, popped two, considered it and popped a third, then dry-swallowed them.

He waited for me to keep talking, and I shrugged again. "I left at eighteen, married shortly thereafter, and never came back. I couldn't afford to, there was no money." I paused and stared at my mostly empty plate, thinking about Gran, about the few times I'd seen her between then and now. We'd talked on the phone at least once a week, always when Himself wasn't around. Life was easier that way. "When I stepped into the graveyard last night, it was like I was ten years old again. I could see the monsters."

There, I'd said it out loud. Notice I didn't mention the prayer I'd muttered at the gate, or the additional training that Gran had arranged for me over the years I'd lived with her. I had to have some ammo for later.

"Like the skeleton," Sarge said.

"Yes! You saw him?"

He raised a hand to the left side of his head. "He bit my ear off. I saw him just fine. But Louis is right, they don't have names."

"Well, maybe they'd be nicer if you gave them a name."

He brushed his hand over his intact ear. Of course, there was no missing ear there now. It had grown back, I guess. Half-men were known for their superior healing abilities. "So why are you here peppering me with questions instead of Eammon? Isn't he supposed to be my Obi-wan Kenobi?"

He winked. "More like your Yoda if we're basing it off looks and age. And normally, yes, he would be here. But...as you saw, my trainee about shot me last night, so Eammon and I are going to switch trainees for a few days. Which means you've got me to go shopping with." He turned his arm over as if checking a watch that didn't exist, and even went the extra mile and tapped his bare wrist. "Speaking of, we need to get going. The market is only open for select hours each week."

I shoved the last of the toast in my mouth, cheeks puffed out with too much food. His eyebrows stayed up as I spoke around the partially chewed toast. "Two minutes." He might be hot, but I knew I had no chance with him, so I didn't really care what he thought of me. And I loved perfectly toasted toast. I hurried back to my room to gather up the money I had. I left the thousand bucks that was my first week's wages.

I'd have to give most of it to Corb for staying here. And eating his food. And making his date run off before he could get any. I grinned. This day was looking up. I was about to go on a shopping date with what I could only say was a very handsome werewolf.

Back in the main room, Sarge stood with his hands tucked into the pockets of a pair of jeans. He'd found a white T-shirt that I was sure was one of Corb's and a pair of boots to go with the clothes.

He crooked his finger at me. "Let's go get you stuff."

Stuff.

Equipment. Right. If only I knew what all I was going to need.

Go with the flow. Don't freak out. Change is good.

I hurried after him down the stairs, his long legs easily outstripping mine. "Sarge, what is it we do exactly? What am I being trained for, because I'm pretty sure it's not a new kind of ghost tour?"

He held the door at the bottom of the stairs, and I stepped into the humid air that could only be springtime in Savannah. I drew in a big breath, feeling a rush of fondness for this place I'd loved so much as a kid. The smell of a heck-a-lot of flowers coated the air in sweetness that some people might find cloying. I loved it.

I shook my head. "Sarge? The job, what does it entail? Because the shadow world is a lot more than ghost tours." How much would he tell me? Did I trust him? The answer to that was not really.

I was not some high-school girl ready to trust a big strapping man with flashy white teeth and pretty eyes. More likely I'd end up kicking him at some point in the day while I enunciated a big word for him just to see if he knew what it meant.

I could be mean like that when cranky and sore.

"Well, it's kind of like an odd jobs company. We do a little of this, and a little of that. Get paid on a job-to-job basis. That can be good, it can be bad. If you get a good reputation, more jobs will come your way with bigger paydays attached to them. Get a crappy reputation, and not so much." He pointed at a big motorcycle propped up against the curb. No helmets on it that I could see.

"Safety first, I guess?" I couldn't keep the sarcasm out of my voice.

He grunted. "I don't break if I fall. And the cops won't bother us. They know me."

But I *would* break. I had a moment there on the sidewalk where a rush of panic bit at me, reminding me that I was not twenty. I wasn't even thirty. I'd been out of this world a long time, and it could be dangerous.

One of Gran's friends had been a cop back in the day. He'd done a little work with me. Taught me a few things about clearing spaces, guns, basic safety around bad guys. Or, in my case, the shadow world. Officer Jonathan would have a fit if he saw me riding without a helmet.

Sarge sat first, and I snapped myself out of it and scrambled up behind him, feeling every bit as self-conscious as one does when pressing her rapidly overheating lady parts against the backside of a very hot guy who is easily ten years her junior.

He leaned the bike so that he was taking the balance and I got my feet up on the footrests.

"You better hang on!" he said as he started the engine. It rumbled up through my butt and along my spine in a not unpleasant way. I reached around his very tight waist and locked my fingers together, my nose pressed against his back. I turned my face to the side and found myself looking up at the windows of Corb's loft.

Corb was standing there in shorts and not much else. Yup, he could give Sarge a run for his money. I kissed my fingers and wiggled them at Corb as Sarge's bike rolled forward. I leaned my cheek against his back and hung on as tightly as I could as we rode away, and just about every dirty fantasy I could think up rolled through my less than virginal mind.

Yes, it was going to be a good day. That's what I thought.

Except that's not what the fates of Savannah had in store for me.

7

The store that Sarge took me to was not really a store so much as a bazaar down on the waterfront along the river. River Street was loaded with tourist shops, and it was not where I'd expected to go.

Not that there was a proper entryway to said bazaar. I'll get to that in a minute.

He parked the bike on the water side of the street and popped the keys into the front pocket of his jeans as he stepped off the bike.

I sat there looking around as casually as I could, then slowly slid off. My knees hurt from being cramped up even for that short ride and I fought to keep them from dropping me onto the cobblestones.

"You okay?" Sarge held out a hand as I stood there with my knees fighting me. Finally, the blood flow got going and I reached out and took his offered hand.

"Yup, fine. But you can hold my hand if you want."

He blinked down at my fingers that he was currently holding. I thought he'd fling my hand away—Himself had done that more than once—and I was secretly pleased when he lifted my hand and tucked it into the crook of his arm. "Southern charm is not dead after all," I said.

Sarge flashed me a grin. "No, it just takes a wolf to remember how old he is and that ladies like to be treated as such."

Wait, what? How old was he? He looked younger than me.

"What?"

He leaned close. "Do half-men age like the rest of the world? I think you know the answer to that."

My gran's book had said not so much. A 1-10 ratio. My jaw dropped. Depending on when he was turned, he could easily be the oldest mentor of the group.

He laughed as he led me across the road to the storefronts teeming with tourists. Candy and toys, clothing, mugs, and everything in between. There was no shortage of kitschy stuff. I barely saw it as I let my mind drift along the fact that Sarge could easily be over a hundred. Again, depending on when he was turned into a werewolf.

I tried to slow him down, the questions burning on the tip of my tongue. But the direction we were going distracted me completely. "Really, this is where we need to buy stuff?"

With a flex of his bicep, he tightened his hold on me. "It's a trick of the eye, just stay with me."

A set of stairs led up from the waterfront—straight up. I grimaced and tried not to think about the stairs even while I was trying desperately not to huff my way up them, one hand still locked against his arm, which made it all that much harder. Near the top, he was almost dragging me up each step, and I'll be honest, I let him.

At the top of what were too many, and too big of stairs, even with his help, my legs shook like crazy jelly once more. Sarge didn't seem to notice as he dragged me along to a storefront that I was not terribly shocked to see.

Madame Trebon's Tarot Readings. Tarot card readings in Savannah are like casinos in Vegas. One on every corner.

Sarge let himself in and a soft chime went off. An older-than-me woman stepped through a set of beads hanging in a doorway leading out of the main room. Her long gray hair was braided to one side and hung over her shoulder. Crisp blue eyes stared not at Sarge, but at me.

"Who did you bring in now, wolf? I just saw Eammon and a new one that won't last a week if I'm seeing things right. Poor lad."

Sarge grimaced and muttered under his breath before he tipped his head to me. "This is Breena. Breena, this is Annie."

He took my hand and showed me off to her, even sending me into a short twirl. I grimaced as I fumbled through the turn but managed to stay on my feet.

I couldn't resist flipping my free hand out and backhanding him in the abs. "Knock that off. I'm not yours to be showing off. Or Eammon's, for that matter."

Annie let out a laugh that turned into a full-blown cackle. "Oh, Sarge, you're in trouble, pup. This one has teeth."

She took a few steps forward. I had to give her credit; she was dressed the part of a classic tarot reader in a flowing, deep burgundy dress that covered whatever shape she had underneath. Thin and gauzy, the material floated around her as she moved. Her clothes were likely far more comfortable than anyone else's in the growing heat.

April it might be, but that meant nothing in the South. I had acclimated to Seattle weather, and now Savannah's early spring felt like summer to me.

Annie tipped her head to one side, a silent request that I recognized as she motioned for me to move to her table pressed up along the wall. I barely glanced at it, then back to her as she spoke. "I do a single pull for every trainee that comes through for the Hollows. Once you get your gear, you come on back up, and we'll do that for you. See if we can figure out your path."

"Long as you only pull a good card," I said.

"Oh, honey, they're all good. Just depends on what you make of them." She gave me a wink with oversized false lashes. As she smiled, the lines in her face showed that she'd done a lot of smiling in her life. I'd take that as a good sign. I paused, thinking about my gran's two best friends, Hattie and Missy. For some reason, this Annie made me think of them—likely it was the tarot cards as Hattie had often done readings for me when I'd lived here.

It struck me then that I could stay with Hattie instead of Corb. Maybe he'd go easier on me if I wasn't in his house. At least it was an idea.

Sarge gave me a tug, pulling me out of my thoughts, and I followed him through the beads, feeling Annie's eyes on me. We went through the back room which smelled like too many herbs and not enough fresh air, to a set of descending stairs. And I mean straight down.

"Seriously?" I pointed at the impossibly steep stairwell. "Why is there not a ground-level entrance?"

Sarge shrugged and flicked on an overhead light. "Don't ask me. I just shop here."

I sighed and followed him down. "This would have been easier as a ladder."

"Not when you're hauling a hundred pounds of stuff up the ladder."

He had a point.

At the bottom of the stairs—such as they were—was nothing but a six-by-six space in front of a cobblestone wall. The stones had a variety of images on them, thirteen to be exact. A few stood out, like the four elements—water, wind, fire, earth. There was a raven as well as a sword. Some were more faded as if they'd been inscribed a long time ago and hadn't been kept up.

Some of the images were painted rather than engraved.

Sarge grinned and tapped on the cobblestone wall just under the raven symbol. The stone depressed, completely disappeared, and there was a low clunking noise as if it had dropped into a metal barrel.

"Harry Potter much?" I muttered as the cobblestone wall slid out and sideways on silent casters that had either seen a lot of grease or were far newer than the wall looked. Again, Sarge led the way, this time into…I shook my head and blinked a few times at the enormous space that stretched out in front of us. We were still inside, but the ceiling had been mocked up to look like a night sky, complete with glowing stars, the moon, and even a few dark spots that had to be bats.

And then one of them moved, and I realized they *were* bats—bats on leashes.

Jaysus Murphy on a three-legged donkey.

Gran had never mentioned this place. Maybe it was after her time? Somehow, I didn't think so. Maybe this was one of those things you get to see after you're inducted fully into the shadow world. That last was more likely.

Vendors sat at tables arranged along one side of the "street," a stretch that had to go the length of the entire street outside. Behind each vendor was a door. If I had to guess, I'd say they each led into the back of a ground-level shop.

No way was I doing those stairs again.

A distinct smell of herbs, grease, wood fires and something I couldn't quite put my finger on floated on a breeze that was not possible. I mean, it wasn't like there were air ducts. This was a full-on breeze blowing my hair back.

Sarge motioned for me to go ahead of him. "Pick out what you like."

"How about what I need?" I said.

"Whatever you like." He waved a hand at the vendors. "Whatever you can afford."

Damn it, so he wasn't going to help me.

"What do I *need*, half-man?" I asked again.

"Why do you keep calling me that?" Sarge frowned down at me, a glimmer of too-white teeth showing in the starlight.

Okay, fake starlight. Real bats. It was a trip.

"My gran used to call those who could slip their skin half-men. Fitting, don't you think?" I looked up at him with one brow slightly arched more than the other.

"Makes me think it was an insult," he grumbled.

"You mean like you only have one ball instead of two? Or can only get it up half the time?" I shrugged. "It's possible she meant that, she was a wicked woman in her own way." With that, I left him standing there, his eyes a little too narrowed and his breathing a little too quick. Irritated he might be, but damn him if he was going to make this more difficult.

I went to the first vendor and looked over what he had, not really understanding what I was looking at. Trinkets? There were nicely decorated boxes of all sorts and sizes, but I doubted they'd help me at my new job. I waved a hand at them.

"What have you got here?"

The vendor leaned forward. "Name is Bob-John. And I sell powders. Mostly clearing powders. A few others too, communication and such."

That rang a bell, but I didn't think Gran had covered it with me, or if she had it had been brief. I didn't think clearing powder would help me with training. "You get many trainees for the Hollows Group come through here?"

Bob-John nodded. "A few. You want to know which tables they visited?"

"That would be great, thanks."

"It'll cost you."

No surprise there. I narrowed my eyes. I wasn't about to give him money for nothing. "How much is your clearing powder?"

He blinked. "Ten a box."

"I'll buy one, and you'll tell me where the others went." I pulled a ten out of my pocket and held it out to him. He took hold of it, but I didn't let go.

"You don't need his stuff!" Sarge yelled.

I kept my eyes on Bob-John. "Think I should listen to him? Or are you smarter than the wolf over there?"

Bob-John puffed up a little under what he no doubt assumed was praise. "Weapons, armor, spells, all the attack stuff," he said. "But if you ask me, a few books wouldn't be a bad idea too. Maybe a bit more smarts in you than the usual lugs they bring through."

I let the ten-dollar bill go and held my hand out. He plunked a rhinestone-encrusted box into my palm, and I tucked it into my other pocket. "Thanks, Bob-John. Nice doing business with you."

Bob-John slid back into his chair which put him into the shadows a bit, and I continued on down the street.

I passed by a table with a lot of dried dead things on it, including several chicken feet and a stack of mummified mice. The next was a table with piles of tarot cards and crystals, none of which I considered necessary for my training. But the next table and vendor were interesting, and I found myself pausing there. The table was strewn with leather of all colors and shapes, along with chunks of a variety of metals, none of it in any particular order.

"Scraps?" I ran my hand over a particularly soft piece of leather that felt more like velvet than something that had once been an animal hide. Light tan in color, it could be dyed to be any shade under the rainbow.

A slim woman stepped forward. The hard lines around her eyes told me she was at least my age, although more likely in her fifties. "You are not the usual type they bring through." She tipped her head toward Sarge trailing me by about fifteen feet. Watching, but not helping.

I looked over my shoulder at him, still irritated by his unwillingness to help. "Sit. Stay."

He hunched his shoulders and glowered at me but didn't come any closer. The woman laughed softly, though there was some grit to her voice, like maybe she didn't smoke now, but used to.

She squinted one eye at me. "You are interesting. I would like to make you something. You need all of it."

"All of what?" I frowned at her. "You want to fill me in?"

"Stupid men thinking they are being smart by keeping secrets. Do they not know that women are like badgers? We will find all the secrets and then share them with each other."

Yup, I liked her already. I leaned forward.

"Right? Seriously, how long do they think they can keep us from knowing…stuff?" Stuff, yes, that was about as pithy as it came.

"Hold out your hands. I must measure you for this."

I did as she asked, without knowing why, and she stepped around her table, a piece of string between her hands. She held it up to me, across my chest, around my waist, from my hip to the ground, around my neck.

"You will be good for them, I think," the woman said. "My name is Geraldine; my friends call me Gerry. I will make your workwear for you. Boots too." She pointed at my runners. I looked down.

"What will it cost?"

85

"What did they give you to spend?" She cocked her head to the side.

"Not enough." I smiled.

She sighed. "It is never enough. But you will show them how this is done. I want it to be in my clothes. Five hundred."

"For one outfit with boots?" That seemed cheap for something custom-made.

"I cannot go lower. And you are a fool if you think it is acceptable to cheap out on this portion of your equipment."

I held up my hands. "Actually, I thought it was too low."

Her lips quirked. "Excellent. Five hundred then?"

I held out my hand and we shook on it. I gave her the money even as Sarge groaned behind me. "How soon can you have it ready?" I asked.

"An hour."

My eyes about bugged out. "An hour?"

"It will be done before you are finished shopping for the other things you need." She shooed me away with her hands, all but pushing me down the street.

As I moved away from her, Sarge draped an arm over my shoulders, warmth flowing from him all the way through me. It was nice, until he opened his mouth. "Now that is such a typical move for a woman. Clothing? You spent a quarter of what you have on clothing. You should have spent it on weapons."

I snorted and pushed his arm off. "Such a typical move for a man. Maybe if *someone* was helping me,

86

I would have. But I like Gerry, and she's going to do an excellent job. I have no doubt."

He snorted. "Gerry is not your friend."

I snorted right back at him. He wouldn't understand how it could be between women. We had each other's backs, especially when large, egotistical men were involved.

The next vendor I stopped at had the biggest setup in the street.

Four tables full of weapons from the tiniest of knives to some seriously big guns that looked as though they could take down an elephant. I paused there. The shadow world was dangerous, but more so when you drew attention to yourself, which meant quiet weapons were best.

More for defense than anything else in my opinion—which was really Gran's opinion.

I drew closer to the first table and let my hand drift over some of the steel blades. And frowned. There were hairline cracks in several of them. In fact, every weapon I looked at had some terrible flaw that really didn't impress me. Maybe this was the cheap stuff, though, maybe the good stuff was in the back.

Moving to the next table of weapons, I looked for the vendor. Make that vendors. A pair of twins, to be exact.

Both were quite beefy, almost as wide as they were tall, and they had matching blond beards that hung to their chests. The pair of them looked rounder than the Vikings in documentaries and movies, but otherwise they fit the image, down to metal chain-mail they wore over their tan shirts.

One of the other trainees was already there, haggling with them. The girl who'd been making eyes at Corb as if he were the last man on earth and she was ovulating and eager to pop out a mini-Corb.

"Hey!" I called out to her. She looked at me and quickly turned her back on me. As if I didn't exist.

It was going to be like that, was it? I did a quick scan for her trainer and found Corb hanging back in the shadows. I frowned. "How the hell did they get here ahead of us?"

Sarge snickered. "They probably used the street-level doors."

I spun and punched him in the chest, right in the old breadbasket. He let out an oof and took a couple of steps back, and my clenched fist immediately throbbed as though I'd punched a wall rather than a block of muscle. But it was worth it for the low chuckle that rolled from Corb as he drew close.

"Sarge, seems you've pissed her off already. I have to say, well done. She hasn't even taken a swing at me yet."

I shook my head. "He's lovely to look at, Corb, but really, your friend is kind of a dick. And not the good kind of dick. A bit on the limp side."

Corb would have made a better poker player than most, except that I saw the smile in his eyes while his lips fought it off. He cleared his throat. "We aren't allowed to help, Bree. You have to do this on your own too. All part of seeing how you can handle things as they come up."

"Yeah, well, that would be great if I knew what the job really entailed, right? Different jobs require different tools," I said, my voice sharp. Damn it, there was a bit of Gran in both words and tone. I shook off a wash of nostalgia and started toward the weapons vendors. Fine, if they weren't going to tell me, I needed to get items that would work across the board. "All right, what have you two got for me?"

The two oversized Viking-esque vendors ignored me and kept on fawning over the pretty young thing beside me. I snapped my fingers in front of me. Nothing. "I might as well not even be here, hey?"

There had to be more than one way to skin this cat. They had to have competition.

I turned and started down the false street, walking to the end looking for said competition, but there was none. I snagged a great leather bag to replace the one I'd lost out in the graveyard and a new set of lock picks that I got for a song. At another table, I snagged a new flashlight that apparently was good under water for a mere fifteen bucks.

I'd passed a book vendor, which I planned to return to, but I needed to get some protection before I bought any books.

But there were no more weapons vendors. Not a single knife on any of the other tables. Really?

I had a hard time believing that. I went back to the beginning, to Bob-John. "Hey, BJ."

Bob-John lifted his head and stepped forward. "More clearing powder?"

I shook my head. "Only one weapons table?"

He looked past me to Sarge. I turned around to see him narrow his eyes at Bob-John, making Bob-John shake his head quickly. Then he mouthed one word. "Later." Interesting.

"Thanks." I slid another ten to Bob-John, and he passed me another rhinestone-encrusted box of something that I put in my new bag, and then continued on my way, thinking about just what I was going to do about this. I needed weapons—something I was still wrapping my head around—and I didn't like the thought of buying one of the knock-offs sold by the Vikings.

I paused at the one table near the end of the walk loaded with books. This was Bob-John's suggestion, and even if he hadn't encouraged me, I would have come here, drawn by the stacks of books. Books upon books, piled high and spread out all around on the ground as if they'd just poured out of the wall behind the table. I bent and picked up a thin book.

I read the title out loud. "*Avoid Becoming A Vampire*. Really? Is it that difficult?"

A round little man no taller than Eammon stepped around the table. His cheeks were bright pink, and his eyes had a deep purple tone. He moved in a way that reminded me of Eammon, kind of a strut with his chest puffed up. "Yes, not been a problem in a few years, but doesn't hurt to be careful."

Jaysus. My gut did a funny little twist that made me feel like the ground was moving again, right under my feet. What the hell, were vampires real? Gran had not mentioned vampires in any of our discussions. Maybe like this place, she wasn't going to mention the really ugly stuff until after I agreed to stay, or whatever it was she had been waiting for.

Little idiot, you're hanging out with a werewolf and talked to a living skeleton last night. Of course there are vampires!

Right, I had to remember I most certainly was not in Seattle anymore. I was in Savannah. Land of the dead. Land of the supernatural, despite what the upper crust might want the world to believe.

I cleared my throat. "Well, what would you recommend for a newbie?" I said. "Working at the Hollows Group is the plan."

"Ahh, here, I have a few. You are the first in a long time to ask. Most just get weapons and armor and think they be done." Yes, there was some Irish in his voice for sure. "Smart of you. Then again, you got a few years on most."

"Thanks for noticing," I said dryly.

He rifled through a pile of books that was taller than him, and pulled out three thin books, plus one that had to be a thousand pages that he set aside. The bigger book was wrapped in red leather with moons and stars embossed deep into the spine and front cover. I *knew* that book.

It was Gran's. My heart picked up speed and I fought to quell it. "Where did you get that one?"

He pushed it under the stack and handed the rest to me. "These will give you great insights into world of grave magic and shadows." I took note that he didn't answer the question about my gran's book.

I didn't want to seem too eager. I took a quick glance at the titles now that they were in my hands. They would be good. One was about all the things not to do in the shadow world—basic etiquette, if you will—the second one was all about finding loopholes with various creatures, and the last was a guide to understanding curses.

I could almost hear my gran cackling with excitement. She'd have loved these books.

But not as much as she'd loved hers.

Time to bring on the negotiations. I'd seen Himself mediate enough divorces with a skill that even I had to give him, that I knew I could make this happen.

I crouched down in front of him and tapped the three smaller books in my hand. "How much? I'm not sure my trainer will care if I have them or not."

He curled his lips up and stroked his face as if he wore a mustache that was most obviously not there. "The three smalls? Let's say twenty. There are many of them out there, nothing special about them."

Fair enough. "Okay, that's doable." I paused in handing over the twenty. "What about that one, there? The one with the red leather?"

He turned to look at it. "That big one, that one is expensive. One of a kind, written by a great woman.

I bought it when she died. Mind you, you'd never need another book."

Shortly after Himself had forged his way to the deed of her house, he'd sold everything he could right out from under me. You see, I wasn't making up the bit about him being like a demon. The bastard was all about greed and selfishness.

"That one…fifteen hundred." He put his hand on it. "One of a kind, I can only sell it once."

I rocked back on my heels. "It's special to you? Did you know her?"

His face was thoughtful before he answered. "She was a friend. Much knowledge is in there." His pudgy fingers gripped it a little tighter and for just a second he narrowed his eyes at me, but it happened so fast, I'm not sure if I was seeing things or not.

"I'll make you a deal," I said. "Half the price, and I'll let you come and read it if you're stuck on something. I'll lend it to you."

"Half price? That is not a deal for me."

I shrugged. "How many people are going to let you have a look at it when you need it?"

His eyes narrowed and I could see the wheels turning with what I'd said. "Twelve-fifty."

I grimaced and turned partially away, paused and looked over my shoulder. "Eight-fifty."

His hand stroked the cover. "My bottom would be eleven hundred."

My guts twisted up because that was a lot of money still, but I knew it would be worth it for Gran's book. That was the book she'd trained me from, in which she'd taken notes, journaled…everything. Everything she knew about the shadow world was in there.

It was the closest I'd come to getting her back.

I made another face and tried to think of something I could offer him besides money. "What about…eight hundred"—I held up a hand as he spluttered, understandable seeing as I'd gone down with the amount— "and a favor once I'm all trained up."

His eyes lit up. "A favor?"

I nodded. "Once I'm trained. One job that falls under my training, free of charge."

"Eight hundred and one favor," he said. "That's still a deal for you."

"It is not a deal." Sarge came up behind me—too late—as I counted out the bills and handed them over. "And you're a fool to think of it as such."

The little man huffed and puffed and scurried right up to Sarge's legs, shoving his barrel chest against the bigger man's knees. "You are the fool, wolf boy! This one at least knows where to spend her money."

Sarge snarled and I took a few steps back as they parried words.

"Shrimp."

"Dog brain."

I ignored both of them and picked up the book. I flipped open the red leather cover. I was a reader, after all, and the book called to me not just because it was Gran's. I breathed in the scent of old paper and a hint of perfume. Lavender and sage. It smelled like Gran, and that brought a lump to my throat that I struggled to breathe around.

"Lovely," I whispered. The first few pages were written in calligraphy, and as I flipped through the book I marveled at the precision and detail within. A thousand pages all done by hand, all done by Gran's hand.

"Here, you sign this." A piece of paper was shoved into my hand along with an ink-dipped quill pen.

I _____ do hereby give Oster Boon a single favor to help cover the cost of the book of Celia O'Rylee.

I filled in my name in the blank spot and signed beneath it, impressed that he'd done it up so fast. Then again, it was likely a leprechaun thing. As a part-time law clerk for Himself, I could see there was nothing funny about the paper. It was a simple contract.

He held his hand out, and the paper floated through the air to him, reminding me of that scene in *The Little Mermaid* where Ariel signed her voice away for legs. "Good deal. I look forward to doing business with you again." He clenched his fist and the paper disappeared with a burst of sparkles, as if it had burned up. Yup, he was definitely the Ursula here. I could only hope that he wasn't as bad as the sea witch in my story.

I kept my face blank, even though a slight chill rolled down my back. I mean, the last time I'd signed paperwork, the a-hole had screwed me over. That was different, right?

At least, that's what I told myself until the book-seller smiled at me, showing off tiny fangs. When did leprechauns gain fangs?

What the hell had I just gotten myself into this time?

8

Sarge was not impressed that I'd bought the big red-leather-bound book off Death Row instead of a weapon, and I wasn't about to tell him I was having second thoughts after the little display that Oster Boon had put on back there, burning up the paper. And since when did leprechauns have fangs? What was this new kind of garbage? I made a mental note to run it by Eammon, to ask him if he knew the book seller.

To ask what the heck Oster Boon was while I was at it.

"You have less than seven hundred for weapons now! You can't get nothing with that! The bulk of your money should have been spent on buying protection, not your nighttime reading." Sarge flipped his hands into the air. "I'm glad I'm not your trainer."

I shrugged and hugged the book to my chest. I hadn't said why it was important, or who had written it. That knowledge was for me, and me alone. There was no way the little book seller could have known who I was, or that I was related to the author.

"Well, I'm glad too. You can't see past the end of your too-long nose to realize weapons aren't the only thing that can keep you safe," I said. Sarge frowned and touched his nose. I just shook my head. Pretty, but dumb as far as I could see, no matter how old he may or may not be.

A quick glance showed that Corb and his protégé were off to another of the vendors, rendering the weapons wonder twins finally available. I tucked my books into my new bag, noting that there wasn't a lot of weight to them, even Gran's magnum opus, and the thick strap across my shoulder felt light and easy.

I sauntered over to the Viking twins, and they saw me coming. Left elbowed Right and pointed at the bag at my side. "She got hosed. She bought that book from Oster."

"Sarge, can you hold this for me?" I held the bag out to him, and he took it with a sigh.

"I should take the books back and get your money for you."

"NO REFUNDS!" yelled Oster Boon from the other end of the stalls. How the hell had he heard us? I did not want to know.

Because my head said vampire leprechaun as if that was a thing. I didn't think it was, but I'd be asking Eammon.

I shook my head. "Listen, you two," I put the palms of my hands on the table and leaned forward, "I have four hundred bucks to go toward a weapon of some sort. Whatcha got?"

"You got more than that. Last chick had two thousand and she spent most of it here," Right said with a grin that showed off several missing teeth and one that was gold-capped.

"I can't help it if she got hosed." I smiled right back at him, using his own words against him. "Let's consider this, shall we? I need a weapon of some sort, and you need to make sure that the Hollows Group stays happy, because without their recruits buying on a regular basis, I'm guessing business might get slim for you."

They exchanged a quick glance and I realized that Left was actually a woman. Just very hard in her features. And bearded. I didn't focus on her, though. I suspected she wasn't running this show by the way she kept bending her head toward her brother.

"Not much for four hundred," Right said. "Nothing really."

I shrugged. "Then I'll find another seller."

They laughed at me as I walked away, waiting for them to call me back, but they didn't. Laughter followed me. I gritted my teeth to keep from…oh hell, why not?

"Hyenas, the pair of you!" I threw back at them.

They only laughed harder, but I ignored them and walked all the way back to Gerry. She held a package up for me, wrapped in a tight piece of twine, topped with a pair of boots that looked like they would come up to my knees. "Here." She handed me the bundle.

"Thanks." The predominant color was dark gray, and I saw flashes of black here and there. The smell of new leather curled up my nose. "This is great."

She nodded. "It will change with you."

Sarge grunted, and I looked at her, not understanding. "Excuse me?"

"The leather will mold to you as you change. So, no need for another set. And I stitched the Hollows Group logo into the top, so you have your badge with you always." She smiled, and her face softened for just a moment. I looked down at the logo of a triangle with a crescent moon inside. That was the Hollows logo?

I held out a hand and she shook it quickly before letting it go. "Thanks."

"Good luck. You are going to need it. Things are happening here, not good things."

"Don't, Gerry," Sarge said with a growl.

That was interesting. She snapped her mouth shut. "Not my problem if you don't mind your people dying. But I like her. I'd like her to survive a little longer than the last few. Perhaps we will have tea together some time."

Sarge strode out ahead of me, heading straight for the stairs, all but tossing my bag back at me. I caught it and slipped my new clothes into it. The bag swallowed them up, holding everything as if it were nothing. I eyed the steep stairs.

I was not doing those again. I glanced at Bob-John and then tried to peek behind him. "Hey, you got a door out?"

"Goes through the candy shop," he said. I pulled a ten out and he shook his head.

I handed it to him anyway, as I passed by, but he touched my elbow, stopping me.

"Another place to get weapons. A bit on the darker side, but better made. I think you've got the guts to go get something. Maybe." Bob-John held out a card and I took it without slowing much. Then I was through a door, and inside an explosion of color and smells that made my mouth instantly fill with saliva.

The candy shop was all sugar and no spice, and I couldn't resist buying two large handmade suckers. Purchases in hand, I was out the door in under two minutes. I found Sarge by his bike, glowering until I held out one of the sweets.

He blinked a few times. "Really, you bought it for me?"

I grinned. "They didn't have any dog biscuits, so I figured this would have to do."

I thought he'd growl at me.

He laughed and took the sucker and popped it into his mouth, speaking around it. "Smart ass. But we aren't done here. You have to talk to Annie still."

Annie? My brain stuttered a minute as I tried to connect the name to a face, and when I remembered, I wanted to groan. Not because of her, but because of where she was. At the top of the freaking stairs.

"The lady who runs the tarot card shop?"

Sarge took my new bag that had all my goodies in it and put it on top of the seat of his bike. I stared at him. "I don't want to leave my stuff out here."

"No one will touch it, I promise."

I put my hands on my hips. "Why, because you have a protective spell on your bike?"

"Exactly."

Well...damn. I didn't know what to say. That was not really what I'd been expecting.

And just like that, I ended up having to do the stairs again after all.

"Carry me," I yelled at Sarge as he jogged ahead of me this time. "I bought you sweets!"

I was gasping as I tried to keep up, not because I had to, but because a small part of me wanted to be able to do it effortlessly. I wanted to be that girl.

That woman who could run the guys into the ground.

I mean, I wasn't, but I wanted it.

His laughter carried back, and I silently cursed him and the long, muscled legs that made this so easy for him. By the time I reached the top, I was huffing again, hating that I'd let myself put on that extra weight, and vowing that I'd do the stairs without puffing next time. No doubt my face was bright

red too—curses of the Irish blood and the strawberry blond hair with pale skin. When I was hot, it
showed.

We headed back in through the front door, the
small chime announcing our arrival, and again,
Annie met us. Her eyes were wide. "You went out
through a different door?"

I shrugged and tried to answer around the stitch
in my side. I pointed at my cheeks and the sweat
dripping down. "You see my face? You see the sweat
and the redness?"

There was no answering smile on her face, no
female understanding in that moment. Maybe she
floated up and down the stairs. Maybe she never had
to do them.

Annie pointed at the stool with a gesture that
would have made Vanna White jealous. "Sit, we will
pull your card."

Sarge gave a gentle shove to the small of my back
when I hesitated, which made my shirt stick to my
skin. I grimaced and pulled it loose. "I'm going.
Don't be so pushy."

I lowered myself onto the stool that was on one
side of a small square table made of wooden planks.
The smell of saltwater and old rot rose off it, and
I made myself put both hands flat on the surface.
There was nothing on the table except a small incense
cup, not yet lit.

Annie sat across from me in a far more comfortable chair, then lit the incense with a single match.
The smell of sage floated around us on a literal curl

of smoke. She reached for a deck of cards and handed them directly to me. "You done this before, darling?"

I took the deck in my right hand and shuffled the cards slowly. "Not for a long time."

The last person to read my cards had been my gran, just before I left Savannah. She'd told me that Himself was going to be the death of me, not in the literal sense, necessarily, but in every other way. She'd been right, the cards had been right. I'd let so much of myself die in that marriage for the sake of keeping the peace, for trying for a child that was not meant to be.

Yet another reason I'd run home to Savannah.

I sighed and closed my eyes as I shuffled, waiting for that one card to reach out to me. That's what Gran had always said, that one card would just feel different and that was the one you needed.

My hand brushed over a card that stuck to the tip of my index finger. I slid it out, face down, and pushed it across the table to her.

"That was impressive," she said softly.

I shrugged. "Like I said, not my first time."

"That's what she said," Sarge mumbled. I shot him a look and realized Annie had done the same thing.

He clamped his mouth shut around his sucker, and those big shoulders shrunk an inch or two. If he'd had a tail in this form, I suspect it would have been tucked between his legs. The more I interacted with him, the surer I was that he was not some ancient wolf in a young man's body.

He was just too much of an idiot to be anything but a young man.

I don't think it was my glare that had chastened him, though—it was Annie's.

I put the rest of the deck face down on the table and waited for her to give me the card and tell me what it meant for me.

She slowly turned it over, and I found myself staring at a dragon's head. Though that wasn't quite right, the dragon's head was in fact a skull. The colors were blues and greens, and the card was obviously hand-painted. An original if I ever saw one. The number thirteen was etched into the top corner. I reached out and slid a finger over it. "You did this? It's beautiful."

"The card, yes." Her tone tugged my eyes to her face, which was quite pale.

I looked back at the card, *really* looked at it, and then I grimaced. "Damn it, not again."

The Death card looked back at me. People usually freaked out when they got it, but it rarely meant that someone was going to actually die. It usually meant something in life was going to change. In my opinion, that was a big enough deal on its own.

"Again?" She leaned forward. "How often do you pull the Death card?"

I leaned in, too, and pulled a grimace, hiding it from Sarge with one hand. "More often than I care to share."

You would think her already pale face couldn't get any paler, but you'd be wrong. "This card is not just any death card, honey. It is…death is coming for you in a way that I can't understand. It is going to be all around you, and you are somehow the balance between life and death. Not a good place to be for someone so new to the shadow world." She slid the card across to me. "Take it with you. To remind you to be careful."

I picked up the card and stood. "Thanks."

She crossed herself, then lit a stick of sage on fire and smudged the air around me as I stood waiting for her to be done. Sarge leaned forward. "What card did you get?"

I already had the dragon death card tucked into my pocket. "You didn't see it? How could you not see it?" And wouldn't his wolf ears have heard every word we said?

"She puts a block on anyone trying to peek." He grinned. "What did you get?"

"Never mind." I pushed past him and headed down the stairs. Once more out in the hustle of the pre-tourist season, we made our way over to his bike. Just like he'd promised, my bag was still there.

I thought about the card in my pocket from Bob-John, and the weapons dealer that I was pretty sure Sarge wouldn't take me to. And I thought about going to see Hattie, my gran's best friend. That tugged at me more than anything else. That old lady was like a second grandmother to me.

But I couldn't do either of those things unless I ditched Sarge.

Which meant I needed a surefire way to get him to leave me on my own. Himself had always been totally freaked out by anything related to "woman's time." I was banking that Sarge would feel the same way. Especially if he was as young as he looked.

I made a face. "Look, I have to pick up some pads and tampons. That time of the month is coming, and I'm totally starting to feel the cramps, like right here." I pointed at my lower abdomen. "Do you mind leaving me here? I can walk back to Corb's place. And the bag isn't heavy."

The bike started before I was finished speaking, and Sarge was backing away, his eyes looking anywhere but at me. "Yeah, no problem. Just be at Corb's by five-thirty."

The engine grumbled as he revved it and did a tight turn into the slow-moving traffic before I could even wave goodbye. Leaving me to find trouble all on my own.

Just as I liked it.

9

First, I headed for Hattie's place. Her home was between the riverfront and Corb's loft. I was there in under five minutes, and as I stood at her front gate, I wondered how she'd made it this long without being stuffed into an old folks' home. Only a couple of years younger than Gran, Hattie would be entering the triple age digits soon, and she still lived alone. Her home hadn't been in great shape the last time I'd seen it, and twenty-plus years hadn't much improved it.

Suddenly, I was glad I hadn't come here first to stay with her. I wasn't sure I would have lasted the night.

The pale blue paint peeled off most of the siding, chunks of it scattering the ground here and there, attached to splinters of wood. How she and the house had survived the last few years of flooding and hurricanes that came off the Atlantic was beyond me. Unlike Gran's three-story brick house, Hattie's was small, one story, and had only a few windows. Two of which were boarded up.

I went up and knocked on the door. "Hattie, it's me, Breena."

There was a shuffle and a creak, and the door slowly opened to reveal my gran's BFF.

Hattie Estella Creston-Marteau was not much taller than my gran had been, barely coming up to my chin. She had a perfect puff of white hair that distinctly reminded me of a Q-tip. I smiled and resisted the urge to pat her on the top of the head. I'd done it once and she'd ignored me for a month.

Not a good thing when she was one of the best bakers in town. "Breena?"

"Hey, I was in the neighborhood, thought I'd drop in for a visit."

Her smile cut through the years and she laughed as she tugged me inside. "Oh, my girl! What are you doing here? Are you visiting long? Or finally come to pay respects to Celia?"

I followed her into the house and tried not to wrinkle my nose in horror. The messiness didn't faze me—the place had always been messy—but the smell was making my eyes water. The sharp tang of saltwater and something fishy that was brutally strong.

Like the smell of burning oil, it clung to the inside of my nose. "Hattie, what is that?"

"Oh, I'm doing some canning. Fish." She pointed at the kitchen and indeed I could hear the bubbling of water.

I grimaced, but followed her to her "sunroom," which was really just a space off the side of the house where she'd put one of those cheap tents up as a roof. Another person waited for us there. My stomach clenched and I had to fight not to grimace through my words.

"Oh, I didn't know you had company. I can come back."

"No, darling girl, you stay. Missy here was just leaving anyhoo." Hattie made a shooing motion to Missy. Not quite as aged as Hattie, Missy was the third in Gran's trio of friends.

I put a hand to my butt cheek involuntarily. The fierce old lady had smacked me more than once with the sharp walking stick she carried around but didn't actually need—always when Gran wasn't looking, never hard enough to leave any evidence.

My eyes narrowed as I forced a smile to my tight mouth. "Missy. How lovely to see you on this side of the grave. I'm surprised." That someone hadn't killed her yet.

Missy returned the look in spades. Her hair hadn't gone a solid silver, like Gran's, or a perfect white, like Hattie's. No, Missy's hair was streaked, and the jet-black strands that made up most of it were still as dark as ever. Her eyes were a light brown that I'd always had trouble reading. "Funny," she drawled, "I was thinking the same thing. Living in the big city must be mighty dangerous. Surprised a mite like you could make it out alive."

"Now, girls, be kind. Celia would want you to be kind," Hattie whispered.

"My Gran preferred I stuck up for myself," I said. "Especially against bullies."

Missy pushed to her feet, using that wretched stick, her eyes on me even as she spoke to Hattie. With a bit of a hobble, she walked around the table, keeping it between us as though she didn't want to be any closer to me than I did to her.

"I'll ring you tomorrow, Hattie. We can finish our conversation then," Missy said. I watched as Hattie visibly withered under her gaze.

"Of course. I'll be here." Hattie waited until Missy was gone before blowing out a slow breath and lowering herself into one of the folding chairs. I matched her movements, moving carefully so as to not knock over the rickety table that was holding up the pitcher of sweet tea.

"Have some." Hattie waved a hand at the pitcher.

"Missy probably poisoned it while you were getting the door," I said with a laugh. Hattie didn't laugh with me.

Instead, she poured a glass for herself and then poured it onto the grass. A hiss rose through the air, smoke curling from the liquid. My jaw dropped. "I was just kidding. Hattie, you can't let her come back!" What the hell had happened since Gran had died to put these two at such odds?

Again, she waved a hand at me. "This is not new. She wants me to agree with her, and I don't. She's getting desperate if she's using…well, again, never mind. Tell me why you're here. What brought you home?" Her face changed in an instant, lighting up. "I've missed you, more since your gran passed…" She closed her eyes and a tear leaked out of one, sliding down her cheek.

I sighed and tried not to get caught up in my own emotions. "I'm divorced. And I had nowhere else to go." And it was time to come home. I didn't say that, but I knew it in my gut.

"The city called to you." She bobbed her head, then leaned back in her chair, which made me tense. They were the same chairs that I remembered from my last visits, over two decades ago, and they'd been cheap then. "This is home."

I nodded. "Hattie, I've got a job, but I could use some guidance."

"Tell me, darling girl," she said. "Tell me."

So, I did. I told her about Himself, everything he'd taken from me, and his plan to sell Gran's house. I told her about staying with Corb, the interview with Hollows Group, and the crappy weapons.

She listened quietly through it all, letting me vent. I finally ran out of steam, and she pursed her lips, no doubt wondering just what I'd gotten myself into.

"And you want my advice?" She tipped her head to one side.

"I…yes, if you have advice." Truth was I wasn't sure that was why I'd come. Maybe I'd just needed a friend I could trust. Gran had loved Hattie like a sister.

"The Hollows Group…they are dangerous. Not to the world, mind you, but to their own. They tend to have short life spans." Her eyes locked on mine. "Dangerous, Breena, and you need to think twice about getting tangled up with them. My advice would be to go, maybe to Charleston if you want to stay in the South, but don't stay here. Something is happening to this town that makes it more of a war zone than ever before."

I put a hand on my bag, thinking of what I'd seen and done so far, and how I felt about it. Gerry's words came back to me. "I heard rumblings from someone else that something is going down."

Her eyes darted away and then back to me. "Demons, girl. Someone is bringing demons to Savannah."

The urge to vomit rolled right up through my belly to the back of my mouth. Gran and I had covered demons in a very simple manner. Do not call on them for help, do not bring them to this side of the veil, and do not make deals with them. They were the harbingers of all that was wrong with the world, infecting people with their hatred and generally piss-poor mojo.

I swallowed hard. "Why would anyone do that?"

She shook her head slowly, and touched the top of her hair, pushing it down a little. "Power. Demons can act as a battery for some spells." She almost seemed to be talking to herself and she shook her head. "Not that you need to know that." Hattie waved a hand at me. "You should leave. It's not safe, and your gran would want me to tell you the same."

I snorted. "Gran trained me for the shadow world, Hattie. You of all people know that."

Her eyes softened with something akin to pity. "Twenty years ago, I'd have agreed with you."

Those words were like a slap in the face, a bathtub full of ice water, or a smack from Missy's stick. My reaction was sharp. I stood up. "I've been getting that garbage from a heck of a lot of people, Hattie. I'd expect better from you."

I turned and headed out around the side of the house. No need to go through it and get that fish oil up my nose again.

"Breena, wait." Hattie followed me. "I want you to be safe. There comes a point where you have to understand that you aren't twenty anymore. That you can't do it all."

I knew in my heart she meant well.

But I wasn't ready to just…give up on life because I was too *old.* I grimaced. "Thanks, Hattie."

Her hand touched my wrist, turning me back to her. "Wait…did your gran leave you anything? A note, something?"

I shook my head. "She left me the house, Hattie, but that rat bastard took it from me."

Hattie sighed. "If she could, I'm sure she'd tell you to walk away. To be safe."

"I spent the last twenty years walking away, being safe." I pulled out of her hand, and spread my arms wide. "And look where that got me."

A divorce.

Buckets of debt.

No job.

And a fear that I'd let my life slip by me.

My inner voice agreed with me. Being safe had done me no good. Time to get a little reckless.

Outside of Hattie's place, I dug around in my bag until I found the card Bob-John had given me.

The Smiths

66 Factors Row

"Not ominous at all," I muttered to myself as I headed back toward the riverfront. I turned back once to see Hattie watch me go with sorrowful eyes. I lifted a hand to her, and she blew me a kiss. So at least there were no hard feelings. I shouldn't have been shocked that she'd tried to talk me into leaving. Of the three friends, she'd always been the most timid. It was Gran and Missy who used to butt heads over sweet tea and discussions about how best to use this herb or speak that spell.

Factors Row took me in behind the buildings on River Street. Restaurants and tourist shops filled the upper level, bridged with wide walkways and paths that created a sort of ceiling above Factors Row. The lower level, tucked beneath the boardwalk? Well, that was a different story. Needless to say, there were no nice tourist shops there. I hurried down a set of stone stairs that were narrow, steep, and probably a couple of hundred years old.

I gripped the iron railing as I went down. I was not falling.

"Hurry up!" someone barked from behind me. I came to a complete stop and looked over my shoulder at a man who was probably in his early twenties. Swarthy skin, earrings running up one side, and more tattoos than I could count.

"Hurry up, old lady," he barked again, and this time I turned around completely.

I had no weapons per se, but let's be honest, I didn't need a weapon to deal with this little idiot. I took a step down, then another and another, taking my time. "Bless your heart, you aren't from around here, are you?"

"Nope. Now move it. I'm late."

"Lack of planning on your part does not constitute an emergency on mine," I drawled, letting the Southern twang I'd grown up with slide back into my voice. Right where it belonged.

I smiled as I reached the bottom, and he pushed by me, using his shoulder to give me a parting shove. I braced my legs wider than necessary, and he caught a foot on one of my ankles and did a stumbling dance down the cobblestones until he couldn't hold his balance any longer and fell flat on his ass, skidding across the stones.

"Hurrying is bad around here. Take your time, breathe it in." I waved a hand over my shoulder as he cussed me out.

Such language. I grinned and put a few of the more creative curses aside for later usage.

But now that meant I had to focus on where I was.

The sloped cobblestone path wrapped down and around the back of the big riverfront buildings. Despite the number of people on the river road, there were very few down here.

Pretty much none. I had a feeling that "The Smiths" would not be on the usual tour guide route. If what I remembered was right, there was magic around some places to keep the unseeing away. Unseeing. The words floated to me on a cloud of memories.

Humans who couldn't see those in the shadows were called the unseeing. Which constituted most of the population. Those who had magic in their blood-lines could have the veil lifted and the shadows would show themselves. Like me. And of course, the other recruits.

My thoughts distracted me for a moment until I let myself see Factors Row, really see it.

The bright spring day didn't look so bright as I stared down the shadowy, wet alley that led away from the main thoroughfare. I'd been here before with my gran, but it had been a long time ago.

What had it been for? Hadn't she needed a repair of some sort to one of her cast iron spelling pots? I vaguely remembered it as though the memory was just out of reach.

I started down the cobblestone opening that was just wide enough for a single vehicle to drive—if you were very careful—checking the numbers on the buildings when I could. Not every door was numbered, not every building had doors.

"62," I muttered, my fingers brushing against the nearly rusted-over digits hanging crooked on the brick building. The next door was boarded up and had been for a long time. But the address after that was 67. I backed up to the boarded door. No sign, no number.

I closed my eyes, thinking back to that memory with Gran. I'd been younger than ten, and I could just see the edge of a proper door, of which this was not. Of course, a lot of things could happen in thirty years.

"Damn."

No harm in knocking. Right?

I lifted a hand and rapped my knuckles on the door. Nothing.

Not even the whisper of feet on the other side.

A whiff of something curled out from behind the boards, the smell of coal fire and a metallic tang. This was the place and they were playing shy.

Fine.

Fully not expecting them to answer unless I made a big enough scene, I kept on knocking and started talking. "Bob-John said to come see you. I'm working with Eammon at the Hollows Group, and I didn't want that crap weaponry that was being offered at the..."

I didn't know what to call it. Diagon Alley wannabe? A market? "That place with the idiot twins who think they know how to make weapons."

118

Lame, I sounded lame, but there was a creaking sound, and the boarded-up door opened a crack.

A hand stretched out, and a super high-pitched voice whispered, "The card. And hush. Too much noise. Boss is sleeping."

I flopped the card into the palm of a hand covered in the strangest skin I'd seen. Ever. Yellowy green and very fishlike in appearance, the skin had a hint of scales across the top of the knuckles.

The hand and arm disappeared and then the door creaked open a little farther, showing off a pair of eyes that glowed in the shadows. Eyes that matched the yellow-green skin. "You alone?"

"I have a big bad wolf waiting for me, but he's not here right now," I drawled, and the eyes narrowed. I smiled. I needed a weapon, and I was going to get one.

One way or another.

10

The door—if the boarded-up plywood could be called that—to 66 Factors Row was peeled back and I took my fancy new flashlight out of my bag. A girl cannot be too prepared, and after the previous night, I was not taking any chances. I flicked the light on and stepped into the shadows of the dark room.

"You are who?" that whispering voice asked.

"Breena O'Rylee."

Another low grumbled question. "Daughter or granddaughter?"

I took a quick guess that this person knew Gran, which meant I was in the right place at the very least. "Granddaughter."

"Ah. Right, daughter dead."

My guts clenched, thinking for a moment it might be a threat, but no, whoever this was seemed to have a thing for pointing out the obvious. "So, are you the Smiths? You make weapons?"

"Ah, yes, he makes lots of weapons. Comes with me." There was a clicking sound, maybe those long fingers snapping at me. I swung the flashlight around and got a glimpse into the darkness. There wasn't much to see, just more shadows, boxes, shapes that weren't really anything.

I followed the narrow-framed, fishlike person, who led me deeper into the room. I did a quick look behind me and could still see the door, so there was no—oof. I bumped into the body in front of me.

"Sorry."

"Clumsy," the voice grumbled. I couldn't decide if it was male or female. Though I guess it didn't matter. What mattered was getting a weapon so I could do my training.

Another click like a snapping of fingers, and four huge urns lit up, flames rolling out of the top of them. And yes, I meant urns when I said urns. They were all black, and I could just make out some sort of inscription on them that looked like birth and death dates. A faint smell of burning hair filled the air, making my nose crinkle and my skin crawl.

I could only too easily imagine what the flames were being fueled with. I grimaced. Then I took a good look at the rest of the room. There were weapons on all the walls, from the smallest of daggers to swords that had to be eight feet long, arrows, bows, axes, and a flail that was pinned high to the wall with a sign that said, "Do not touch, will eat your soul." Comforting, that one. I would be sure to pick something else.

The figure in front of me slowly stood upright and faced me. I bit down on the inside of my cheek to keep from letting out a squawk. The face was kind of human, but there was a reptilian nature to it with tiny scales across the super high cheekbones, and the eyes still glowed somewhat in the light. "I sell for my boss."

"You mean you didn't make these?"

Fish shook his head (I was going with him for now). "No, boss sleeps during day, makes weapons at night."

"Night owl, huh." I dragged my eyes away from Fish and looked around the room. "How much for a dagger?"

"Which one?"

I didn't think it wise to tell my newfound friend that I wanted the cheapest weapon they had. I pointed to a small dagger on the wall that had a bright turquoise handle. It reminded me a little of the colors on the death card, which seemed fitting. "How about that one?"

"Five thousand dollars."

I blew out a sharp breath. "I have…" I peeled out the last of the cash I'd brought, or at least most of it. I needed room to negotiate. "I have five hundred and sixty dollars."

The reaction was immediate. And rather unpleasant.

"You get out! You cheap whore!" Fish shoved at me with those long fingers, and I shoved him right back, making him stumble.

"Hey! I am not a whore and it's rude to speak to a customer that way, Fish lips!" I yelled.

Fish gaped at me. "You hit me!"

I put my hands on my hips. "I pushed you, you liar. And you started it!" I pointed a finger at him. "I came here to get a weapon, and I'm not leaving without one."

Fish's eyes drifted just above my head, widening. "You go ahead and talk to boss then. Boss kick you out if you won't go." Muttering under his breath commenced that sounded like "cheap whore" again.

I turned around and found myself looking at a rather wide chest, and when I looked down, the wide chest dipped to a narrow waist wrapped in a sheet. A barely there white sheet.

Eyes up, Breena, eyes up!

I forced my eyes upward much as they wanted to linger on those perfectly sculpted abs.

The boss, whatever his name was, looked down at me, the exhaustion on his face doing little to disguise the irritation there, or the sharply handsome features. His hair was so black that the light gave it little colored highlights. Blue eyes flecked with gold stared down at me. "What the hell is all this noise about?"

"She is cheap whore," Fish said. I spun around.

"Listen here, you knock it off or I'll turn you into sushi!" I snapped the words, using my best imitation of my grandmother.

The boss blew out a breath behind me. "I'm not getting any sleep until you leave. What is your budget?"

I swallowed hard. "Low."

"How low?"

I fanned out what remained of my money. "That's it."

He frowned and seemed to wake up a little more, and I looked down at my graveyard dirt-stained capris, and the shirt I'd pulled on that morning that had a few holes along the bottom hem. "You look like a tourist who got lost. How did you find this place?"

"BJ." I smiled and then frowned. "What is that place with all the vendors called?"

"Death Row," the boss said. "You were on Death Row and you didn't get a weapon there? Why not?" His frown eased off his face and I found myself staring hard at him. It was hard not to look, given his beautifully formed features and body. No one should be allowed to be that perfect.

Which only made me think of just how soft I was, so very imperfect. I pulled my head out of the mental beating I was giving myself and propped a hand on one hip.

"You mean besides the fact that the twins are about as charming as a pair of turds doing a tango? Their metal looked thin, and when I touched it...I didn't like it. There were small hairline cracks in everything. I don't want something that's going to break the first time I use it." I shrugged. Look at me go, throwing twenty-plus years of being normal out the window. *If it feels off, listen to your gut*, Gran had told me time and time again. And for the first time in twenty-some-odd years, I was doing just that.

I'd felt that warning the first time I'd held Himself skin to skin, and I should have listened then too.

The boss rubbed his face again. *Big hands,* my mind whispered. *Bet he's good with them.*

Yeah, so again, that libido thing? Totally out of control. I mean, not like anything was going to happen. I knew my place on the hotness charts, and he was well out of my category.

Those strange blue and gold eyes closed, and he drew a slow breath. Almost as if he was smelling me. Which was quite possible in the shadow world. "Feish," he said gently, "go get some tea ready. I can see this is not going to happen quickly, and I'd like to get some sleep today."

He walked to his workstation.

There was an anvil blackened with usage that had to be at least several hundred pounds, four kinds of hammers of varying sizes, chunks of metal in various stages of being made, and a thick table behind it all which was where he pulled up a chair and sat. With a quick gesture, he pointed to another chair, then pulled a thick apron of leather off the table, leaving it bare. "You're new to our world, then? The Hollows Group is bringing you in?"

I shook my head as I sat on the hardbacked chair. "Yes and no. My grandmother raised me believing and seeing. I left for twenty-plus years, and now I'm back. But also, yes, I'm with the Hollows Group."

I'd given up thinking I was crazy. I mean, hell, maybe I was crazy, maybe this was some strange side effect of early menopause, and I was really just walking around the streets mumbling to myself, but I didn't think so. Menopause might have physical side effects—like the libido issue—but the rest was just a woman who'd given up trying to please everyone.

And the world didn't know what to do with a woman who'd run out of ducks to give.

I was that woman. I held out one hand. "Breena."

He eyed me up and down once and didn't give me his hand. "Crash."

I grinned, thinking it was a nickname. "Clutzy much?"

He shook his head and scrubbed at the stubble on his chin. "No."

Feish—damn, I knew I'd been close, my guess had been pretty much spot on—brought a pot of tea and one cup. Crash shot him a look. "Another cup."

Feish snorted and strode away, muttering under his breath.

"She's a bit weird when another woman comes in here," he said. "Protective."

She? Well, damn, I'd been wrong on that count. He poured me the first cup of tea, and I picked up the fine china. Feish brought another cup, paused when she saw that I had the first one, then disappeared again.

"Poison or some such in that second cup, I'm betting?" I asked as I took a sip of tea. After my run-in with Missy, I wasn't taking chances. I let the flavors linger on my tongue. Hints of honey, ginger, cardamom. Sweet with a little bit of spice.

Crash nodded. "Probably just something that would make you shit your pants. She doesn't harm those she doesn't like, just embarrasses them."

Lovely. I made myself go through my memory banks. "Is she a river maid?" River maids were different than mermaids, or nymphs like the one I'd dealt with on the riverbank of the graveyard. Not as pretty and no siren songs in their repertoire. They were more like the fish they were created from. Territorial, that was the only trait I could come up with from my rusty memories, and it looked as though she thought her boss was part of that territory. Good enough.

He nodded. "So, you do have some knowledge then."

Feish brought a second cup—different than the first—and set it in front of Crash. I lifted a hand, knowing just how to defuse her hatred of me. "Good tea. I'll have to get my boyfriend to pick some up for me. Where did you get it?"

Feish squinted at me. "You have a man?"

"Half-man," I conceded. Sarge wouldn't mind.

Feish's eyes bugged open. "Half-man? You brave, they bad in the bedroom. All bark, no bite."

I choked on the tea, laughing. Oh, it was going to be fun to hold that one over Sarge. "I'll remember that."

She gave a funny half bow from the waist. "I get Boss tea from Death Row. Cranky old lady vendor."

I gave her a wink. "Thanks."

She melted back into the shadows and I turned to find Crash watching me. "What's your last name?"

"Does it matter?" I suddenly didn't want him to know I was connected to Gran, even though I'd already told Feish.

"I can guess, because you look a bit like your family. But more like your gran. And your hair is the same as when you were here as a child. All fly-away edges as if you can't manage to tame it." He dropped two sugar cubes into his cup and stirred it around. Damn, so much for keeping my identity free and clear. Was it weird that I was having tea with a guy wrapped in a sheet, who knew my gran, remembered me as a kid, in what I was pretty sure was a secret hideout full of weapons? Yup, totally weird.

And I loved it.

I grinned. "Will you give me a better deal on weapons because you knew my gran? Because I still look like that sweet kid?"

He grunted and I think there might have been a chuckle in there. "Maybe."

"O'Rylee," I said. "Not that you didn't know."

He leaned back and nodded. "Thought so. I'd heard you married and left town."

I grimaced. "Divorced and came back to lick my wounds." Damn, that maybe sounded too bitter.

Crash lifted his tea and downed it in one big swig of a gulp as if there were a shot of something else in there too. He leaned forward and the burning urns threw light over a very nice set of shoulders, and some rather well-defined biceps. Of course, it made sense that he'd have sculpted arms given he was swinging a hammer around all the time. I lifted my teacup between us and watched him over the rim of it as I took another sip. Mostly because I wasn't sure I could talk right in that moment.

Too busy drooling.

Corb and Sarge were lovely to look at, but they were…pups. Annie was right about that much. They were young, and still thought with parts other than the head on their shoulders.

Crash, on the other hand…I wouldn't kick him out of bed. I mean, assuming I could get that far with him. That dark hair had a few silver strands at the edges that only added to the urge to run my fingers through his thick locks. I had to clench my fingers around the teacup to stop myself. Himself had pretty much no hair anymore, and what was left was short and stubbly. Not an ideal playground for a woman's fingers.

I pursed my lips. "The wonder twins, they mostly had guns, and the blades they had were poorly made."

"Because guns don't take a lot of skill," he said softly.

I pointed out the pair of pistols above us on the wall. "You have guns too."

"Those are special." He didn't lean away from me. "You don't like guns, do you?"

I shrugged. "I know how to use them, and in the right place and time they are worth having. But they wouldn't be my first pick, no. Too much noise, too much attention."

I must have said the right thing because he gave me a look that had me squirming. He liked what I'd said. Agreed even.

Crash tapped his fingers on the table. "Two blades, one for each thigh, not too long. No guns for you, not yet."

A rush of excitement whipped through me. "Really? You'll sell me two knives?"

He stood and reached for a pair of knives mounted on the wall, retrieving those as well as what looked like some sort of holster system for them.

One was the turquoise-handled knife I'd been drooling over; the other had a silver handle that was shaped perfectly for my hands.

"I'll take four hundred for the pair," he said. When Feish gasped, Crash smiled and added, "And then I'll take ten percent of your first bounty."

I blinked a couple times at that, not sure what he meant. "Bounty?"

Sarge had said something about payment being on a job-by-job basis, but that word hadn't come into it.

He didn't take his hand off the table, or off the knives. "The Hollows boys didn't tell you much, did they? Figures. They like to keep people in the dark as long as they can. It's a trademark of theirs, as though it gives them the upper hand with their trainees. The truth is it ends up getting their people killed a lot quicker because they do stupid things."

Unspoken between us, I could almost hear him say, "like going into Factors Row by yourself."

I wasn't sure just how much I could trust this guy. I mean, I was reasonably sure that he was a shady fellow and there was some sort of weirdness going on with him and the fish chick, but if he could fill me in on things that Sarge and the others were not telling me...then wasn't it like figuring things out in my own way? Them's the rules according to the Hollows boys.

"It might be cheating if you tell me." I smiled. "But if you don't tattle on me, I won't tattle on you."

His lips curved upward. "Just like your gran."

I raised my teacup, partially saluting him. "I take that as the highest form of compliment."

He poured himself another cup of tea, throwing a few more cubes of sugar into it. "The Hollows Group takes on odd jobs that are sold to the highest bidder. They specialize in all things weird within the shadow world. That's pretty much everything. As long as it pays." He gave me a pointed look and I motioned for him to go on. I'd figured out the weird part all on my own. "You could end up doing a bounty hunt for some supernatural that didn't pay debts. Or you might be paid to do a recovery—I had them recover one of my weapons that was stolen a couple years back...they didn't like that

I wouldn't give them the full amount when my item was returned broken."

I didn't disagree with that thinking. If they broke it, then they shouldn't get full payment.

He looked at me with a slight frown. "Basically, it could be anything that comes up that someone can afford to pay."

I frowned. "So almost like a cop for critters?"

Critters was a word in the South used to refer to anything paranormal—ghosts, aliens, monsters, demons. All under one nice little word that didn't sound so scary.

He barked a laugh. "Critters. Haven't heard that in a long time. But yeah, kind of like a cop for critters, but without the rules. No rules for you, and no rules for the ones you're being asked to hunt and keep in line. They won't hesitate to hurt or even kill you."

I wanted to ask him more questions, I really did. But we were interrupted by a loud banging on the door. I grimaced. "I think I've been found."

Only it wasn't Sarge. It wasn't even Corb or Eammon.

It was my first taste of just how ugly the weird could be, and just how deep into it I already was.

11

Feish let out a squeak from her thin fish lips, and she scurried across the room that belonged to the Smith, out toward the front of the warehouse, her feet scuttling across the floor, clicking. Did she have crab feet? Damn, she was a strange one.

Crash stood and his sheet slipped lower over his hips, a slide that I watched with absolute fascination and possibly a bit of drool that I struggled to swallow down. "You need to go."

"I didn't sign anything for our deal. Here." I flipped the money he'd requested onto the table. I didn't really want to go—I wanted to just sit here and talk with this man. And have tea with him. And maybe touch that body and run my fingers through his hair. Maybe a few other things too.

He put a hand on my shoulder, the heat of his palm against my skin notable enough that I fleetingly wondered if he had a furnace burning inside of him, and steered me ahead of him. Not toward the entrance I'd used earlier, but in the opposite direction.

"I'll know when your first bounty comes through," he said. "And I'll take my ten percent then. Verbal contract is fine. I know your gran. She wouldn't let you get away with breaking it." He spoke like he still talked to my gran.

"Okay, but—"

He pushed me through an open door. "In here, be quiet."

I turned as he shut the door. He'd put me in his bedroom. Hot damn. All thoughts of Gran fled.

A few steps in and I found myself at the edge of his rather large and still rumpled bed. I put a hand on the mussed-up side, and it held some heat from his body. He really had to have a furnace going under his skin.

I had no doubt that he was deep in the shadow world, which indicated he probably wasn't totally human.

But what was he?

Voices floated through the air—the low, calm rumble of Crash's voice, plus an answering voice that fell in the mid-range. Male, I thought, and irritated.

I made my way back to the door and pressed my ear to the wood.

"You said you would consider making the item I requested." Yup, definitely male.

"I did consider it, and I asked a single question which you didn't want to answer. So that means my answer is no. Talk to the twins if you need it made."

A slap as if a hand had hit the table. "You and I both know their weapons are cheap. They ship them from China half the time! They have no skill, and you do."

I grinned. I'd known those weapons looked shoddy!

"Answer the question," Crash repeated. "What use have you for an item of that nature?"

Damn, it was almost like…he knew I was listening? Yup, that had to be it. He wasn't naming anything.

"Why so cagey…ah, did I interrupt you and a lady friend? My apologies, I understood that you had sworn off women. Evil creatures that they are." The "guest" laughed, and I frowned. Evil? Another slam of a hand on that table. "I am not asking now. I am telling. Make me the item. One week, or I will make your life uncomfortable. My overseer is not a patient soul. You know this."

Silence from Crash for a full minute. "It can't be made in a week, and you know it."

Was he giving in to this a-hole's demands?

"How long will it take?"

Silence again. "Three months. Certain cycles have to be considered in the making of it, you know that."

The other voice let out a huff. "Fine. Here is your down payment for the crucible."

Oh, so that's what it was? Why would it take three months? My curiosity was at its height, which was why I was slow on the uptake of what happened next.

There was a heavy thud and then the sound of footsteps leaving the space. No, not leaving, heading my way. Toward the bedroom.

Shit!

Why did I get the feeling that if I got caught now, my job at the Hollows Group would never happen? Because this person would kill me for overhearing their business with Crash. I dropped my bag and ripped off my clothes, flinging them onto the floor as I stumbled toward the bed, snagging a thick blanket bunched up at the foot of the bed as if it had been too hot for anything but a sheet.

I grabbed the cover, yanked it up and slid under it, closing my eyes as the door creaked open. I fought to keep my breathing slow and even—not an easy feat after that little sprint across the room. There was an upside: Crash's leftover warmth and smell wrapped around me. Damn, I'd take that any time. I all but sunk into the mattress with a heavy sigh.

Footsteps came closer, then stopped beside me. I feigned sleep. "Crash, I'm disappointed," the other man said, not bothering to keep his voice quiet. As if he didn't care if he woke me.

"What?" Crash's voice was wary. He was no doubt wondering what the hell I was doing in his bed.

"She's rather old and…less hardened than I would have thought you'd choose to break your fast with. Soft. Feminine."

Old? I was forty-one! Not a hundred and three! And soft? Some men liked…

"I like a woman with some curves on her," Crash said. "I like to have something to hold onto in the bedroom."

Jaysus lord in heaven, my heart rate shot through the roof. Don't start panting. That would give me away.

"I can see that." His words dashed my growing heat.

I deliberately took a big breath, mumbled "ass-hole" under my breath, and rolled so my back was to the both of them. The blanket shifted down to the curve of my waist and I had to fight not to pull it up. Someone lifted it to cover my shoulder.

Their footsteps receded, but I stayed put. Just in case they came back. Which was a good thing since they paused at the door.

"And Crash?"

"What?"

"Consider your new friend's life on the line if you don't get the crucible to me in time."

The door clicked shut, and I was plunged back into a semi-darkness that smelled like a wood-burning fire, the salty ocean, and something else I couldn't quite put my finger on.

I waited quietly until the door creaked open.

"He's gone," Crash said as he stepped into the room. "And what are you doing in my bed?"

"What?" Feish strode in past him. "You said you have a man already!"

I sat up and the blanket slid down a little. "Yeah, well, it saved your butt and mine, didn't it?"

"No, it didn't." Crash stared at me hard and I stared right back, unblinking under those lovely eyes of his. "If he'd thought you were just a lost tourist, which was what I was going to tell him, he would have sent you on your way. Now he thinks you're important to me because you were in my bed, which means he'll—"

"Kill me if you don't make a mysterious crucible for him?" I slid my legs out from under the covers, holding one knee to my torso as I reached for my bra on the floor. "Yeah, I heard him. Who is he, anyway?"

"Your dog is going to be mad!" Feish glared at me as she threw my shirt and pants at my face. "Get out of his bed! Out, out!"

I got my bra on under the covers and then pulled on my shirt. "I'm going, Fish Lips! It was an act. I wasn't trying to get into his bed for real."

Crash just watched me dress the whole time. If he thought I was going to blush and get flustered, he had another think coming. How many doctor's exams had I had up to this point? Too many to count, and most had involved a speculum, which meant now a little bit of skin showing was nothing.

"Thank you for the weapons," I said, yanking the last of my clothes on. "I'll come back when I get my first paying job."

"It'll be months away," he said. "Maybe a year. You won't have a reputation until then. That's how this goes."

I didn't want to hear that. I couldn't afford to wait that long. "I tend to break rules as I go, so we'll see about that."

I brushed past him, my arm bumping up against his side. I took note of a tattoo that curled around to his back, something I hadn't seen before because of the way the sheet was wrapped. Flames, just flames winding around his torso. Feish harried me all the way to the front door, pushed me out, and slammed it shut behind me.

I stood there in Factors Row thinking things couldn't get any weirder, any worse.

That was a terrible way to test Murphy's law, in case you were wondering.

I checked my watch. Five! How could it be so late? The walk back to Corb's place was easily twenty minutes. I had to hurry if I didn't want to be late.

A tapping on the cobblestones behind me turned me around.

There was Robert, watching me, swaying where he stood. "Robert, what are you doing here?"

"Warning."

Just that one word, and then he was gone between one blink and the next.

Warning, huh? Warning for what, though?

I turned in the direction of Corb's loft, then let out a shriek as I stumbled backward from the literal horror in front of me. A spider of enormous size,

139

perched on long, hairy legs. The size of a freaking horse, legs stretched out a good ten feet in either direction.

I hated spiders.

Almost as much as I hated Himself.

"Oh, fresh meat." The spider ducked its head under the bridge that led into the walk and scuttled toward me.

"You can't be seen!"

"You're right, I can't be. Trick of my magic keeps the unseeing from seeing me or my victims. Only allowed to chase those who can see me now." The fangs that flicked out from under its mouth were the size of my thighs. As thick as them too.

The spider stretched them one at a time, flicking a bit of venom toward me with each movement. The droplets hit the cobblestones with a splat and smelled of death.

I backed up and banged on the door I'd just stepped out of. "Feish, open the door!"

"No, go away!"

"I'm sorry. I didn't mean to be sassy!" I yelled, my voice creeping up to an octave I hadn't known I could achieve until that moment. "There is a spider out here!"

"Crash sleeping, go away!"

I banged harder, but then I had to step back because the big-ass spider was closing in on me.

Weapons, I had weapons! For what good they'd do, I pulled both short knives out of their bundle and slung my bag around to my back. I pointed both tips at the ginormous spider, thinking that it had been too long since I'd actually sparred with weapons. The moves would be clunky at best.

But here I was, pointy parts directed at enemy, check.

Enemy laughing.

Check.

"You don't know how to fight, do you? Excellent." The spider lunged at me so fast that I didn't even see it move—I blinked, and it was on top of me. I had my back pressed to the cobblestone walk and was staring up at the hugely hairy underbelly.

"You should consider waxing," I spat out as I kicked up with both feet, hitting the belly hard. The spider flailed.

"Right in the lady bits!" it screeched. Okay, *she* screeched. I scuttled backward on my ass, through puddles of water, dragging the knives with me as the spider lurched around, wailing, legs flailing. This was my chance.

I pushed to my feet and ran for all I was worth down Factors Row, racing for the stairs at the far end. If I could get above, the spider wouldn't follow.

I hit the stairs, stuffed one knife into my bag and grabbed the railing with my now-free hand, pulling myself up as much with my arm as with my legs, which had once more turned to jelly. I got to the top of the stairs and bent at the waist to catch my breath. A quick glance over my shoulder proved I'd thought wrong about the spider's supposed limitations. Those long, hairy black legs were following me.

"Gran, you never warned me about this!" I yelled to myself as I moved with speed down the streets that would lead me back to East Perry. I had to believe Corb was still at the loft. Or Sarge.

Something splooshed into the building that I'd just circled around. I looked back at the oozing hunk of what had to be web stuck to the old brick building. Only it wasn't light and airy, but thick like mucus spit.

I stuck my head around the corner to glare at the still oncoming spider. "Seriously? You're spitting at me?"

The spider let out a snarl—yes, a snarl!—and opened its mouth. I squeaked and ran all the way to the Colonial cemetery, which was just kitty corner from Corb's loft. I ran with all I had, which left me once more sweating and red-faced. I didn't care. I stumbled into the park and tucked down behind one of the larger tombstones. My legs were done, my heart was done, I couldn't go any further even though I had probably a block left at best. I slid down, still clutching one of the daggers. What the hell was I going to do with it anyway? The stupid spider was right, I didn't even know how to...the sound of a rumbling bike engine snapped my head to the left.

Not exactly a knight in shining armor, but I'd take Sarge in a heartbeat.

A dog on a hog.

Laughing hysterically, I burst out from my crappy hiding spot (okay, burst is maybe a bit of an oversell; more like crawled quickly, stumbling as I tried to look behind me) and headed across the grass, between a pair of tourists who scrambled away from the crazy lady holding an oversized dagger and laughing like a maniac.

"Sarge!" I hollered for all I was worth, and thank God, he heard me. He stopped, turned, and then just stared at me as I crawled toward him. The fence was in the way, which meant I had to pull myself over it. I did manage to get my dagger back into my bag first, so I didn't end up impaling myself on the tip.

Why wasn't he helping me? I got caught up on one of the sharp points, my shirt tore, and I fell to a heap on the other side of the fence, my bag clutched to my body. I landed on it, and the items within the depths of the bag did nothing to soften my fall. I was pretty sure I could feel the point of Gran's book jab against one of my ribs. A scattering of applause rose from behind me from the tourists. I twisted around, totally expecting to see the spider waiting there to scoop me up.

Nope, just Robert, watching me go, and a few tourists shaking their heads as they stared at me. How the hell was no one else seeing him? I lifted a hand and waved, and he waved back.

The tourists cringed as if I had yellow fever.

Sarge crouched beside me. "Do I dare ask what that is all about?"

I blew out a breath. "Do I get a pass on tonight's training seeing as I just ran for my life from a giant spider?"

Sarge squinted one eye. "How did you piss off Jinx?"

"You know the giant spider of which I speak?" I pushed to my feet, Sarge holding me under one elbow as I limped over to his bike. He got on, and I slid on behind him with a whimper.

"She's a trickster. She wouldn't have really hurt you," he said. "She likes to tease those who can see her."

Maybe it was the kick to her lady box that had pissed her off. "She said she was allowed to eat those who could see her."

That seemed to give him pause. "No, she was just teasing."

"I don't like her teasing." I wrapped my arms around his solid body and held on as the bike rumbled forward. I closed my eyes and tried not to think about the big spider. If she was a trickster, what would it be like to face down something that actually wanted to eat me? I mean, it had been a long time since I'd seen any of the monsters in the shadows and...

"There weren't many monsters in the shadows in Seattle." I shouted to be heard over the whoosh of air around us. Even when I'd been still seeing them, they had been few and far between.

"You don't have to shout, my ears are good," Sarge said. "And the answer is simple. There aren't many monsters in Seattle. Not of the supernatural kind, anyway. Certain places hold a bit of a lure for the shadowed ones."

Shadowed ones. That name rang a loud bell in my head. Gran used to say that, she used to say that the shadowed ones weren't all good, they weren't all bad, but a whole lot of gray, just like people.

"And Savannah is one of those places?" That felt right too, again like something Gran had said.

"New Orleans too, Salem, Gettysburg, Chicago, just to name a few. Lots of bloodshed, lots of suffering. Makes for good breeding grounds for a lot of the monsters out there."

I had nothing to say to that. My mind wouldn't shut off, though. All those places had monsters lurking in the shadows like Savannah did. Really?

Sarge drove us back toward the cemetery where this had all started. It was hard to believe the interview had been the night before. Felt like a week at least.

Maybe Eammon would give me the night off, maybe I'd get a break.

Yeah, I didn't think so either.

12

Sarge pulled up to the cemetery with the address 696 Hollows Road stamped on top of the gate. Night had just started to creep up on the horizon, and it made some of the gravestones almost glow with that last bit of the sun kissing their tops.

The gate opened wide by means unknown and Sarge drove us through. At least we didn't have to walk all the way to the entrance to the…"What do you call this place?"

"A cemetery."

Under my hands his body shook. Laugh at me, will you? I grabbed a bit of flesh over his abs and twisted it. "You know what I mean. Do we call it the lair, the training grounds, palace of death, Hogwarts 2.0?"

146

He smacked my hand away. "The Hollows, that's what we call it."

Great. Everything was called the Hollows. The group. The training place. The road it was on. Lack of imagination if you asked me. Which of course, no one had.

Two minutes later, we were once more underground in the main room of the Hollows's training area.

We were the last to arrive, and everyone watched as I stumbled in after Sarge. Corb's jaw hung open. "What the hell happened to you?"

"I left her behind to get…some girl things." Sarge grimaced. "She had a run-in with Jinx. And she spent all her money on books and clothes, so she has no weapons. Good luck with that, Eammon."

Eammon took one look at me and motioned for me to sit next to him. I started to lower myself but then saw that no one else was sitting. Damn it. "I'll stand, thanks. And I have a weapon. Two, actually."

I patted my bag and the two daggers clinked.

Sarge snorted. Then sniffed the air. "Wait a minute, where have you been?"

I'd sat behind him on the bike, but it occurred to me that he wouldn't have smelled me then, with my butt sitting behind him. I grinned. "You tell me."

Eammon clapped his hands together. "Enough, both of you. Training begins now. Put on your working clothes, get your weapons on, and start with three laps of the graveyard."

147

My turn for my jaw to drop. "I just ran across half of downtown with a giant bug chasing me!" I spluttered.

"Then you're all warmed up." Eammon's green eyes twinkled at me. Yes, I knew eyes were not supposed to twinkle, but they did, and I wanted to smack him for it.

Damn leprechaun.

I glanced at the other trainees and laughed to myself when I saw that they were all standing there, not moving.

The girl put her hand up. "I didn't buy any clothes. I just bought weapons."

Corb gave her a push. "Then put them on and get running."

I, on the other hand, stripped to my underwear where I stood and pulled on the new clothes Gerry had made for me. The soft, supple leather clung to every curve, but wasn't hard to get on. Some subtle netting strips ran down the legs of the pants, which would help with cooling me off—a necessity not only for the heat, but for the fact that I was going to sweat like crazy. The top was actually a snug-fitting jacket that I reluctantly pulled on over my tank top, buckles cinching it shut.

"Gerry does nice work," Eammon said. "Expensive, but the best."

I nodded. "I like her."

Then I pulled my two knives and the leather strapping out of my bag. "Can you help me with this? I'm not sure how it goes on exactly." I held it out to

Eammon, and he recoiled as if I were offering him a snake. "What?"

"Where did you get that?" His finger shook as he pointed at the worn black leather. "And those!" Now he pointed at the two short knives I held in my other hand.

I put the knives on the ground and started fiddling with the straps, trying not to freak out along with Eammon. "I got them from a vendor."

He put his hand to his head. "I should never have sent Sarge with you. He just let you run off, didn't he?"

"Probably not." I shrugged. "But I got a better deal on these—"

"No, you probably didn't. What did you sign?" Eammon helped me get the harness across my hips, attaching the straps for the sheaths around my upper thighs.

"Nothing."

"What?" That slowed him down. "Feish didn't make you sign anything?"

"See, you knew exactly where I got these." I patted the leather, bent with a small groan, and picked up the daggers. I slid them into the sheaths and there was a soft click, like they'd locked in place. Nice. I put the turquoise one in the right sheath, and the silver in the left.

"Feish never lets anyone out without signing a contract."

I shrugged. "I didn't deal with Feish. I dealt with Crash directly."

Eammon swayed where he stood and then sat with a thud on his stool. "Go run. We will talk when you get back."

The other trainees had already taken off, and I realized then that I was the only one left with the five trainers. I looked to Corb but couldn't read the look in his eyes. Tom and Louis were not laughing anymore, and Sarge looked green around the gills.

As I pulled my sorry butt up the stairs, he was already apologizing. "Eammon, she said she needed girl stuff. I left her on River Street. I didn't think she'd be pulled down Factors Row."

I didn't understand the fuss about the weapons. Crash seemed perfectly normal, and far more helpful than any of the men here. Sure, he was probably shady as hell, but he'd done nothing to me.

A deep breath and I broke into a slow jog. The other four were well ahead of me. I didn't bother to catch up. I just ran. If experience had taught me anything, it was that you couldn't be the best at everything. It had to be two miles around, easily, and I wasn't even halfway through the first lap before I slowed to a walk. A tap of bones to the right of me caught my ears.

I didn't have to look. "Robert."

"Friend."

"You scare that spider away at Centennial Park?"

"Yessss."

"Thanks."

"Friend."

I gave him a thumbs-up. "Friend. One of few, I'm sorry to say." I didn't have many friends in Savannah. My gran had been the center of my world here, and I'd never really socialized with kids my age. I'd been too busy learning about the shadow world when I wasn't at school.

I looked over then, feeling a sudden gush of fondness for Robert, but he was gone, and I knew why as one of the boys lapped me. He didn't bump into me, but the next little turd did—on purpose.

Just a bump of shoulders. Enough to throw me off balance—physically.

He flipped me off as he ran backward. "You're going to fall pulling a stunt like that," I said.

Robert crawled out behind him and the kid yelped as he went flying backward. Robert melted into the ground, and I winked in his direction.

Lapped again, and again, I kept jogging and walked only when I couldn't do it anymore. It was of mild consolation that the leather was comfortable, and about as breathable as leather would probably ever be.

I finished an hour after the other trainees, and things just went downhill from there.

They did rope climbs.

I hung from the ropes and prayed I could just hold on.

They sparred with each other, using their weapons.

I wasn't allowed to touch mine.

They did squats holding weights; I just squatted and prayed I wouldn't pee my nice new pants. Part of

151

me wished I'd been doing Kegels more regularly—or at all. Weren't Kegels supposed to make it so you didn't pee yourself?

Six hours rolled by, and at two in the morning, the physical part of the training was finally over. I lay flat on my back on the floor, staring up at the under-side of a graveyard. I'd only puked twice. Go me.

Corb leaned over me. "You ready to give up?"

I looked straight up his nose. "You missed some hairs in the left nostril." His nose flared. I pointed. "That flaring business is just making the long ones flutter. I mean, if you care about stuff like that."

Eammon cleared his throat. "We will break early for the night. Be here at six p.m. tomorrow."

The others cleared out. None of them were limping. Their names were muddled up in my exhausted head, but I forced myself to name them as they walked by my carcass on the floor. Brick was the one who'd bumped me and then gone down—shaved head, tattoos up his neck. The girl was Suzy and she barely looked like she'd sweated at all, her hair still perfect. The one whom I'd stopped from shooting Sarge was Luke, and he gave me a quick thumbs-up as he walked by. The last guy was too quiet. He had dark blond hair and bright blue eyes that were super intense. Something about him made my skin crawl.

"What's your name?" I made myself ask as he went by.

"Chad," he answered with barely a look in my direction. Chad it was, then.

I noticed the two people who'd watched over the group the previous night, who were presumably full-patch members of the Hollows Group, were not there. Maybe out working cases?

Crash's words came back to me. Based on what he'd told me, they could be doing basically anything, so long as it was both weird and dangerous. I rolled to my side and put a hand on my hip, fingers resting near the handle of the knife.

"Don't touch those," Eammon barked. "Maybe we can get you out of the contract."

"I'm telling you, I didn't sign anything!" I snapped. "Eammon, perhaps you forget that I'm not a child like the other trainees you brought in here." I pushed up to my feet, mostly so I could look down at him. I put my hands on my hips. "So, unless you're willing to tell me why I should exchange these perfectly good weapons for the crap those twins were selling, you can just knock it off!" I paused. "Maybe because you think you should have gotten more out of Crash for returning a broken item?"

Eammon threw his hands in the air. "I was wrong. She's going to be dead before the week is out!" And he stormed off. He damn well stormed off!

I looked at Corb, who just shrugged. "I warned you not to get involved."

Anger lanced through me which made my eyes burn. "Well, maybe if your cousin wasn't so busy trying to screw me out of my gran's house, I wouldn't have to whore myself out to a group that basically wants to use whatever life I have left to chase around critters!" My voice snapped through the air with a sharpness that Gran would have indeed been proud of.

Corb stared at me, and there was just a small amount of softening in his gaze. "He's trying to take your gran's house?"

I blew out a breath, and some of the anger went with it. Not all, but some. "He transferred my signature onto papers that made it look like I'd willingly signed over everything—Gran's house included—and taken on all of our combined debt. Because, according to him, I stepped outside the marriage with a man he took to calling 'Harry' in the paperwork."

Tom and Louis hadn't moved a step. Sarge, on the other hand, was cringing. "And were you?"

I shot him a look, thinking that at least the irony of what I was about to say would not be lost on him. "Harry was a chihuahua I worked with. So basically, he was accusing me of cheating on him with a dog."

Sarge grinned. "Maybe I know him."

"He shouldn't have been able to move your signatures," Tom said. "Any lawyer worth their salt—"

"I tried," I said, shaking my head. "He'd had it notarized and everything. Either he has more friends in high places that I don't know about or he found someone to put a spell on the paper, so I didn't know what I was signing." Which didn't make sense, because he didn't believe in magic. But what...what if the person he hired was from the shadow world, and was just that good? Maybe Himself didn't even know? Because what other possible reason could there be to have a judge and every lawyer who looked at the paperwork for me say I had no recourse?

As soon as the words flipped out of my mouth, my jaw dropped. "Oh my God. That's it. He had someone spell the paper." But who would do that, and who would he trust? I spun and stared at Corb.

He held his hands up. "Don't look at me. My cousin doesn't believe in anything that isn't tangible in his world. You know that."

"You were there when this was all going down," I said, trying not to freak out.

Corb looked up at the ceiling of the training room. "And I did that all because I wanted you to move in with me? Because I wanted you to try out for a job that I don't want you to have? None of what you're saying makes sense, Breena. Alan has—"

I held up a hand. "Don't you dare say his name in front of me."

He sighed. "Look, I'm sorry he's such a dick. I really am. But he does have lots of friends who would help him with this. And with you out of the picture, no one is challenging his right to anything."

I held both hands in the air. "Never mind. I'm here now and I'm not going anywhere." I paused and changed directions. "Look, will anyone tell me what the issue is with the weapons? I swear I didn't sign anything. Is this all because of the fallout of the bounty the group did for Crash?"

Tom approached me slowly. "Did you agree to anything?"

I nodded and the four of them groaned in unison. I touched the handles of the two knives attached to my thighs. "I agreed to a ten percent cut of my first bounty to pay for the blades. I gave him four hundred as a down payment." Or something like that. I mean, honestly, a lot had gone on. I didn't think this was the time to tell them we'd agreed to the deal over tea, while Crash was wrapped in nothing but a sheet, and then I'd ended up pretty much naked in his bed. No. I'd save that for another day.

"Crash is...temperamental." Tom seemed to be picking his words carefully. "I can only think that you caught him on a good day."

"I woke him up," I said.

Tom pulled a face. "And he still gave you the weapons?"

I thought back to the few quiet moments I'd spent with the big blacksmith. "Yes. He said I'd need them. And he agreed with me that the twins have shoddy work, and really, why would you send us all there?"

"The twins' work is fine for someone just learning," Louis said. "We all have weapons from Crash. But on a bad day, he can exact a terrible price from those who bother him. I think Eammon was just worried about you." He smiled, which did a lot to lighten the severity of his face. "And you are right, at the moment Eammon and Crash are not friends. Eammon has banned all of us from going there until Crash pays up. No doubt he thinks Crash is using you to get to him."

I frowned and even that hurt my face. Damn it, I was going to need to double up on the Advil tonight. "Which actually worked quite well, seeing as Eammon buggered off."

"Eammon and Crash have fought before," Tom said. "Similar backgrounds. They don't get along on good days."

That helped a little, but I doubted it was the whole answer. "So…but I'm guessing they're not both leprechauns?"

Louis shook his finger at me. "You are too smart. How did you know he's a leprechaun?"

Okay, now that it had been confirmed, I wasn't sure how I felt about it. Leprechauns were devious little monsters. They could be good luck, but they could also steal your luck from you if they wanted to. "I am right?"

Louis stroked his narrow chin. "You are far too good at guessing. That will get you into trouble when one day you guess, but are very, very wrong."

"One day," I said as I started up the stairs, "but that one day is not today."

13

Eammon did not speak to me the next week except the day after my first night training, which was fine because even speaking hurt muscles I hadn't known I possessed.

"You can keep the daggers."

"Spoke to Crash, did you?" I asked.

Eammon glared at me. "He said you were in his bed."

I grinned. "Yup, had my clothes off too, Dad. You going to ground me now?" Eammon's eyes about bugged out, and I leaned down to give him the talking-to that he needed. "Eammon, you don't get a say about my love life, or lack thereof. You can complain about anything that pertains to this job, but the rest of my life is off limits."

"When you are humping the leg of a…" He clamped his mouth shut and then continued on. "…a man with a bad attitude, that pertains to this job! He is a sometime customer." He jabbed a finger toward my shoulder. I took a step back, not because I was afraid, but because Eammon clearly knew what not-human thing Crash was and had almost let it slip. Interesting. Nor did I fancy a poke in the shoulder. "You do not need to owe him ten percent of your bounty. The weapons are good, but they're not worth that. He took advantage of you."

I opened my mouth to say, "He can take advantage of me anytime," but was yanked away by Luke, who pushed me toward Sarge. Luke was shaking so hard I wasn't sure how he was even still standing.

"I can't spar with him," he said.

And that was the end of my conversation with Eammon and the start of my werewolf obedience lessons with Luke. "He's just a big dog. So, don't make eye contact unless you want to challenge him, use a firm voice, don't turn and run." I rattled through some dog-training basics. "And when he's bad, use a choke collar." I grinned and Sarge did not.

Neither did Luke. "How do I get close enough to get a choke collar on a werewolf?"

I grinned at Luke and pushed him forward. "Offer him a treat."

That first week, I spent my evenings reading through the book I'd spent so much of my money on. Reading through Gran's handwriting, remembering slowly the things she'd taught me when I was a child. Which shadows I should fear, and which I should befriend.

Jinx was in there as a potential friend and sometime ally. Oops. I snorted when I found a particularly interesting passage about the trickster. "Loves *Charlotte's Web*, does she?"

The memories this city stirred; I knew that I should probably be more afraid of some of the things that I'd told myself for years were just my childhood imaginations. I knew any normal, rational woman would be terrified or feel like she was losing her mind. But I couldn't seem to get enough of this shadow world, soaking in the words, taking my own notes in a simple lined notebook I'd found in the closet.

Part of me was looking for a way to help out with Himself and the sale of the house. The more I thought about it, the more certain I was that he'd had some sort of magical help to make my signature be on papers I would never have signed. But did he know? Did he know that there was someone helping him knowingly? "Son of a bitch, did you actually use magic after making me give it up? After letting me think I was crazy?" A whole new level of anger surged through me at that thought that he'd gaslit me all those years.

I couldn't help it, I sent him a text.

You ducking bastard! Magic isn't real, huh? That's why you got someone to magic up that paperwork? Duck you and your ducking friends who helped you screw me over!

I hit send, and then turned my phone off. If he could play dirty, so could I, and I was going to find something to help me in Gran's book, I had to.

But so far, though, the best spell I could find was one that made the recipient's breath smell like death warmed over. Gran's words, not mine.

Morning of the eighth day, I was up and making breakfast by two in the afternoon. Bacon and eggs with some wilted Swiss chard. Corb strolled out. "Smells good."

"Thanks, there's extra if you want it." I pointed at the half-full frying pan. He picked up the pan and ate straight out of it.

I eyed him up. "You look nothing like Himself."

Corb paused and a grin washed over his face. "Thanks. It's a compliment to hear that I don't look like my balding, overweight cousin who is a complete moron."

I snorted. "Not so dumb. He got me good."

"Yeah, he did." Corb took another bite. "Something else is going on with you. I get that you want to start fresh, and I get that you want your gran's house back, but shouldn't you be able to hire a lawyer?"

"With what money? Do you see piles of money in my underwear drawer?" Which was funny, seeing as I didn't have a drawer. I waved my fork around. "Besides, I'm uniquely qualified for this work. You must have realized that by now." A part of me thought the answer would be in Gran's book. Something, maybe a memory, but hope said to keep looking. To keep digging through the pages and I'd find it.

He shrugged. "Maybe. I...I don't want to see you get hurt."

"Too late for that." I took a bite of bacon and chewed it. "Nowhere to go from here but up."

"Or under a gravestone," Corb pointed out.

We ate in quiet for all of thirty seconds. "What is it about Crash that is so bad? I mean, he was kind to me, far kinder than Feish, who tried to give me a teacup poisoned with a ramped-up version of Ex-Lax."

Corb scooped up the last of the food in the frying pan. "He's strong in his...abilities, let's call them, and has very little to do with the community other than to make weapons. And he's old, so he's got a lot of knowledge and could do plenty of good, but he doesn't. He just shuts everyone out. That you even saw him is shocking, to be honest. I've never met him, and I've been here for almost fifteen years."

"He knew my gran," I said, thinking about what Crash had told me. "He talked about her like they were old friends."

Corb put the pan into the sink of soapy water and I cringed. Damn it, I'd been seasoning that pan all week. "Look, if Crash likes you, that's not a bad thing. It's only a bad thing if you get on his bad side. I'm guessing he doesn't know you're working with Eammon?"

I shook my head. "Not working with him directly. He knows I'm with the Hollows Group."

Corb went on. "Then you'll be fine. Don't worry about it."

"Thanks," I said. "This is the nicest you've been to me since I got here."

"I was trying to make you leave, but you seem to have taken root. And I won't turn down a few good meals here and there." He grinned, and there he was, the Corb I'd first thought was pretty nice despite the reputation Himself had told me about. Then again, Himself didn't like my gran and she was amazing. Maybe Corb would turn out okay too.

Corb left me in the kitchen, and a moment later, the shower came on in his bathroom. Which left me sitting there alone, stewing in my thoughts. In the time I'd been here, I hadn't even gone by to check on Gran's old place. Mostly because it would be torturous to stand outside a place that had been my home and not be able to go in, to know a stranger owned it.

But the time had come to put on my big girl panties and check the place out. Maybe I could do that before training started. Yes, that was what I'd do. Catch one of the trolleys and head to West Harris

Lane. Check on the house, see if the For-Sale sign was up.

Himself had said he'd sell it fast, and I had no doubt he meant it. He'd sell it for nothing just to spite me.

You'd think I'd been the one to end the marriage. I seriously didn't understand him. Anger curled through me. I mean, I didn't have the funds to maintain a home either even if I was able to buy it.

I found myself hesitating over whether or not I should take my two knives. I wouldn't need them, unless, of course, I ran into another trickster type like Jinx. Call me crazy if you want, but luck hadn't exactly been on my side lately despite hanging out with a leprechaun. I slipped the knives inside their sheaths, of course—I wasn't a savage—and then into my bag. Not that I'd been allowed to use them. Nope, Eammon had made sure of that.

But I could aim the pointy ends at a monster. I could do that much, and really, I needed to just start practicing at home. Maybe I could find some sort of yoga-with-knives on the YouTube or the Google. I sighed, slid the purse over my shoulder, and a mere two trolley rides later, I stood in front of my gran's house. The For-Sale sign was indeed on the lawn of my childhood home. The brick was streaked in places where the water had run, and the yard looked overgrown to most, but I could pick out Gran's favorite plants that she'd used to make her different teas. I grabbed the sign and yanked it out of the ground, holding it in one hand as I entered the gate and let my hands drift over the plants, naming them quietly under my breath.

Was it just my imagination, or did they perk up a little as I brushed my fingers over them? I smiled at the thought. At this point, anything was possible.

A loud throat-clearing turned me around to see a woman in a slick business suit holding a clipboard in one hand and a dangle of keys in the other. The realtor? Maybe my luck was shifting. "Excuse me, can I help you?"

"I am here to see the house." The words popped out of me before I thought better of it. And I held up the sign as if that somehow made it better that I'd pulled it out.

Her eyes narrowed on the sign. "Did you make an appointment?"

"No. I'm sorry, I just saw the sign," I gave it a shake for good measure, "and was hoping to peek in the windows." I smiled at her, though, she didn't thaw for a second. "But you can show me around now. I'm sure you know all the nooks and crannies of the place."

She plastered on a smile. "My name is Monica, and I am the realtor." No surprise there, but I nodded and smiled. "I'm actually here to show another client this place," she said. "You'll have to come back another time. We can book right now if you like?"

"I don't mind if she joins us."

I looked past Monica to the rather broad-shouldered man with the short-cropped dark hair and…

"You look good with clothes on." I tossed the sign to the side as if that was where it went. Best to act casual when you got caught red-handed.

Monica gasped and Crash just stared at me as though I'd sprouted another head. Maybe I had.

"Stars in the heavens," Monica whispered. "I never in my life!"

And then it hit me that Crash was there to buy my grandmother's house. That he'd only known it was for sale because of me and my big fat mouth. My eyes narrowed, and if I could have shot him dead on the spot, I would have.

"Sure, I'd love for you to show us both around," I growled, suddenly thinking that maybe I would become one of those man-hating women who said they all could find a place to rot together. I could bury him next to Himself after I was through with them both.

Monica huffed and brushed past me on the path so she wouldn't get her shoes dirty by stepping into the garden. Crash took a few steps and then was right behind me.

I deliberately widened my stance. "Seriously? I tell you about my gran's house and then you go behind my back to buy it?"

His eyebrows shot up. "Behind your back? We are not friends."

"Sure we are." His face clouded over and I leaned toward him. "It gives me something to hold over Eammon."

I was hoping to make him crack a smile.

I wasn't banking on a full grin. His eyebrows went even higher. "You'd hold it over Eammon that we're *friends*?"

Shrugging, I started after Monica in the Suit. "Someone told him that I ended up in your bed with my clothes off, and that I'd made a deal with you. He lost his marbles. Went all white in the face and I thought he was going to pass out."

Crash's laughter buoyed me up the steps, and I let the sound carry me into the home of the woman who'd been more of a mother than a grandmother. Her smell was still there as I stepped through the doorway, and it wrapped around me, not unlike her ridiculously tiny arms.

She'd been so thin her whole life, like a bird. A tiny chirping bird with the sharpest of beaks if you stepped out of line.

Monica prattled on, and for the most part I ignored her. I knew this place inside and out, better than any realtor ever would.

Crash walked around the bare entry room, the wood creaking under him with pretty much every step. I left them there and made my way to the kitchen. The smell of herbs and dried flowers still permeated everything. I ran a hand over the butcher block countertop, feeling the grooves from countless times she'd chopped up roots for spells on the same surface she'd then use to chop up chicken. I could still taste the grit on the chicken if I put my mind to it. Honestly, it was shocking we hadn't ever gotten food poisoning with the cross-contamination I was certain happened.

I missed her so much. What I wouldn't give for her to hold me one more time, especially this last year, especially now. My throat tightened and I curled my fingers against the wood, scraping it lightly.

"That could easily be replaced," Monica said, bringing me out of my slip into melancholy.

"I like it," I said, noticing the catch in my throat and clearing it quickly.

Crash's footsteps approached and I made my way out of the room and toward the stairs that led to the second floor so they wouldn't see the emotions on my face. Color me cautious, but I suspected he'd be able to read me far easier than Monica, and I had no desire for him to see me cry.

Monica's voice cut through the air as she told Crash all about the kitchen, how it could be easily updated. I hurried up the stairs, gripping the familiar banister, the wood warm under my palm.

For just a moment, I was ten years old again, and I could hear my Gran talking to me.

"Hurry up, honey child!"

"Coming," I whispered as though she were really there.

I paused at the top of the stairs, and movement to my right tugged me in that direction. A swoop of long silk sleeves, bare feet, and a long skirt that swirled. My heart picked up as I chased the image of Gran into her bedroom.

She spun and smiled at me. "Took you enough time." Her long gray hair was loose, wildly messy as it hung in waves to the middle of her back, and eyes the same light green as my own blinked back at me. That was the only part of her I'd inherited, despite what Crash had said.

"Are you really here?"

"Can you see me?"

"Yes, but I can also currently see a skeleton named Robert from time to time. I just figured it's because I'm so close to dying, advanced in years as I am," I drawled.

She snorted and waved a hand at me. "You're saying that because of the death card? It's always been attracted to you, since the first time you had your cards read." She sighed and beckoned me to come farther into the room. "Nothing is what it seems here. There are dangers at play that you can't possibly understand, and that I'm not able to speak of. They slip in and out of my memories like fireflies."

"Of course not, that would be totally logical and helpful." I couldn't help the bite of sarcasm. "Don't worry, if some crazy maniac comes after me, I'll be sure to lock myself in a basement where he'll never find me. You know, like all the smart girls do in the horror flicks."

Her glare was sharp. "Don't sass me. I might be dead, but I can still put you in your place."

I laughed at her. "Pardon me if I'm not terrified of my ghostly gran. I'll be with you soon enough—you can smack me around then."

A frown flashed across her face, there and then gone. "What in God's name is that supposed to mean? I've read your lines; you'll be long-lived, just like me."

I didn't want to dissuade her of the idea. Funny how this felt more normal to me than my life had been back in Seattle. Like that had been the dream for nearly twenty years, a fantasy that wasn't real.

But here, talking to a ghost in what was now one of many haunted old houses in Savannah, accompanied by a guy named Crash, who I was pretty sure was some sort of critter…that felt normal. I sighed. "Gran, Himself is selling the house. If it's the last thing I do, I don't want it to end up in the wrong hands."

She put her hands on her hips. "I would hope not. I left things for you here, but you have to live here to get them."

I stared at her, feeling my face tighten with irritation I couldn't hold back. "Couldn't put them in a safety deposit box? Or tell me where they are, and I can get them now?"

"No. That's not how this works," she said. Of course it wasn't.

"Or leave them with someone for me? What about Hattie?" My voice was rising. Footsteps clattered up the stairs. I didn't care. "Gran, you are going to be the death of me!"

She sniffed at me and disappeared as Crash and Monica reached the doorway. Monica's eyes were wide. "Who were you talking to?"

"A ghost," I said.

Monica's eyes lit up. "Oh, that's perfect. I was just saying to Mr. Crash here that I would like to try something new with this place. And it being haunted is perfect! You know that in Australia they sell houses completely different than we do here."

Crash looked past me, but it was pretty obvious there was nobody there.

I nodded as though I cared to hear how she was going to sell the house that I wanted so badly to save.

Monica all but beamed at me. "It will go on the live auction block."

14

Sweat and rain ran down the middle of my back as I tried to work through the anger that had caught me by surprise when Monica had announced that Gran's house was going on the auction block.

The training grounds were slick with mud from a sudden rain, and the dark made the run that much more treacherous.

I did my laps slowly, still walking part of the way. But it was better than the first run. Kind of. The anger pushed me forward, and by the end of the run, the worst of it had passed through me.

"What's got your knickers in a knot, lass?" Eammon asked as I clumped into the underground training area.

"You're talking to me now?" I shot him a look. "Very mature of you."

Eammon beckoned for me to follow him. I considered ignoring him the way he'd ignored me most of the week. Then again, he was supposed to be helping me get through this training so I could make enough money to buy back Gran's house. Something I wanted more than ever. An auction maybe wasn't the worst thing. If no one wanted the house it could go cheaper than a list price. Of course, the opposite was true too, and I had no doubt that Crash's pockets were deeper than my own.

Yes, I had a crap ton of debt, but the debt wasn't really mine, and I needed to save Gran's house. I needed to. That was all there was to that.

I sighed and followed Eammon to a smaller room off the main larger one. Eammon sat at a desk that had clearly been made for him, owing to the size, and he pointed to the chair across from him. "I have an idea for how to get you out of Crash's debt, in a reasonable manner. It will cover the true cost of the daggers and sheath, so as to not offend him, without overpaying him."

My eyebrows went up. "Really?"

He nodded. "We were approached last week by a client who thinks he's being stalked. We did a cursory look into it, and there's no evidence anything is stalking him. He's a bit paranoid."

I leaned back in the chair. "He needs a babysitter from nothing?"

Eammon nodded. "We were going to turn him away, but if you take it, it'll technically be your first bounty. It won't be a big payout, so you'd only need to give Crash far less than a bigger bounty." He smiled and again that twinkle was there.

"You're a bit of a sneaky leprechaun." I smiled and shook a finger at him. But I could use the money. Maybe I could even go to the auction for Gran's house. Maybe...

Shoot, it was a dream, but sometimes dreams were what kept you going through the mud and the rain. "Okay, I'll take the job. When does it start?"

"You'd go now, work for him for four days, $500 a day, that's two grand." Eammon slid a paper across to me with a name and address on it.

I skimmed it quickly. "Eric Pine. He's way out in the boonies. Wait, is that the Eric I met last week?"

Eammon grimaced. "Yes. He prefers the quiet. He's a half-man and completely out to lunch. He's had us watching him off and on for the last...well, I guess nearly a year. But there is no one there. Nothing."

Like Sarge, then, a werewolf. I could handle that. "You're sure that he's just being paranoid?"

"Absolutely," Eammon said. "We've bodyguarded for him before, but there are other jobs coming through that are frankly worth more."

My cut with the Hollows was a 70/30 split. That would leave me with fourteen hundred for the four days, and only another hundred and forty for Crash. That didn't seem right, but for the moment I held back mentioning that Eammon was being rather stingy. The turquoise knife was priced at five thousand. If I'd negotiated, I bet I could have gotten it for four thousand at the highest. Really, I should have paid seven to eight thousand for the pair. I swallowed hard, knowing already that I wouldn't let Eammon dictate how much I would pay Crash for the knives.

Then again, Crash was no doubt going to be at that auction for my gran's house so maybe I didn't need to be so generous with him. I folded the paper. "Okay. So, I go out there and then what?"

"Do some perimeter checks, take this handbook with you—the Basic Bodyguarding section will walk you through it. Your main function will be to talk him down, basically." Eammon tapped the desk. "Don't stay more than four days."

I frowned and took a handbook that would have been mighty nice to have from the beginning of the week. "The contract is four days, why would I—"

"He'll try to talk you into it." Eammon sighed. "He's like a hypochondriac always going to the doctor. But we're the doctor. I'm about sick of seeing his face around here, and if not for the fact that he's got some cash squirreled away and he always pays, I wouldn't bother."

"But a good first job for the newbies." I nodded. "Smart. You should keep him on the client list for sure. Use him with all the trainees."

Eammon gave me an appreciative look. "Good business sense in you, lass."

I shrugged. "I've been around the block a few times. I'll see if Sarge can give me a ride out."

He waved both hands at me. "Ah, no, don't do that. It's going to be bad enough that I'm sending you. No cell service, and Eric doesn't like Sarge. Them shifters can be weird around each other."

"What about Corb?" I wasn't sure Corb would take me, but he was an option.

"No good there either," Eammon said.

I narrowed my eyes at him. "Does Eric hate all of you?"

Eammon snort-laughed. "Not hate, no. But he's scared of those two."

I pushed to my feet. "Fine, I'll find my way out there. I should go now?"

"Yeah, off you get. You're ahead of the others in all the written work, so I'm not worried. The physical stuff will come to you, lass." He winked. "Here, take this phone. Anything comes up, you call me. I don't expect anything, but still good to be prepared." Then he shooed me out of his office.

"Out there" turned out to be an hour drive easily, if I'd had a car. Walking would take all night. I grimaced, my legs hurting already.

Eammon saw me out, and I felt the others' eyes on me. They probably thought I'd been kicked out.

"I'll be back! Don't get killed without me!" I gave them a cheery wave that struggled not to turn into a one-fingered salute. Up the stairs, I went into the still-drizzling night. Robert sat across from the tombstone stairwell, swaying next to a tree. I lifted a hand to him. "Hey, Rob, how's it hanging?"

"Friend," Robert whispered, and I nodded.

"I've got to go on a job. Want to come?" The words slid from me, bypassing my filter.

"Coming," Robert whispered, sidling along a few steps behind like he wasn't quite sure it was a good idea. Hell, he was probably right. I still wasn't a hundred percent sure I wasn't already losing my mind. Maybe…nope, I wasn't going there.

I walked through the graveyard to the main road, and then kept on walking. All the way back to Corb's place, I walked. That alone took a couple of hours that was no small feat after running in the muddy, rain-soaked cemetery training ground.

I needed to take the whole bottle of ibuprofen with me.

"You stay in the cemetery," I said to Robert when I reached the house. "I'm going to get some sleep."

I climbed the stairs to the loft, pulling myself up with each step. "What the hell are you doing?" I asked myself repeatedly.

This was all crazy, insane, stupid. I could hear every word as clearly as if Himself were standing right there shouting it. I mean, if he had been standing there, I would have kicked him in his useless nuts. But you get the point.

I smiled as I let myself into the loft and tromped to the bathroom.

Showered, clean, and warm, full of some great over-the-counter drugs, I went to bed. Seeing as my client wasn't in any real danger, I would go in the morning when I was ready to face the world.

Besides, I had an idea of who was going to give me a ride out to the boonies, and I needed to catch him when he was sleepy and amiable.

I smiled as I fell asleep, thinking that I had it all planned out.

Boy, was I wrong.

The next day I made my way down to Factors Row. I wore my leather pants that Gerry had made for me, paired with a loose white T-shirt instead of a tank top. The sound of Robert keeping pace behind me helped me not freak out about the possibility of running into Jinx.

The mere thought of the oversized spider had my guts twisting into knots and I had to stop once to use a public washroom, sweating as though my insides were going to remove themselves on their own.

Sure, I had my daggers and my bad-ass leather outfit, but honestly there had been no real training I could lean on. Nothing recent. I needed to tap into the training Gran and Officer Jonathan had given me, and it was so long ago, I could only remember bits and pieces.

Eammon seemed inclined to let me just stumble through the tests that the other mentors had been setting up. I'd done plenty of exercising and reading, and not a whole lot else.

Under the shadow of the walkways, I knocked on the boarded-up door.

"Feish, open up," I said. "I need to talk to Crash."

There was no response at all. I pushed on the door a little and the wood groaned, opening just a crack. "Hey, I'm coming in, you'd better have clothes on!" I grinned as I pushed a little more and squeezed myself through the opening. Robert slid through behind me, his skeletal fingers clutching at my shirt for just a flash of a second.

The darkness was absolute, and I fished around in my bag, pulling out my flashlight. A single click and it was on. I swept the room with it, took a few steps and paused. "Hello?"

A whisper of cloth turned me to the left. I panned my light in that direction, but no one was there. Chills skittered up my spine, but I shook them off. "Come out, come out, wherever you are," I whispered with as much menace as I could. I mean, if they wanted to play the scare-the-poop-out-of-you game, I could do that too.

I kept moving forward, hearing that cloth rustle to my right now. I didn't bother to pan that way—my eyes were drawn straight ahead to where I'd sat with Crash and had tea. The space was bare, the urns gone, the weapons nowhere to be found. He'd left, apparently.

Which meant I was in this place with a critter of indeterminate breeding.

Well, crap. The chills that I'd pushed away as nothing to be worried about came back full force. "Jinx, that you?"

The rustling came faster now, and with it, the sound of something metallic sliding across the floor. Still to my right.

I turned to my left, away from the noise, and bit back a scream.

Robert stood there, swaying, his head down, his skeletal hand pointing at the exit. "Jaysus," I breathed out.

"Robert," Robert said, correcting me. Because, of course, he wasn't Jesus. He was Robert.

Not a time for laughing, though the urge ran through me in a rather quick, so-scared-I'm-giddy moment. I walked as normally as I could toward the barred-up door. I stuck the flashlight in my mouth and ran my hand over the edge of the door to let myself out. Only the edge was not an edge anymore.

The whisper of cloth and sound of metal being dragged on stone drew closer.

A litany of curse words flowed around the flashlight in my mouth. Where in Sam Hill was the edge? Having no other choice, I turned and pulled a dagger out. "Seriously, I am not the woman to test today."

The flashlight wobbled, the light bobbing in the empty room. No one was there. I locked my elbow to stop the shaking and gripped the dagger with my other hand. I stepped back to press up against the door, to keep my rear covered.

Only there was something already there waiting for me.

Arms wrapped around my middle, and a low chuckle rumbled in my ear. I screamed and snapped my head back—a knee-jerk response. Let me tell you, nothing about that movement had been thought through. But it saved me.

A roar erupted and the arms let me go. I spun and slashed blindly with the knife as the flashlight hit the ground, spinning around uncontrollably like I was in some sort of B-grade horror movie. "Not in the mood!" I yelled, following whatever it was as it spun away from the door.

I took a second swing at the stumbling, snarling creature that I only caught glimpses of here and there in the shadows.

It kept backing up.

I could have taken another go at the door.

"Out of ducks," I whispered as I bent and scooped up the flashlight, my arms still pumping with adrenaline, but I wasn't scared. Okay, I was scared, but I was irritated too. The critter snarled and flung something toward me, just a blur. I ducked and a set of chains rattled behind me.

The critter pulled the chains back in an attempt to net me. I jumped, like doing skip rope, and the chains slid under me. Before it could take another swing, I ran at it.

Yup, *ran at it*.

Tackling it to the ground, I used my body weight to pin it to the floor. Back when I was a kid, I'd wrestled with plenty of smaller critters. Gran had said they wouldn't hurt me, but they'd always bit and scratched. We crashed to the ground, and I held it down with my forearm across its throat.

181

Robert sidled up beside me, a shadow in the dying light of the flashlight. "Demon."

The critter snapped super sharp teeth at me, teeth that were more shark than human. You know, you'd think there would be hesitation in me, being that this was the first time in a long time that I'd truly faced a monster. Its face was sort of human, but not really with narrow slits for eyes and nose, and a mouth that took up far more room than that was needed for anything, as far as I was concerned.

Demons didn't do well with silver knives, and their eyes were sensitive. I'd read that this last week in Gran's book.

I had the silver knife in my hand—thank God for that—and plunged it into the left eye of the critter, sliding it through the narrow slit on the first blow. It flailed under me, bucking and screaming as its body slowly went to ash until there was nothing but the set of chains.

Just like that, the critter was gone. I sat back on my heels, breathing hard. "Robert, that was not fun."

"Demons." He shrugged as if that said it all.

I laughed and slowly pushed to my feet. "I hope the demon didn't eat Crash."

I picked up the flashlight as I headed back to the door, just as Feish pushed her way in.

Her greenish-yellow eyes went wide as saucers. "You...what are you doing here?"

"Oh, just killing demons and looking for a ride." I put my knife back in its sheath, ridiculously proud of myself.

"DEMON?" Feish clutched at her heart and dropped her basket of goods to the floor. "Oh boy, Boss is going to be pissed."

She rushed past me and I did a slow turn. Crash was here? How had he not heard me yelling? Even asleep…unless he was hurt? No, he wouldn't be hurt. He was some big scary dude that even the Hollows Group had a healthy respect for. As quick as my concern came, it was gone in a flash of understanding that Crash didn't need me to protect him.

I grimaced and did a quick look for Robert, but he'd slid away once more. The room changed as Feish hit the lights—so to speak. The urns lit up, but they were scattered on the floor, smashed to the ground. Feish started doing quick little turns, cleaning up.

I put a hand on her shoulder, stopping her. "You should check on your boss. I'll clean up out here."

She gave me wobbly, tear-filled eyes. "I don't want to wake him. He will be so angry."

I rolled my eyes. "Fine, I'll wake him up. I was yelling and screaming earlier, and he heard nothing."

Mind you, there was a small part of me eager to wake the blacksmith. He'd only have a sheet on again, no doubt.

One small perk. With what I would only say was a bounce in my step, I headed for the back room I'd been stuffed into on my last visit.

The door was shut tightly. I knocked once. "Crash?"

Nothing. I put my shoulder against the door and pushed. The base of the door screeched across the wood floor, as though splinters were being pulled up.

The room was lit with a few candles, which was completely unsafe, especially in a sealed-off room like this. No one would know it was burning down until he was dead as a doornail.

"Crash," I called to him from the open door, secretly hoping he wouldn't wake up.

No movement from the bed though there was the distinct shape of a body under the sheet. He was breathing, the rise and fall of his chest obvious even this far away. So not hurt, not dead.

Good day for me. Grinning, I strolled across to the edge of the bed and bumped the mattress with my knee. "Wakey, wakey." Nothing. "Really? Jaysus, you sleep like the dead."

I reached down and put a hand on the bend of his knee, shaking it lightly. Much as I wouldn't mind getting another look, I was wary enough to recognize that if Feish was nervous, I'd be smart to take it careful.

This deep sleeping, though, it was more than a little ridiculous. I clapped my hands together, shouting his name as I did. That did the trick.

Only I wasn't expecting him to grab me.

15

Crash grabbed me by one arm and flung me across his bedroom so fast, there was no way I'd have been able to avoid it if I'd even tried. That's what I got for waking the grumpy blacksmith up. There was a moment of perfect suspension where I knew I was flying, and I knew the impact was going to hurt like a son-of-a-bitch.

My only thought was *so, this was why Feish hadn't wanted to wake him up.* Damn, he was a grump.

There was a roar of anger, a jolt of pain, and then Feish was babbling rapidly while the room spun around me.

The last thing I remembered was Robert whispering *demon* in my ear. Which was my only explanation for what happened next.

A looming figure came toward me, my eyes fuzzy with the blow, and I was up and slashing with both knives before I even realized I was moving, the movements flowing through me as if I knew what I was doing.

"Easy. Breena, easy."

I blinked up at Crash and the blades I had crossed at his throat. His image came into focus. "Morning," I said.

"You mind dropping the knives?" He arched a brow at me in a perfect lift that I envied.

I slowly lowered them, managed to slide them into their sheaths, and then wobbled back on legs that were not steady. "Who ate your bowl of sunshine this morning, thundercloud?"

Feish gasped. "Don't make it worse!"

Crash grunted, but he didn't yell. "I was up late working. And yes, I sleep deep and wake poorly."

He stepped forward and then he picked me up. Not like over his shoulder, but like you see in the movies, scooped up like he was going to walk me across a threshold, and oh my God, it was as good as you might have imagined. I felt tiny, and feminine, and... he gave a grunt. "Been building muscle, have you?"

"Put me down." I bit the three words out.

He carried me out into the main room, set me on a stool, and pushed a cup of tea toward me. "Not poisoned, I hope?"

Feish touched my elbow. "No, it will help with the head knock."

The head knock. I lifted a hand to the bump on the back of my head which felt as though it was growing even as I palpated it. "Damn."

"Feish said there was a demon." Crash let out a slow breath and I noticed he didn't have tea. The pulse in his throat was hammering away, and the flush to his skin was subtle but undeniable.

He really was a grump when he woke up. "That's what Robert said." I took a sip of the tea and the familiar bitterness of it made me grimace even as it took me back to Gran. "Feverfew tastes like crap, works like a charm on headaches. Thanks, Feish."

"Wait, who is Robert?" Crash growled with a sharp look around the room.

"Friend of mine. He's kind of like Feish, but with bones." Yes, my words were not really stringing together well. "Feish, did you put something else in this?"

"Yes, I put kava kava in it," she said.

I groaned. "I get high on kava kava. It's like... it makes me goony." And then I giggled. "Thanks, Feish, you rock."

Feish bobbed next to me. "No, thank you. Sleeping master doesn't wake easily."

I squinted at her. "You mean someone sent the demon to hurt him?"

"Waited for me to leave for supplies," she whispered, cringing. I could feel Crash's eyes on me as heavy as a weight.

I pointed at her. "Smart, you are *so* smart! They have your Achilles' heel figured out." I took another sip of the tea, forcing more of the bitter stuff down my throat. Already the ache in my skull faded, even as the room spun a little more. "Look, I didn't pop by for tea. I need a ride out to the wildlife reserve. I've got a job!" I pumped a fist in the air for good measure.

Feish tugged on my arm. "I'll take you. Boss, you good?"

"Fine. Take her." He stood and strode from the room, and damn it, there was no sheet this time. But I only just noticed, which meant I saw only the back end of him leaving. The kava kava had disintegrated my filter, and as he strode away, I couldn't resist.

"Nice ass!"

He paused in the entryway to the bedroom, just a split second, but I couldn't help it. I laughed. "That's right, work it!"

The door slammed shut behind him. Feish let out a sigh of relief. "Come, I take you on my boat."

"Wait, you have a boat?"

She tugged me along toward the door, guiding me out, and I let her. Because I had my tea in one hand, and I wasn't letting it go for anything. "You know, this is the first time my body hasn't hurt in like a week?"

"Training is hard on older ones." Feish linked her arm with mine and let out a heavy sigh. "Especially us women."

"Yes, right?" I squeezed her arm. "I like you, Feish. Maybe we can be friends."

She startled. "I have no friends."

Maybe it was the kava kava running through my veins, but I was feeling all soft and squishy, "That's not good. I don't have friends either."

"Friend," Robert said from behind us. I waved a hand in his direction.

"I'll amend that to girlfriends. I don't have a girlfriend."

Feish looked sideways at me. "I'm ugly to humans."

I shrugged. "I'm overweight and apparently past my prime. So, they don't much credit me either."

"You are pretty to humans," Feish said.

I frowned. "No, I don't think so. Especially not to the men. I speak my mind. They say they want that, but that's not really true. That negates any amount of straight teeth or green eyes." I pointed at my own eyes and jabbed myself. "Ouch." Note to self, don't poke yourself in the eye. Yes, the kava kava was definitely kicking in high gear.

She sighed. "Men are strange. Men of the river or men on the land."

I lifted my teacup and downed the last of it. From there on out, things got rather blurry. Feish loaded me into a boat (I think), and then we drove down the river at high speed while I sang "Row, row, row your boat" (I think), and then we glided down a small tributary where the trees hung low over the water's edge where the Spanish moss was almost within reach.

"Stay in the boat," Feish snapped, grabbing my belt and yanking me back into the seat. "You want to fall in with the alligators?"

189

I blinked a couple times and a splash of water to the face snapped me out of the worst of it. "Was I singing?"

"Yes. And talking about the boss's ass." Feish grimaced. "Please don't do that. I don't like seeing it on display."

The kava kava must still have been in play because my mouth opened, and a question popped out. "Are you two a couple? You and Crash doing it?" Yup, definitely the kava kava working overtime. Who said "doing it" anymore?

The boat motor slowed as her hand eased off the throttle. Her lips twisted into what I suppose would make for a fish grimace. "Me and Boss? Gods of the sea, no! He's very ugly to me, and I don't like his temper. Too mercurial."

"But you're all protective of him," I pointed out. "I thought it was because I was a woman in your territory?" Damn, I was getting bad at reading people apparently.

Feish docked the boat against a log, stepped out and held it steady. "Here is your drop-off point. Follow this trail. But watch for booby traps."

"No, you tell me, why didn't you like me?" I kept my butt in the boat. "Poison, remember?"

She sighed. "Many women come to Boss. Many want to hump him because he is handsome, but more seek him out so they can use him. He has many talents. You obviously don't want to hump him. You didn't even fix your hair."

I put a hand to my hair, feeling the ponytail and every strand that had been pulled out of it in my match with the demon. My jaw dropped. "I killed a demon, didn't I?"

Feish smiled, which was frankly a horrible look, like she was a fish struggling to breathe on land. "You did. My friend killed a demon. And you make the boss a little bit crazy. That's good. Keeps him from getting overconfident."

And then she blushed, which was a strange shade of orange on her yellowish-green skin.

I grinned back and pointed at her while I tried to wink. Maybe the kava kava hadn't worn off as much as I had thought. "Hey, I am your friend." I wobbled across the boat and she held out her hand. I took it and then I was on solid ground. Or kind of solid ground as my feet sunk into the shoreline.

Feish got back in the boat, paused, and then held out her hand to me. I reached back, my boots sinking deeper in the water and muck, well over my ankles. She turned my hand palm up and placed in it a small, smooth blue stone. "When you need me to come get you, put this in water. I find you."

She gave me her version of a smile and I grinned back. "You got it. And you know, Feish, it goes both ways. If you need help, or just want to complain about your job, you can talk to me."

For just a moment, I thought she was going to cry. Her big yellow-green eyes seemed to wobble full of liquid, but she blinked it away. "I go now. Be safe, new friend."

She backed up the boat and I waved as she pulled away, disappearing down the river on the first bend. I turned and sloshed my way out of the sloppy water and muck and onto a well-worn path that was likely maintained by the city. The nature reserve was a popular tourist destination with lots of walking paths.

I wondered why the big guy was out here. At the gates of the cemetery, where we'd first met, he hadn't seemed like the kind to live in the bush. He'd had on very nice shoes, far too clean for tromping around in the muck, those tailored pants, a clean dress shirt, and a bow tie, for goodness' sake. I'd taken him for a lawyer, or maybe a doctor, or a professor. I looked down at my very nice new boots and grimaced at the layer of thick mud on them. They were going to need a solid cleaning after this.

The path was quiet as I walked, a few birds, nothing more than the usual animal noises. At the end of the path, I took a quick look around to make sure no one was watching me, then stepped to the left, as had been indicated in my instructions from Eammon.

Left was a shadowy bush trail that was barely visible from the main path, even though it was nearly noon. I pushed the bushes out of the way, knocked aside a few long strands of Spanish moss, and kept on the little bit of path I could see.

A guess, but I'd have laid money this was the way to Eric's house.

From the corner of my eye, Robert suddenly appeared. Maybe he'd been there the whole time? I didn't think so.

"How are you doing that?" I asked.

"Friend," he muttered, swaying as he walked. I sighed.

"I doubt I'll get any clear answers out of you, huh?"

Just as I thought, there was no answer to that either.

After an hour of pushing through the bush on a trail that was barely there, the path became more obvious, clearly laid out as a route and not just a bush trail. A few rocks lined the sides of it here and there, and I caught a whiff of wood smoke. Really? Who would have a stove on this time of year? The heat was already climbing into the eighties most days.

"Must be getting close."

That's what I said, and then a snap of a twig behind me stopped me in my tracks. That and the point of what felt like a gun in my lower back.

Slowly, I put my hands up. "Don't shoot."

"I can't guarantee that."

16

A growling voice rumbled behind me, competing with the normal sounds of the marshy forest around us, the sound not all that different than Sarge's when he was in his wolf form. The gun pressed into my back dug in a little harder and a bead of sweat rolled down my neck. "Who are you?"

"I'm Breena. Are you Eric?" I asked. "I met you a couple weeks ago at the Hollows Graveyard?" I didn't move. It didn't sound like Eric, and I had a hard time imagining the lanky fellow with a gun in his hand, never mind using it on someone.

But if he was as paranoid as Eammon thought, it wouldn't take more than an itchy trigger finger for him to end up blowing a hole in me.

Maybe not the worst way to go, but I didn't plan on dying just yet. Of course, that was assuming this was indeed Eric.

"I am not. But I am with the Hollows. Joe." The gun left my back and I looked over my shoulder. The man was the beefier of the two observers I'd seen on my first night, the night of the interview. "They sent you out here to take over?" He frowned.

I frowned right back. "I'm here to look after Eric, yes."

Joe's face broke into a grin. "Ah, Eric. Gotcha. Sorry, I thought you were here to…never mind. I recognize you now." He tipped his chin in the direction I'd already been heading. "His place is out there, not far. Have fun."

I couldn't put a finger on it, but I didn't like him. I didn't like the fact that he was out here, either. I mean, sure, his explanation—such as it was—made sense, and I had no reason to doubt him, and yet, there it was.

"Thanks. I think." I took a step back, turned and continued on down the path. He'd been doing his job, stopping me and making sure I was no danger. Still, I didn't like him. I paused. "Who trained you?"

"Corb. He's the best," Joe answered.

I looked over my shoulder. He was almost out of sight and moving fast through the bush, though he made very little sound.

Nope, didn't like him at all. I itched to call Eammon and ask him if Joe really was on an assignment, but I had a pretty good idea that he wasn't.

All ideas of phoning Eammon slipped away as I turned the last corner, pushed some low-hanging moss aside, and got my first good look at Eric's home. One story and built sturdy with brick—something of a surprise this far out in the reserve—it had one door and four small windows, tall and narrow, two to each side of the door. They couldn't even have let in much light.

I did see movement behind one window, like someone twitching a curtain maybe. "Eric? It's Breena. We met at the cemetery a couple of weeks ago. Eammon sent me to…" I wondered how to word this. I didn't want to say I'd been assigned to babysit him because he was a pansy. "…to hang out with you for a few days, make sure things are good."

The door opened a crack and the big dark eyes I remembered from that first night peered at me through the gap, his glasses making them even bigger, just like that first meeting. "Oh. They don't think much of me, do they, that they'd send someone untrained."

He wasn't wrong. I shrugged. "Let's make the best of it. I'll do a perimeter check, then I'll check the house and you can tell me what's going on. Okay?"

He shut the door and I let out a long sigh. "Yeah, this is going to be fun." I made my way around the house, touching the brick here and there. I even pulled out the handbook on bodyguarding that Eammon had given me, but there wasn't much in it that wasn't common sense. The tall, narrow windows were on every side of the house, and there was another door at the back. I ran my hand over it, feeling the wood, and then noticed a ding in the upper panel.

I squinted and peered closer at it. A bullet hole? We hadn't covered it in training, but I'd seen my fair share of cop shows. I pulled a nail file and tissue from my bag and pried the bullet bits out of the door and wrapped them in the thin paper. Maybe not the best forensics, but it was worth keeping. Maybe Eric wasn't wrong about people stalking him.

Or whatever he thought was going on.

Hell, maybe he'd put the bullet holes there himself to get people to believe his story.

I walked around the house a couple of times, going farther out with each loop. On the last pass, when I was easily a hundred feet out and searching the ground for I-had-no-idea-what, something caught my eye. Not much of anything, just a piece of metal, but it was partially buried in the ground and not rusted, which in this environment meant it was fresh. I pushed the metal with the toe of one boot and it pulled out of the loose soil.

The first link in a series of chains that pulled farther and farther out.

It looked just like the chains on the demon at Crash's. Was it possible that its buddies were following me? The chains grew cold as I held them, until they iced over and started sticking to parts of my skin. I dropped them to the ground, and they slithered back under the dirt like a snake.

"Not weird, not weird at all." I opened my bag and peered in there. I had that clearing powder from

Bob-John; maybe this was a good time to use it. It was supposed to clear away negative energy and if those chains were attached to another demon, I'd say that was about as negative as you could get. I opened the rhinestone-encrusted box and began sprinkling the white powder that smelled like sage on the ground.

The marsh grasses fizzled and popped, and the new smell that crawled up my nose had me backing up. Forget that, I was here to do a job, even if Eric wasn't impressed that I'd been sent. I leaned over and poured the clearing powder on top of where the chains had sunk themselves. A massive metallic shriek cut through the air as the ground rumbled. The white powder sunk into the ground and then the chains spit themselves back out, trembling and shaking. Did I dare take them?

I bent and pulled the silver-handled knife from its sheath on my left side and pressed the tip against the chains. Nothing happened. I reached out and touched the chains, but they didn't move, so I picked them up and stuffed them into my bag. Which still didn't add to the weight I had to carry. Three cheers for magic bags that carry everything, and don't turn into an abyss.

I took a step back, considering just what might be going on here. Eammon didn't think it was anything, Eric thought he was being stalked, and I'd found evidence that maybe there was something strange out here. Maybe not after him specifically, but still out here. The demon chains were interesting. Especially for me to find them twice in one day. What was that about?

I made my way to the house and knocked on the back door. "Eric, can I come in?"

I heard the sound of bolts sliding and then a heavy thud echoed through the wood before the door creaked open. A hand shot out, grabbed me and dragged me in. Just as quickly, the door was slammed shut and bolted tightly.

The interior of the house was sweltering: the fireplace roared, and flames licked the top of the firebox. Rough hardwood floors, and rougher planed wood on the walls, that was my first impression of the room. We stood in the kitchen, a high farmer's sink set in the counter on my left, next to a small cooking stove. No microwave. No fridge. *Rustic* was the only thought that came to my mind. The little light that came in the narrow windows was not enough and he had several candles lit in various places which only added to the heat. Gawd in heaven, I needed to get my questions answered and get out of here before I melted into a puddle.

I pointed at what could only be a handmade table. "We should sit to discuss your situation."

He shivered and I frowned.

"Are you cold?"

"The heat keeps them away." Eric kept his voice low. "They don't like it warm."

Sweat already slid down my sides and dripping down the inside of my pants, which was impressive considering they were leather. I cleared my throat and moved to sit at the table. "Tell me what's going on here. Then I will have a better idea of what we're up against."

"You believe me?" The shock in his voice was heavy. "I mean, they've sent out others, but they don't believe me. They just hang outside and watch the grounds and then leave as soon as they can." He shook his head.

"You shouldn't have paid them if you didn't think they were doing their job," I pointed out. Like Crash. Maybe they would have taken Eric more seriously if they'd been having to work for it.

Eric pushed his glasses up on his face and touched the top of his head. His auburn hair was wildly messy, and he looked a bit like a mad professor, even more so than the first time I'd met him. "You don't want the Hollows angry with you. They're a very powerful group. And I can't protect myself from these things, so I need them."

I shrugged, and my clothing stuck to every movement. "Tell me what's going on, in your own words, then I'll tell you what I'm seeing out there."

He pulled out the chair opposite me and sat with a heavy sigh. He was a big guy, like I'd noticed that first night, easily over six and a half feet tall. Leaning forward, he motioned for me to do the same. As if we were conspirators about to share secrets.

"They want me dead."

I pulled a notepad and pen from my purse and motioned for him to go on. His hands lay flat on the table as he whispered across to me as if he thought *they* were listening.

"It started maybe a year ago. I noticed I was being watched. Nothing serious, just someone always there out of the corner of my eye. With my background, that's not a big deal." He waved a hand in the air, and I paused him there.

"Wait, what do you mean with your background? Because you're a half-man?"

Those big eyes blinked at me through his glasses, more like an owl than a werewolf in my estimation. "You…they didn't tell you what I am, did they?"

"You're not a werewolf like Sarge?"

"A werewolf wouldn't need protection from someone like you," he said with a snort.

I put the pen down. "What do you mean, *someone like me*?" He was not used to women, that much was clear. Maybe he was the perpetual bachelor, because even a man who didn't know women well wouldn't have missed the warning in my voice.

Even Himself would have backed down at that point.

Not Eric. He just kept on going, oblivious to the current danger he'd put himself in.

He touched his glasses, adjusting them. "Well, a woman for one thing. And you're rather long in the tooth. Obviously not fit, given the way you're sweating, and I can smell the hormones on you, which means you're coming up on some powerful menopausal symptoms which will work to impair your thought processes based on the articles I read. Not what I'd call cream of the crop when it comes to being a bodyguard. No werewolf would so much

201

as glance at you, let alone think he needed you to protect him."

That's what Sarge thought of me too.

And Eammon.

And Corb.

All of them pitied me because I was *old* to them, old and useless.

The thing was there wasn't an incorrect statement in any of Eric's words, and *that's* why they hurt. Because just like that, I'd been dismissed, and for reasons I couldn't really deny. I was older. I was a woman. I was out of shape. I *was* gliding into early menopause.

Hell, I wasn't even fully trained for this stupid bodyguarding gig, no matter that I'd had training as a kid.

I sat there, all those words rushing through me, leaving as much of a sting as if he'd physically hit me.

Old. Weak. Woman.

Was this going to be my life from here on out? Was every man, critter, and child going to assume I was incapable based on my age and the fact that I didn't have a rock-hard body? I slowly stood, knowing I was about to blow my job right out of the water. But did I care in that moment? Not really.

I refused to be labeled. I refused to let the world tell me what I could and couldn't do based solely on my gender and age.

My eyes narrowed. "Go fuck yourself."

I turned on my heel, and let myself out, almost booting the door open. Rage pushed me forward like a wounded animal. Eric didn't follow me as I strode out with all the indignant fury of a woman who was done being cast aside for not being better than she was. For not somehow denying time its ravages on my body and soul.

My lower lip trembled, damn it all, and I almost ran all the way to the water's edge. Breathing hard, trying not to cry, without a second thought, I threw in the blue stone Feish had given me. I paced there while I waited for her, my ego and heart aching like I'd been slapped repeatedly on the back of my head, even while I raged that I would prove them all wrong.

A soft touch on my elbow turned me around. Eric stood there, his head hanging, *tears* dripping off his long face. "I'm sorry."

I glared at him. "Sorry isn't going to cut it, Eric."

He bit his lower lip. "You are the first person to believe I'm in danger, and I was unkind to you."

"Unkind," I drawled the word and he flinched as though I'd hit him.

He clenched his hands together in front of him. "I know better than anyone what it feels like to be put in a box and thought of as useless. Please. I don't want you to go. If you're willing to help me still."

The sound of a motor cut through the air. Feish was quick on the draw, I had to give her that. I stared at Eric. "Convince me before the boat gets here."

He went to his knees in front of me, adjusting his shirt, then clutched his hands at his chest as if he were begging. "Look, I think something's happening, and not just with me. Savannah isn't what it used to be. It used to be safe for us in the shadow world, one of the safest cities, and now it's not. I think someone wants me dead, maybe as part of a spell? That's my best guess, but I don't know. They've watched me for almost the whole last year. I had the Hollows help me try to track them down, but there was never anyone there. So, they labeled me as paranoid, and you're the first person to come out and actually believe me. And I was a jerk to you."

The motor was getting closer.

"Why do you think it's a spell?" I asked, choosing to ignore the part where he said he was a jerk. He needed me; he'd say anything. The part that made me sit up and take notice was that he thought it was for a spell. This was Gran's specialty.

His eyes darted around me as the boat drew closer and he spoke faster. "One day, about six months ago, I woke up in the bush with a dart in my side and a bunch of my fur clipped off." He cringed. "That's when I moved into my house on a more permanent basis."

A lot of spells needed fur, or spit, or just a little blood. "So, if they have your fur, then maybe they don't need you—"

"The next dart took me out two months later, and that time I had puncture wounds up and down my arms, I looked like a junkie. Whoever they are, they're progressively getting more aggressive. If my fur and my blood wasn't enough, there's only one other thing that they might want for a spell."

His eyes pleaded with me to understand, and I did. Only too well.

Death magic was not unknown to me, or to Savannah for that matter. Hoodoo and voodoo were not unheard of here, sister religions that could literally go either way. Sometimes toward the white magic, but more often than not toward the blacker magic that stained souls and stole lives. Getting caught out in a cemetery in Savannah near midnight was a dangerous activity, especially when you could see the shadows and all they hid within them.

Gran had made no bones about avoiding the cemeteries at that time, and in fact the one time she'd caught me out past midnight, I'd regretted it for days. I put a hand to my butt as if I could feel the sting of her switch even now. I loved her to pieces, but she'd not been a gran you could cross and hope for cookies the next day. She was old school granny who had more spells up her sleeve than anyone I knew.

If only I could ask for her advice.

But then, maybe I could. Her ghost was just an hour away. I didn't know how much she'd remember as a ghost, but it was worth trying.

The boat cued up behind us.

"Breena? So quick?" Feish said.

I held up a hand. "Give me just a minute."

Eric's eyes wobbled with tears. "I'm really sorry. Please help me."

The sounds of the waterway stilled as the engine died, and the birds that had been chirping a moment ago went suddenly quiet. Just like every horror movie I'd ever seen, right before the bad guys did something bad. My guts twisted and I found myself tackling

205

Eric to the ground in a move that was stupid. Even as we went down, I thought the two of them would laugh at me.

Except something thunked into the boat behind us and Feish squawked. I rolled to see a dart with a red piece of fluff sticking out its butt end jammed deep into the wood frame of the boat.

"Get in the boat! And stay down!" I grabbed Eric by the arm and half hauled him from the ground and into the boat while a wide-eyed Feish stared at me like I'd sprouted horns. Maybe I had.

I leaned into the boat, pushing it out into deeper water, feeling the strain on my old muscles, and my old lungs, and my old bones.

Yes, that's sarcasm.

I was waist deep getting the boat out as far as I could and my bag suddenly dragged me down, as if it were strangling me. I yelped and clung to the boat as I was slowly pulled under the water.

I reached down to my bag. Something had the bottom of it and was pulling me back toward shore. A gator wouldn't take me to shore, that was some small measure of comfort.

A rattle of chains rumbled under the water, that I heard only because it was so close. The chains I'd pulled from the ground slithered into the water as they slowly wrapped around the hands of a figure as it appeared in front of me, shark teeth and slitted eyes naming it as a demon.

I stumbled back, deeper into the water, and a set of hands grabbed my shoulders and yanked me up and over the edge of the boat with a flop. "Go, Feish, go!" I yelled, unable to take my eyes off the demon.

Oh, my God. I'd just yelled a card game at her. Even that was distant to watching the demon slowly turn in the water and then race outward, toward the bush. The sound of a gun, a man's scream and then we were too far away.

Did Joe just get taken by the demon? They weren't on the same side?

The boat engine revved and then we were flying away from the edge of the water. I peered up over the lip of the boat and scanned the tree line, but there was nothing. Or at least no one I could see with my old eyes. I snorted to myself and sat all the way up.

"Where are we going?" Feish glanced over at me, her eyes still a little wide.

"River Street."

"You can't take him to Boss!"

"No"—I shook my head— "I'm not taking him to Crash." I had one person I knew I could trust no matter what and she was dead. But I knew where to find her.

I just had to convince one reluctant realtor to let us in. That or we were about to do a break and enter.

The realtor's card was still in my purse—bottomless magic purses for the win—and I pulled it out, dialed the number and waited for Monica to pick up. She didn't. I smiled to myself.

B&E it was then, FTW, as the young ones say.

17

Eric and I stood in front of my gran's house, side by side. I slid my arm through the crook of his elbow for good measure, startling him so badly he jumped. I clamped down on my grip. "Here's what's going to happen, my large, hairy friend."

He looked down at me and I stared up at him, still pissed about all the things he'd said. He swallowed hard. "What?"

"You're going to follow me up the steps, and then you're going to cover me while I pick the lock, and then we're going inside." I tugged on his arm and we started up the path together, not really fitting on the narrow cobblestone walkway together.

"I think we should go back to my house," he said. "It's warm there, and the things don't come too close."

"If I'm right, the *things* were not shooting at you." No, I was pretty sure Joe had done the shooting. A Hollows member, or whatever the hell we were called once we were trained. Which would explain why no one had ever found the stalker when they'd gone to watch over Eric.

"Was it Joe who was watching you before me?" I asked.

"Yes, how did you know?" He sounded genuinely surprised.

"I'm a good guesser, but I don't think he'll be watching you again," I said as we reached the top of the stairs and the door. That scream had me thinking that Joe wouldn't be watching anyone ever again. Guns and bullets don't work on demons, I knew that much. He'd have needed a silver knife. Like mine. I shivered, grateful I had the knives Crash had sold me. Without them…well, let's not think about that. "Okay, cover me."

He stood there with his arms spread wide and I just shook my head. "Never mind. Turn around and watch the street. See if anyone notices us here." Which was totally possible. My gran's house was on a side street, sure, but that didn't mean there wasn't foot traffic. Her place was right next to the Sorrel Weed house which was a popular tourist stop with its history of blood, death, and ghosts.

"People are looking," he whispered.

"Wave at them, look friendly," I said as I set to picking the old tumblers. My gran always kept the lock greased, which was about to work in my favor as I picked one tumbler after another in quick succession. The lock clicked open and I stood, reached back for Eric, and dragged him inside with me. "Stay away from the windows," I said as I turned and locked the door behind us. "Better yet, sit there." I pointed at the bench in the entryway, kind of built into the wall. "You should be able to see someone come to the door, but they won't immediately be able to see you."

"You're better at this than I thought," he said. "I'm sorry I doubted you."

I wanted to tell him to stuff it, but instead just went up the stairs, each one creaking under me as much as an announcement of my presence as my voice. "Gran?"

A whiff of her perfume tugged me forward and I hurried toward what had been her bedroom. She paced the room, a bit more transparent than she'd been the other day, but that could be the shaft of sunlight that slid through the arched window behind her.

"Gran, I need your help." I sat on the edge of the bed, a small puff of dust rolling up.

"And I need yours." Her voice wasn't as strong as before either. I frowned, wanting to reach out for her, but I refrained as she looked me up and down. "What have you been doing, playing in the swamp?"

I looked down at my clothing, splattered with mud and bits of moss and other foliage. "Yes." Her eyebrows went up and her body faded a little more even as I watched. "Gran, what's happening to you?"

"Tell me your woes first, honey girl," she said, waving a hand at me to go on.

I took a breath and gathered my thoughts. "Someone attacked a half-man for his fur about six months ago, then two months later his blood, and now they are still hunting him which can only mean they want his death. I have to keep him safe. And I think maybe they are using demons?" That was a stretch there because I wasn't sure, but running into two demons in one day, I wasn't going to discount it, especially since the chains of one had been on Eric's property. Really, it made no sense to me as to why a demon would be after a half-man when it was obvious that a person with a gun was shooting at Eric. But I wasn't as familiar with the shadow world of Savannah as Gran had been, and where the intricacies would lie.

She tapped a finger against her chin while holding her elbow with the other hand. Classic Gran thinking pose.

"Anything else?" she asked.

"The demons have chains of some sort with them."

"What kind of metal?"

I grimaced. "You want me to guess?"

She shot me a sharp glance. "No, as good as you are at that, I think this is not the time for guesses."

I thought about the chains left behind by the demon at Crash's place. "I can find out."

She nodded. "That will help pin down what is happening, and it'll give me time to think on it. Without my book, I…well, it's nothing."

I grinned. "The red leather book? I have it! I bought it on Death Row!"

She clapped her hands together. Okay, she made the motion and my brain supplied the sound that should have issued from her hands. "Excellent. Bring it here tonight, we need it."

I could do that. "Midnight, or the witching hour?"

"Just before midnight, please." Her body faded a little more. "Without the house being occupied, I'm drifting, honey girl. My thoughts are not as clear, and my memories are not as sharp as when I was alive. I'm afraid—"

We were interrupted by Eric coming up the stairs. "I think maybe someone found us, I heard voices and feet on the stairs."

"Get in here." I grabbed him and dragged him into the bedroom. "Gran?"

"The closet. I don't think the realtor knows about it." She pointed at the closet I used to play in as a child. There was a sliding panel within it that led to a secret room. A tiny one. I didn't know how both Eric and I would fit in there, but we didn't have a choice.

I pushed him in first, and there was really no room left for me unless we got nice and cozy. "Don't get any ideas," I whispered as I climbed pretty much on top of him, squeezing my legs around his hips, and slid the panel shut behind us. He gave a squeak because he ended up grabbing my butt when I slipped, and he had to grab me, so I didn't bash backward into the door. We were truly in an awkward position should anyone find us there.

The sound of our breathing was loud in the dark, and I could smell Eric's last meal. It had included fish and garlic.

"Quiet." I kept my voice pitched low as other voices curled toward us from downstairs, getting closer. Not being found was rather important at the moment. Were they the ones looking for Eric?

Crap, I didn't know if I could defend him properly. So far it had been more about luck and timing.

Monica's voice floated up through the house, no doubt as they climbed the first set of stairs. For just a moment, I relaxed. The realtor we could deal with. If it had been demons or one of the other Hollows members, we would have been screwed. Funny how I put the Hollows group into the untrusted...or maybe not, considering Joe.

"Yes, of course, I understand that you don't like the idea of the house going to auction, but Mr. Walker, let me assure you that it will go for a much higher price," she cooed. "More money for both of us."

Himself's voice was hard, exactly as I remembered it when I woke up at night alternately hating him and cursing myself for loving him. "I understand that, but the longer we wait, the more time my ex-wife has to figure out a way around the court order. She's a sneaky cow like that."

I froze in place, my body both freezing cold and burning at the same time as I involuntarily gripped Eric harder. He whimpered.

"Miserable piece of—," I growled. Duck, duck, duck. God, I hated him!

"Who is it?" Eric's hands were huge and held my butt easily, but he was nervous. I could feel him shaking every place we touched, the heat flowing off his hands was crazy—like being pressed up to a furnace.

"My ex-husband is out there, trying to get more money out of my gran's house." I fought not to snarl the words. Eric's life was on the line and I couldn't just blow that because Himself was walking through the house that was by rights mine.

"You're squeezing me," Eric whispered. "Like, very hard, I can barely breathe."

I forced my legs to relax as the voices moved away from Gran's room. I let myself slide off Eric and then pushed the sliding door open. A bit of fresh air was not a bad thing and I needed to clear my head.

"I'd put a hex on him if I could," Gran said. "Little twerp. Steal my house and sell it, will he?"

I glanced at her and noticed that Eric did too. "You can see her?"

"I'm something of a ghost myself—depending on who you ask— so I can see her," he said quietly. "It's one of my abilities."

"But you're solid, not a ghost," I said, letting myself be distracted by Eric's quiet voice.

He shrugged. "Not everyone can see me, Breena. Even in my human form, I can slip by unnoticed.

You didn't see me at the graveyard gate until you whispered your prayer of seeing."

"Oh," Gran cooed, "you remembered."

Himself's voice rose, cutting them both off. "Do the auction this weekend. Put a reserve on it of four hundred thousand."

Monica gasped. "That's very low for the current market."

"I want it gone, and I want the money," Himself said. "Are you telling me you aren't able to sell it? I'll get someone else then."

What an ass. He'd pulled that crap with me more than once. Ask a question and then pull the rug out from under you before you had a chance to answer.

She sucked in a sharp enough breath that it echoed through the house and then she quickly back-pedaled. "No, no, I can sell it. We'll do it on Sunday. That's a good day. I'll start distributing flyers now. I have a couple leads already."

"Good. That's more like it."

Gawd in heaven, I wanted to smack his face on her behalf for the condescension in his voice. I clenched my hands, fingers curling into tight fists.

"He'll get what's coming to him," Gran said. "He will."

The door downstairs clicked shut and I wanted nothing more than to run down there and push Himself down the stairs. Forget hexing him, I'd settle for watching him die on the steps. Slowly. In a great deal of pain.

So yeah, I wasn't so much of a nice girl, after all. I moved to the window and peeked around the edge to watch Monica and Himself go down the path. He was taller than me by a few inches, closing in on six feet, slim with a potbelly-dad body going on. If you didn't look at him sideways and didn't realize that he wasn't a dad, you'd think that he was in shape. Balding on top, he often wore a cap of some sort to hide the spot. Clean-shaven as always, he wore his sports jacket and jeans with crisp lines ironed into them.

He turned back toward the house, and I shifted so my profile was out of the window frame view, but I could still see him. He squinted at the house and then smiled, a slow smile that said it all. He thought he had me.

We'd see about that.

"Here's what's going to happen." I backed up from the window. "Eric, you stay here with Gran. That will give her the energy to stay with us, right?" I glanced at Gran and noticed that she was looking more solid already. She gave me a quick nod.

"Lots of energy comes off a half-man like this one. Plenty extra for me to draw on."

Eric's big shoulders slumped. "They'll find me."

"Not right away," I said. "I'm going to find a set of those chains, grab my gran's book, and head back here so we can figure this out."

Eric cleared his throat. "Maybe could you bring some food too?"

I didn't have a lot of extra cash, but I nodded. "Chicken?"

He gave me a grin. "Extra crispy."

Of course he wanted extra crispy. I hurried down the steps, feeling a strange sense of euphoria even though I should have been scared, tired, frustrated. Gran floated in front of me when I went to the door.

"I want an apology," she said, lifting her chin and crossing her arms. Petite she might be, and a ghost, but she could still stop me in my tracks like I was twelve years old again.

"Apology?" Maybe I could play dumb.

Her scowl deepened and I turned away from her and headed toward the back door. "Gran, I'm in a hurry, can we discuss this later?"

"There might not be a later if he sells this house," she said, and a cold whisper rushed through me as she literally pushed her way through me to get in front of me once more. I stopped and sighed.

"You were right. I was wrong, okay? Is that what you want to hear?" I put my hands on my hips. "Can I go now?"

Again, she folded her arms and stared me down. "You aren't a child, you're a grown woman, and you need to own up to your mistake."

I closed my eyes a moment to compose myself. "Gran, do you blame me? I was trying to make a life with a man who had never been around anything more spiritual than watching his favorite sports team win a game. What was I supposed to do when he stuck me in the psych ward?

"Every doctor he talked to said I was delusional, and that the best thing for me was to never come back to Savannah. That's why I never came home. And yes, I let him convince me that everything I'd seen, everything you'd taught me growing up was just a fantasy. I wish I hadn't. But I…I loved him." I shrugged and spilled a truth I didn't like, but this was Gran, and so I could tell her now, even if I hadn't been able to tell her when she was still alive. "And I thought no one else would ever love me."

Gran's eyes widened. "What?"

I made a sweeping motion with one hand up and down my body. "I'm not tiny enough. I'm not quite pretty enough. I had to rely on my smarts and charm to get anywhere. You don't understand what it's like because you just never gave a flying f—"

Her eyes narrowed, stopping me. "Language."

"Fridge. I was going to say fridge," I muttered. "What any man or woman thought of you. You were always confident." I blew out a slow breath, trying to find the right words. "I thought he was more important than anything else. I put him first."

A wooden floorboard behind us creaked and I turned to see Eric standing there. "But he never put you first." His voice was quiet and soft.

I shook my head. "No, he didn't. He told me I embarrassed him, and I believed him. He told me I was a joke. And I believed him. He told me…" I swallowed hard. "He told me I was a miserable bitch." Oh, that last one was tough. I made myself keep talking. "I believed him because it was easier to change than to admit that the man I picked as my partner was a complete and utter selfish asshole." I sighed.

Gran's eyes were sad. "Why didn't you tell me this before?"

"You mean when you were dying? When the cancer was eating you from the inside out?" I spread my hands wide. "Seriously?"

She frowned and touched her head. "When I was dying, I was so sick. But you should have told me then."

Eric cleared his throat. "We often keep our secrets closer to protect those we love, but then we end up hurting them. It's a common issue."

I half-turned toward him. "Listen here, Mr. Therapist—"

He smiled. "Psychologist, actually."

Well, that was a shock. "Wait. You're a doctor, a psychologist?"

He nodded. "I do a lot of my work via phone calls, mostly for those in the shadow world who need help walking through a transition."

I couldn't help it, my lips twitched. "You help the monsters with the monsters in their closets?"

He gave a shy smile. "Something like that. You can't understand how hard it is for some of them to accept what they are, especially those who started out human. It's on par with any major life change. Divorce. Death. Coming out."

I looked from him to Gran. "Then maybe you can talk to her about why I might have run away from the shadow world. It wasn't right what I did, but as a young woman, I didn't think I had any other choice if I wanted a life. I know now I was wrong, but…I can't change what happened in the past."

"Training," she said softly. "I was training you to be strong and I failed."

I brushed past her, a rush of cold running down my side as I strode to the back door. "No, you didn't fail, Gran. Because at the end of the day, I came back and I'm doing exactly what you taught me to do. To look out for those who couldn't look out for themselves. And, right now, I have a job to do. Eric's life is in danger and I—*we*—are the only ones who believe him. Which I think was on purpose."

"How do you know that?" Eric asked.

I grinned and managed a wink despite my weary heart. "When it comes to guessing, I'm the best."

18

My first stop was not 66 Factors Row, despite the urgency of my trip to find the chains and get them back to Gran. Because every person I walked by gave me big eyes and pointed looks at my shirt. A glance down said it all. I had to change if I wanted to go incognito at all. Mud stained my once white T-shirt, and my leather pants were caked in the same mud that flaked off as I walked, leaving a veritable trail behind me.

I ducked into a tourist shop where I bought a cheap T-shirt and changed it out with the grubby, stained, torn shirt I wore, in a makeshift changing room with one of those curtains that doesn't quite close properly. The white shirt showed every mark of the last few hours, including a few spots of blood that I had no idea where they'd come from. The new shirt was black with the word Savannah etched across it in silver glitter. Not quite as inconspicuous as I'd like it to be, but then again, a tourist would think I was just another tourist, and a local might even skip over me thinking the same thing. I used the dirty shirt to knock the worst of the mud off my pants and boots.

Maybe I needed to rethink my outfits when I was on a job. No more white, that much was for sure.

Hurrying, I caught a glimpse of myself in a shop window. My hair was a disaster, my face had dirt smeared across it, and my eyes had bags under them. Crap.

The closest bathroom was at Vic's Restaurant on the riverfront. I slipped in with the crush of tourists on the bottom floor getting ice cream, slid by and made it to the bathroom. I splashed water over my face; cleaning it off helped a little. I pulled my long hair up into a high ponytail, smoothing back the flyaways as best I could. For just a moment, I looked younger, but it might have to do with the wide doe-eyed look I had going on. Shock was a funny thing but seemed to be working in my favor.

"Crap. You look like crap," I whispered to my mirrored reflection as I leaned forward. And I was going to Crash's and I couldn't help but want to not look like…a mess.

"Oh, here, I can help with that." The voice was followed by a woman who stepped out of the last stall. "Are you going on a date?" She was dressed nicely, pressed pants and a loose blouse that screamed money. She was about my age, but her life had obviously treated her better if the nails, hair, and makeup were any indication. She moved to the sink beside me and washed up her hands, drying them quickly.

"Uh, no. But I'm going to speak with a guy that—" Oh, crap, I had the hots for Crash.

She smiled and opened her purse, pulled out a compact, and turned me toward her. Her hands moved smoothly over my face, and I stood there and let her. Because this was Savannah. You let people help you here.

"Look, I'm a believer that men should love us no matter what, but you want to know the truth?" she said as she swept a brush across one of my cheekbones and then the other.

I wasn't sure I did. "Do I have a choice?" I closed my eyes as she quickly brushed something across the bags under them.

"The truth is, sometimes they need to really *see* us. And they're too dumb to see us without a little sparkle. After that, well, if they still can't see you, then they aren't the right one for you, darling. But without using a two-by-four to hit them upside the head, this is the next best thing." She stepped back and I opened my eyes. She smiled. "See? You just needed a little highlighting, pretty girl."

I turned to the mirror and my mouth dropped open. "Are you a fairy godmother?" My pale green eyes, lined with black and various shades of color, looked as though they'd been turned up in volume by at least ten notches. The bags were gone. Gone. My lashes looked longer than normal, dark, sweeping upward and framing my eyes.

And my cheekbones were accented against the rest of my face in a way that made it look completely natural with just a touch of color to my now kissably plump lips. I could never have pulled the makeup off on my own. "Seriously?"

I turned and squinted at her, suddenly suspicious. "Are you fae?"

Her eyes widened and then she smiled. "I see the resemblance now. You're Celia's granddaughter, aren't you?" I noted that she didn't answer my first question which meant yes, she probably was fae.

I stared at her, not sure what to say. Fae could be… difficult at the best of times. "She was a great loss to the community," the woman said softly. "My name is Karissa." She pulled a card out and handed it to me. "I'd love to have tea with you. When you aren't so busy."

"Breena," I said my name automatically as I stared at the card. Her name and a phone number on white card stock.

She patted me on the shoulder. "Whoever he is, make sure he notices you. Make sure he sees the real you, Breena, and not the woman you fear yourself to be."

She left me there in the washroom. Part of me wanted to wash the makeup off. The other part wanted to seal it on forever and ever. "Damn." I left it on, my vanity getting the better of me.

I tried to remember what I could about the fae in Savannah. Not many of them. None that I knew of went by the name Karissa, so that was probably a knock-off name. They didn't like giving out their names for a reason—too much power in being able to call them. The fact that she'd given me a card was no small thing when dealing with fae. I didn't take it lightly.

I shook it off, left the bathroom, and hurried toward Crash's place. First there, then I'd go to the loft and get Gran's book. We'd figure this out, one way or another.

Once I arrived at Crash's, I took note that it was much later than I'd ever visited there before. Okay, I'd only been there two times.

I knocked on the boarded-up door. "Feish, it's me."

The door opened right away, and she peered out at me, her face lighting up. "Boss is working. You want tea? We have a good visit; you tell me about that one you protecting."

I was about to say no, but the truth was, tea sounded amazing. Tea and something to go with it. We had time and I knew Eric was safe with Gran. "Yes, you get the tea. I'm going to get us something to eat."

Feish gave me a shy smile and I hurried back the way I'd come, not at all suspecting that I might have a problem getting a snack. I had a twenty in my bag somewhere, one of my last twenties. I needed to talk to Eammon about this week's training stipend. I realized then that he'd forgotten.

Looking down in my purse, I didn't notice the scuttling sounds in the quiet of the alley—until a long, hairy leg blocked my path.

I stopped so fast I ended up balancing on my toes for half a beat before I rocked back to my heels. "Oh, Jinx. Hi."

"Who told you my name?" The giant spider's multiple eyes blinked in succession and her fangs did this stretching thing toward me that made me take a slow step back. Then another. "Look, I was reading *Charlotte's Web* last night, and I was thinking—"

She lifted a leg and pointed it at me. "You like *Charlotte's Web*?"

"It makes me cry," I said. That was honest, even if I'd lied about actually reading it the night before.

"The spider dies at the end; you like that part?" She growled. Let me tell you, a spider growling is not a cool thing.

Oh…shoot. "No, that's the part that makes me cry."

"Liar!" She opened her mouth and I dodged to the side as she spat web at me. What the hell? I'd thought telling her that I liked the book would soften her toward me. I pinned myself to the side of the building as she took a swing for me, lunging forward. I ducked down and she hit her face on the brick wall. I scooted out, made myself grab a leg and yanked it hard.

She was over six feet tall at the back and had legs that spread in all directions. I'd expected her to have some weight behind her, so it caught me off guard when I easily spun her off to the side and pretty much smashed her into the wall. She lay there stunned and I used the moment to hurry my ass up.

I'd promised Feish something to go with tea, and I wasn't going to disappoint. "Enough of this, Jinx," I snapped. "Seriously, I didn't bother you. I don't know why you're bothering me."

"Job," she whispered, pushing herself up. Her seven legs wobbled, and she kept the injured one lifted. "You're a jerk."

I glared at her. "What do you mean by job?"

"My job to scare people. That's my job."

"Well, knock it off. Scare someone else." I wanted to run, but I also knew that turning my back on a large predator was a bad idea. Very bad idea. So, I went sideways around her, keeping her in my sights.

I still couldn't believe how light she'd felt when I'd grabbed her leg. Her bristling, furry leg against my palm, ugh, it was like I could still feel it there. I suppressed a shiver as I continued on down the path. A memory attempted to surface in my mind but didn't quite emerge. Something from Gran's book. There'd been something important about her, beyond the *Charlotte's Web* stuff. About…her hair? I blinked a few times and the world did a funny little wobble thing that had me on my knees like I'd had one glass too many of that really lovely Pinot Grigio I'd had that one time at that one restaurant with Himself.

My brain grappled for the information as I leaned against the brick wall of the alley and slid down, so

I was no longer standing, but in a semi-crouch, my head leaned back and my hand throbbing.

A long black leg slid into my vision. I blinked up at the fangs and multiple eyes staring down at me. That long black leg shimmered and shifted into a naked human leg. A woman with hair as black as any I'd ever seen leaned over me, her mouth wide and fangs that made me think of her spider form bared to me.

"You are way too big," I said, and my words were slurring hard. So hard. "Big furry spider." As I flopped my hand at her, a hand shot forward that was not my own and clamped around my wrist. Webbed fingers, greenish-yellow skin, and then Jinx was gone, just like that.

I rolled my head toward Feish. "Hey, you saved me."

"Her spines are in your finger. Slivers. Makes people sick." Feish clicked her tongue several times and then she was dragging me back the way we'd come.

The heels of my boots caught on the cobblestones here and there, and my head lolled back, almost touching the ground, which meant I was looking up at the bridges and some of the tourists looking down. I smiled and waved. No one waved back, except for one little boy who waved and frantically tugged on the adult next to him, trying to get his father to see me. But the man didn't seem to recognize that anything out of the usual was happening. I wondered if he could see Feish at all.

"Good kid," I mumbled. And he was a good kid, trying to help some lady being dragged along by her fish friend. My mumble turned into a laugh, and then I was being dragged through the narrow opening into 66 Factors Row.

As soon as we stepped—okay, Feish stepped and I was dragged—out of the open, the sound of hammering metal on metal rang through the air. Loud, rhythmic, and loud…did I mention loud? How could you not hear that from the outside?

"Loud," I mumbled the word.

"Boss help," Feish said, dropping me in the middle of the floor. I stared up at the ceiling, the timbers of the building clearly visible, the age on them even more so. They probably still smelled like saltwater. So often the timbers used to construct the buildings on the waterfront were pulled off old ships. I lifted a hand as if I could touch the wood and still feel the cool saltwater.

The hand that I lifted was the one I'd used to grab Jinx. Lines ran from my fingertips and palm, creeping down my wrist toward my elbow in a pattern that looked suspiciously like a spider web.

"Cool." I turned my hand over, but suddenly a figure was blocking the light. The hammering noise was gone, and when I looked up, Crash was staring down at me. "I grabbed Jinx." As if that would explain everything.

He took me by the wrist and pulled me up to my feet with little effort. "You have some of her spines still in you."

I closed my eyes and tried, with great effort on my part, not to giggle. "I don't feel anything. I just feel a little...tipsy." A giggle might have slipped out at the end, I'm not sure. I went from standing to being carried all the way to a hard bed that I tried to roll out of, and almost succeeded.

Hands grabbed me. "You need to hold her down," Crash said.

"Okay," I answered. "What's wrong with her? Who do I need to hold down?"

Feish clucked her tongue. "Why is she reacting like this to Jinx?"

"I don't know. But I think it might be an allergic reaction." Crash leaned on my forearm and pinned it to the table, which meant it was pressed against his side. The heat of his body was intense. I rolled my head to see a knife in his hand, poised over my fingers. "Hey, don't be poking me with that. I thought I was holding Feish down for you."

Confusion reigned and then the knife was poking my skin. I yelped and tried to buck, but there was a weight across my legs and lower body. I would have turned my head, but it was feeling heavier by the second.

"That hurts," I said, only I'm not sure whether I said it out loud. "Why are you even helping me?"

"The gods only know," Crash muttered.

"Because you are my friend," Feish said quietly, and with so much sincerity that my throat tightened a little.

"But I'm old," I whimpered the words, "and out of shape, and I can only remember some of the things my gran taught me, and no one thinks I can do anything! Over the hill, no good for anything!" The words turned into a wail of despair.

"Hush." Crash put a hand over my mouth. "Just hush."

The sobs continued, tears spilling out of my eyes and sliding back into my hair. Probably all my grays were showing anyway, so what did it matter if I was a mess?

"She is slipping," Feish said. "Please hurry!"

Crash's eyes had locked on mine, and he seemed to struggle to pull away. He slid his hand off my mouth. "Be quiet while we get these hairs out."

The tip of his knife pressed against my hand. There was a tiny pop, and a pressure I hadn't felt building in my hand eased off a little. Another pop, and another, and with each one the coiling tension that had been gathering in my muscles slid away, and so did everything else. My worry about my age. The fact that Crash was lovely to look at but would never look at me, even with the fancy fae makeup. The knowledge that Eric was waiting for me at my grandmother's house and was in great danger even there.

I closed my eyes, drifted off, and passed out.

19

Warmth surrounded me, and I snuggled deeper into the covers that smelled of fire and metal and something else. I arched my back as I stretched, muscles looser than they had been in the last two weeks. That arching put my butt up against a very hard body that was exceptionally warm. A large hand settled on my hip, tugging me closer to the body it was attached to.

I didn't know where I was—I only knew I didn't particularly want to leave. I rolled and slid my arms around a wide chest and pressed my face against pecs that...wait...I opened my eyes, found myself staring at a chest that I'd seen before. Hell, I'd seen his bare ass before.

Crash grumbled something in his sleep, and I remembered how badly he reacted when woken. What the hell time was it? How long had I been out? I lifted my hand that had grabbed Jinx to see there were still red spots here and there, like tiny little stings all over my palm and fingers. But there was no swelling, no pulsing pus pockets.

That hand on my hip dug in harder, pulling me closer to him. "Go back to sleep," he mumbled.

He pulled me down to the bed, tucking my hip in close to him, and threw a leg over mine as if to pin me there. A part of me loved it, I mean…he was built like a Greek god and had saved my life. The least I could give him was a nooner. I twisted around to see a clock on the bedside table. Hours had slid by while I'd been out cold. Hours we didn't have.

But Eric was waiting, and I'd not brought food back to him as I'd promised, and what if the people hunting him had found him? Hell, I hadn't even grabbed Gran's book yet, and I didn't have time now!

"Crap!" I pushed Crash off me and scrambled from the bed. Only then did I really notice that I was wearing next to nothing. Panties. That was it. Even my bra was missing. "Where are my clothes?"

The room was dim, lit by candles as it had been on my first visit, and I searched around until I found my leather pants. I yanked them on, found my bra and shirt, and was dressed in a matter of seconds.

Socks, boots, bag were next. I pulled out my leather sheaths for the two knives and got those on too.

Crash mumbled something under his breath, and I couldn't resist. I ran to his side, turned his face to me, and kissed him—on the forehead. "Thanks. For getting the hairs out."

He blinked up at me, those lovely eyes of his clearing for just a second. "Come back to bed."

Oh, yeah, that sleepy, sexy man didn't know who he was talking to; I was sure of it. But I winked anyway. "Rain check. I've got a job to do."

I hurried to the bedroom door and shoved it open. My muscles were wobbly as though I'd been working hard and not sleeping for hours.

"Feish," I called out as I shoved the door open far enough to slip out.

She hurried toward me, gave me a look up and down, disapproving.

"I know. I know! I'm not after him, I promise! I didn't—"

She swung a hand up between us, cutting me off. "Get back in that bed right now! Boss said you need to sleep, and you will sleep with him!"

I couldn't help the smile. "You are a good friend, maybe the best I've had. But I have to go. Where are the chains from that demon I killed?"

Feish opened her mouth and then shook her head. "Boss uses them to make something."

Why would he do that? "Do you know what kind of metal it is?"

She motioned for me to follow her to his work-station which included a huge coal forge, two different anvils, piles of hammers, tongs, and other tools I could only guess at. He'd added that second anvil since I'd been here last. Feish pointed to a knife that was on the anvil. There was no handle on it, just a bare tang that had yet to be fitted to something worth holding.

"Yeah, great, but what kind of metal is it? Steel?" I picked up the knife by the not-sharp end, turning it over. There was nothing special about it, but it had been made from the chains that a demon had wielded as a weapon. I frowned and set it on the anvil.

"It's special steel," Feish whispered. "Magic. Nothing that has a name."

Of course, it was so special there was no name. But still, if I took it to Gran, maybe she'd know what it was. "Can I borrow it?"

She shook her head. "No, Boss is still working on it. He doesn't like to send out unfinished work."

I did a quick tally in my head of how long it would take me to get to Gran's place and back. "When will he wake up?"

Feish tipped her head at me, her eyes saying it all despite their strangeness. "He would be very mad if he found it gone."

"But if he doesn't wake up until after we bring it back…then wouldn't that be okay?" Right then, I made a choice that I hoped I wouldn't regret. I scooped the knife and slid it into the sheath with one of mine. "You come with me; we'll hurry."

I grabbed her by the arm, and she didn't resist me, at least not much. "Oh, he is going to be mad if he catches us."

"Yes, but I'll take the blame," I said.

And just like that we were out of Crash's place and rushing back through the streets, dodging tourists and cars, weaving our way through parks. As we neared Gran's place, a buzzing sounded from inside my purse. I flipped it open and grabbed my phone.

I didn't recognize the number. "Hello?"

"Where the hell are you?" Eammon roared. "I sent Corb out to check on you, and you weren't on the reserve! Eric is missing too! Then I be sending you text after text for the last twenty-four hours and nothing!" He was breathing hard, then he let out a deep sigh. "You be okay, lass?"

Holy crap. I thought I'd been out just a couple hours, not twenty-four! It was the *next damn day!*

Checking over my shoulder, I adjusted my bag and motioned for Feish to follow me around to the back of the house. "Yup, fine. Just hunkered down with Eric."

"Thanks be to the stars. Where are you? I'm sending Corb and Sarge to back you up."

I frowned. "What, why?"

"Turns out that Eric wasn't wrong. There's something afoot, something that wants him dead," Eammon said.

236

"Well, I already figured that out, and I'm working on a long-term solution for keeping him safe."

"So, the bigfoot is okay then?" Eammon asked and I stumbled to a stop because I had to have heard him wrong.

The what? Did he say what I thought he said? Traffic flowed around us and Feish tugged on my arm, trying to get me to move out of the way of one of the horse trolleys.

"BIGFOOT?" I squeaked the word, not because I was afraid, but because I was stunned to the core. "He's a *bigfoot*?"

"Well, yes, what did you think he was?"

"I knew he was a shifter, but…not that." I got my feet moving again. Hurrying once more. I all but ran the rest of the way to Gran's house where I ran around to the back and banged on the door. Three knocks, a pause, two more, a pause, one knock. Not exactly rocket science, but I couldn't come up with a better code at the moment, and at least I was making it pretty clear that it wasn't the realtor coming to the door.

And anyone trying to kill Eric wouldn't knock.

Except Eric didn't come to the door.

"Hurry," Feish whispered. "I can feel the boss stirring. Early, he's up early!"

Oh crap! "Eammon, I've got to go." I could tell him about his corrupt co-worker later.

"Who is that with you?" he growled. "It sounds like Feish. It better not be that two-faced—"

237

I hung up on him and put my shoulder against the door, pushing it open while my free hand went for the knives at my sides, pulling them clear.

The main floor was clear, each room empty of anything. So upstairs I went, the steps creaking each time I moved. Not exactly stealthy.

Blood splattered a few spots on the banister. I wanted to hurry but didn't. It wouldn't help Eric if I ran right into the enemy's arms.

"Gran?" I whispered her name and she appeared right in front of me. I squeaked and stumbled back into Feish, nearly taking us both down. "Don't do that!"

"Where have you been? Two of those demons took Eric!" Gran scolded, wagging her finger at me. "I couldn't stop them! If I'd been alive, I could have stopped them, but all the protections on the house have faded with my death."

A stream of profanities lined up at the tip of my tongue, but I bit them back, swallowing them for later. "Look, I have the chains. They've been made into a knife."

I tucked my own weapon away and pulled out the knife that Crash had been making. Gran ran a hand above it and then jerked back as if she'd been burned. "Demon steel. That's very bad." She pressed her fingers to her forehead. "Bree, whoever made this…it's a weapon used in sacrifices. A weapon that could kill a ghost."

My jaw dropped. Eric's words filtered back to me. "Eric said he could see you because he's sort of a ghost too. Is he dead? Have I been hanging out with a dead man and didn't know it?" But how could that be? I'd practically squeezed him in half in the closet.

"Bigfoots are complicated. They're both physical and ethereal. It's why they're so hard to find in their other form. They can literally disappear. But it's also why they are so rare. They don't procreate well." Gran sat on the top step. "A weapon like this would draw blood on him like nothing else would and would ground him here in this plane long enough to kill him. But it would have to be made by a master smith. Someone who has both the physical skill and the magic to bend metal to his will."

I did a slow turn to look at Feish, my heart rate soaring. "Is…" I wanted to ask if Crash was the bad guy. If that demon had shown up to deliver the metal rather than attack him. Was he the one who wanted to kill Eric? Had we been working against each other without realizing it? I just couldn't get the question out. I didn't want to know. I mean, I did, but I didn't.

"I need to take the knife back to him. He's awake!" Feish held out her hand, but I saw the fear in her eyes. I shook my head.

"Feish, he was going to kill someone with this!"

"Not the Boss." Feish waved her hands in front of her, but I saw the uncertainty in her eyes.

I bit the inside of my cheek, thinking fast. "Gran, what's going on, why would someone want to kill Eric, and where would they take him?"

"Grave magic." She shook her head slowly. "You need to talk to Tomas and be quick about it. There is a powerful alignment of the stars and solar system tonight. It would be a good time for a blood ritual if there was going to be one. But if the one who made this knife is dangerous, your friend won't be safe going back to him." She shook her head. "There are only two who could make this knife, and I can't remember them. Damn memories are all jumbled up."

I looked at Feish. "I don't want you to get hurt. Stay here."

She sucked her bottom lip in. "I have to go back. He's calling me."

I nodded. "Tell him that I stole the knife. Tell him that you tried to get it back. That's the truth."

She turned to go, and I touched her arm, then pulled her into a hug. "I'm sorry. You've been a good friend to me."

Her arms came up around me hesitantly. "I don't want Boss to be the bad one."

"Me either."

Except that I think we both knew the truth.

I'd been playing with the enemy, and I hadn't even known it.

20

From the top window of Gran's house, Gran's ghost and I watched Feish hurry away. "How do people not see what she is?" I asked.

"They see a woman with a harelip," Gran said. "That's what those without the sight see. Their minds make up something that fits within their scope of normal. But that is neither here nor there right now. Right now, you have to find Eric. He's a lovely man."

"I'd use that term loosely," I said. I needed a car—I had to get to Tom and back. Backup wouldn't be a bad idea, either, so might as well kill two birds with one stone. "Would a werewolf be able to track Eric? Like if I bring Sarge here, could he smell his way after him?"

Gran nodded. "There's my smart girl. Get the wolf. Bring him here."

I dialed through to Sarge and got nothing, so I swallowed my pride and tried Corb. Nothing there either. I went to make another call and my phone died in my hand, like the battery literally went from eighty percent to nothing.

Gran leaned over my shoulder. "Oops. That was my fault."

I grimaced. "Let me guess. There's no power to the house right now either, is there?"

"No, or I'd have been using that to keep myself together."

I hurried down the steps, pausing at the bottom, a possible solution coming to me. "Is that old bike still in the root cellar?"

And that's how I ended up riding a bike first to the loft—where no one was, but I grabbed Gran's book and stuffed it in my bag, then plugged the phone in and tried a few more numbers. None of the numbers programmed into the phone rang through. Not Tom's, not Louis's, none of them.

"Not good, this is not good," I whispered. I had no choice but to ride out all the way to the Hollows. Not on a hog like Sarge's lovely Harley, but a pedal bike that looked like the last person who'd ridden it was Dorothy in the middle of her tornado episode.

I pedaled hard through the streets of Savannah, going for all I was worth. I was still the same forty-one-year-old with extra weight, serious self-worth issues, and the worry that I was speeding my way toward an early grave, but something important was keeping me going.

I was Eric's only hope of survival. For the first time in I don't know how long I had a purpose beyond just putting one foot in front of the other.

I pedaled harder, and within an hour, I was at the gates of the graveyard. I checked the position of the sun, marked it in my mind to be close to high noon. Graveyard magic would happen closer to midnight. I had time. I had to believe I had time.

I had twelve hours to find Eric and stop whatever was coming for him.

No problem. I pushed the gates open, and there was Robert waiting at the gravestone, tapping his long skeletal fingers across the top. "Hey, Robert." I was totally out of breath and huffing hard, but he didn't care.

"Friend."

I didn't stop to chat, just hopped back on the bike and hurried my way through to the entrance of the entrance. Yes, I know—I said it twice, but my head couldn't come up with another description.

I'm going to blame it on my age.

The opening was open (damn, my brain!) and I braked to a gliding stop, hopped off the bike, and peered down into the tomb under the weeping angel with the broken wing. The flame in his hand was out.

"Eammon?" I called down into the darkness. A groan answered me. I pulled both my knives, clutching them with sweating palms, and hurried down the steps as carefully as I could. The last thing I needed was to tumble all the way down on my ass.

No extra swelling needed there after that bike ride.

At the bottom of the steps the light that flickered was in the middle of the room, a single fire lit, and a pile of weapons thrown into it.

Another groan and I did a slow turn. "Eammon?"

"Lass?"

His voice was broken and sounded wet, which couldn't be a good sign. I found him under a plank of wood. I put both weapons down and pushed the wood off him. "What happened?"

"Crash came here looking for you," he whisper-groaned. "You shouldn't have taken something from him. He's madder than a gator with a sore tooth."

"I'm not sorry," I said as I helped him sit up.

Eammon shot me a look. "No? He killed the other trainees. I couldn't help them, all there was, was screaming."

Horror, ice and fire, roared through my veins. "What about the other teachers?"

"Tom and Louis are out of town. I went down in the first explosion of magic. Sarge fought him off, chased him out of the crypt. No idea where Corb is, he was on his way back from a job that took him to the edge of Savannah." Eammon coughed again, and when I moved to help him, he pushed my hand away. "You've caused enough harm."

I stood and stumbled away from him, forcing my feet to bring me to where the other trainees lay strewn about. Their bodies were still, but I saw chests rising and falling. Triage, we needed triage.

Luke was closest to me, and his body was curled around something. I bent and touched his shoulder, tentatively. Bite wounds covered him. Big bite wounds from an animal with a long muzzle and huge teeth. What the hell was Crash? I turned Luke over, and his eyes stared up at mine, amber gold. And he mouthed one word. A name.

"*Sarge.*"

He shuddered and convulsed under my hand, froth foaming his mouth. One of the other trainees groaned and rolled—Chad by the looks of it. "He's alive!" I yelled. "Eammon, he needs help! They all do!"

A hand on my shoulder all but threw me backward, and I found myself staring up into Corb's very angry eyes. "This is your fault. We lost four good people, all because of you."

I slid backward, feeling the weight of his words like blows, but I pulled myself together. "They aren't dead. And I didn't do this." Crash had, or so Eammon had said, but he hadn't seen Crash. Only assumed. I trusted Luke's word over his that Sarge had something to do with this.

"Yeah? Well, why did he do it? What did you take from him?" Corb pushed me backward with his size and all the anger flowing through him. His hand went to the gun at his side, and he pulled it from its holster. "Give it to me. Give me the knife. I know you have it."

I swallowed hard, looking at Luke as he trembled under the weight of what was happening to him. Sarge had done this to him. He'd *changed* him.

There was no way Corb would believe me. He and Sarge were buddies. But maybe I could get him to believe something else.

"I don't have it with me." How the hell did he know it was a knife if Crash hadn't been here causing this mess? Crash would have come in, yelling for the knife. Trashing the place. I knew he was strong enough, he'd thrown me across the room like I weighed nothing.

"Then you'd better get it and bring it to me. Maybe I can salvage this with Crash. We do not need him pissed off at us." He picked me up by one arm and pushed me toward the stairs. "You're worse than Alan said. You aren't just chaos, you're stupidity incarnate."

I stumbled up the steps and grabbed the bike.

Corb's words stung like blows to my body, and I shook as I walked my bike back through the graveyard. He agreed with Alan.

And every insecurity, every time Himself had said he'd been embarrassed by me came rushing back, dropping me to my knees. I put my hands over my face to block out the light, to breathe through the pain washing over me. Too old. Too out of shape. A woman. A joke. Had I been a joke to Eammon and the others all along? I swallowed hard as a burning core of anger cut through the pain.

"I am not a joke." I all but growled the words. I'd prove it to them if it killed me in the process.

Eric needed me, which meant I had to pull my bigger than average big girl panties up, and get the job done.

I wiped my face of the tears I hadn't meant to cry. Robert swayed next to me and I looked at him. "Sarge had something to do with this. So, I can't use him to track Eric. And Corb would never believe me now." Yeah, that stung. Robert swayed a little faster.

I pushed to my feet. Eammon was out too, seeing as I was his number one on the "You're an idiot" list.

Who did I have left in my arsenal to help?

"Not Feish," I muttered. She worked for Crash and was afraid of him.

Crash was definitely out, seeing as he could very well be the bad guy here. Damn it, I had to be honest, he was the bad guy. He'd made this knife.

Who was there left that I knew? Not Hattie, she was too timid, and I didn't want to get her killed.

I groaned and flexed my hand, feeling the spines of hairy legs stuck into me again as if they were still there. If Jinx was truly a trickster, and a shape shifter, maybe I could get her to play a trick on someone if I played my cards right. A plan formed in my mind, and I started forward again. Beaten down I might be, but I was not beaten.

Not yet.

Turning my bike around, I began the long trek back to Savannah and Factors Row. "Robert, you want to come with me?" I asked as I passed the skeleton swaying against one of the still-standing gravestones.

"Yessss." He stepped toward me and then crumpled into nothing. Well, nothing but a single bone that looked like a finger bone to me. I bent and scooped it up and tucked it into my bag. I was guessing, but it seemed like the right thing to do.

Maybe I needed to get bopped in the head again.

Scratch that, I did not need another smack in the head.

An hour later, I coasted into Savannah and headed for the part of River Street with all the tourists. I was going to start there. I had an idea. Maybe not my best idea, but I suspected if I did things just right, it would work. I hoped it would work.

I headed for a used bookstore at the edge of the tourist strip. I stumbled into the store, dragging my bike with me. "Excuse me, you can't bring your bike in here."

The man at the front desk looked me up and down and tried to wave me out. I glared back at him. "I need a specific book, and I need it now before I lose what is left of my sanity which would result in me making quite the scene in here."

His jaw snapped shut and he blinked at me a few times. "What book is that?"

"*Charlotte's Web.*"

"Oh, we have several copies." He motioned for me to follow him as he stepped around his desk. I propped my bike against the desk and hurried after him as best I could. The exhaustion of the day was catching up to me.

I really was too old for this shit. *Lethal Weapon*, in case you were wondering.

He stopped at the back of the store and pointed to a stack of books. "I have several copies somewhere in there."

I put my arm out as he moved to go by me. "Let me make myself clear. I'm in a hurry, and I'd bet the tourists would not like to see me have a meltdown in here, maybe push a few of these stacks over?" I put my other hand on the tall bookshelf to my left. "Maybe you should help me find the book, and then I can leave, and we can both be happy. M'kay?"

His lips thinned as he pressed them together. "You are being a bitch."

"I'm being a *boss*," I said with a tight smile. "Though I doubt you'd see the difference."

He bent and grabbed a copy of *Charlotte's Web* off the bottom shelf, handed it to me. I took it.

"How hard was that?"

"That'll be 3.99," he growled.

I pulled a five-dollar bill from my purse, using the motion to pull my long shirt up just enough for him to see the knives strapped to my thighs.

He cleared his throat. "I'll get you change."

"Keep it." I brushed past him, stopping at his desk. I scooped one of the pens off the surface and handed it to the shop keeper. "Sign this for me."

"What?"

"Sign as if you were the author." I pushed the pen and book at him and watched as he scrawled "EB White" onto the title page.

"You are crazy," he muttered.

"And dangerous, don't forget that," I said as I took the book and the pen, stuffing them both into my bag and then backing my bike out. Several of the customers were watching me. I waved at them and then yelled, "Look out, crazy old lady on the loose!"

I pedaled the bike along the cobblestone street, to the far end, as far away as I could get from a certain address on Factors Row. That was the problem with the two streets running parallel to each other. The last thing I needed was for Crash or Feish to see me.

At the end, I turned and peeked into the alley between the two streets. I grimaced. "Jinx. I need to hire you for a job."

There was a scuttling above me, and the big spider jumped down but didn't advance on me. In fact, she was still favoring one of her eight legs.

"You have nothing I want," she said, but she didn't walk away. I held up a hand.

"I think I do." I pulled out the battered-up copy of *Charlotte's Web*. "I have a *signed* edition of your favorite book."

She gasped. "Give it to me."

I tucked it into my bag. "I need you to track someone for me. You can change shapes, right? I saw you turn into a person after you stuck me with your hairs, and I tossed you around."

Her eight feet did a funny tap dance that drummed across the cobblestones. "Yes. I can. For the book, I'll track something for you. A shape of my choice, though."

I was hoping for a dog. "You'll have to act like you're my pet. To keep the tourists from realizing that you aren't normal."

Her feet tapped again, rapidly, and I got the impression it was her version of a nervous tic. "Who are you looking for? Boy toy?"

I frowned. "Who?" Then held up my hand. "Never mind. I'm looking for a friend." I didn't give her more than that because I really didn't trust the spider. Tricksy Jinx indeed.

"You touch him recently?"

I nodded. "Yes, you mean you can pull his smell off me?"

Her body shivered and she turned and walked around the corner onto Factors Row. Sure, we were an easy quarter mile from Crash's, but that didn't mean he wouldn't notice me peeking around the corner.

I waited. "Jinx?"

A snuffle cut through the air and then out bobbled a bear. Not just any bear. A great big black bear that smelled of musk and a darkly wooded forest.

I couldn't help my feet from taking me backward. "Holy crap on toast! A bear? Really?"

"Best nose." She rubbed her face against the inside of her leg. "Too good. You smell like a lot of creatures. You get around, huh?"

I frowned, wanting to point out that her words could be taken two ways, but maybe that was what she'd intended. "The bigfoot."

She started out straight away, heading down the length of Factors Row. "Can we take a different direction?" I asked.

"Scent is here."

Oh no.

This was not good.

If Eric's smell was here, then...

Crash really was the bad guy. He'd been the one to take Eric. There went my thoughts of finding my way back into his bed. Damn it, I really did a have a thing for the assholes. Here I'd thought he was different, and not just because he'd been kind to me.

I blew out a breath. "Lead on."

21

Jinx, in bear form, trundled down the path to Crash's shop, her big paws padding along silently with only the occasional scratch of her claws on the cobblestone path. The heat was stifling, weighing down on me as much as the worry of what we'd find. She paused there, pushed on the boarded-up door with her snout, took a deep breath, and then continued on down the path. I walked behind her with my bike. No point in riding it, but I wasn't leaving it behind either.

"He was here?" I asked. "Eric was here? You're sure?" What the hell? Wouldn't Feish and I have noticed if someone had dragged him past us from Gran's house?

Had Crash gone and found Eric when I'd been sleeping and taken him back to Factors Row? I frowned, just not seeing it. When would Crash have had time to get Eric? The timeline didn't fit.

"Yes, bigfoot was here. Gone now. Just dead fish."

Her words hit me hard and a rush of air slid out of me. "What?"

"Smells like dead fish. And the other one. I can't say what he is, not allowed. But he was here too, and angry." Her ears bobbled.

I put my hands to my head, mind and heart racing. Feish was my friend, and if she'd been hurt…If Crash had hurt her, then it was my fault for dragging her into this. "Wait here."

"Sure." Jinx sat and scratched at her belly with her long claws. I pushed my hand against the door and slid through the opening, the edges of it dragging against my bare arms. Adrenaline soared and I struggled to keep my breathing steady. Only one of the urns was burning, but a few candles were scattered around, two on their sides but still burning.

"Feish?" I whispered her name.

A smell I didn't like flowed to my nose. Something dead and something fishy, just like Jinx had said.

Please God, don't let it be Feish.

Step by step, I drew closer to Crash's workstation. The tools that had been carefully laid out had been tossed everywhere, as if a seriously pissed off someone had thrown a tantrum. I found myself pulling out the two knives from my thigh sheaths, taking comfort from the fact that at least I wouldn't be taken by surprise.

"Who are you?"

I shrieked and spun, slashing with the knives toward the voice. The speaker bellowed and fell backward, a hand to his face. So much for not being surprised.

The man stumbled back a few more steps, breathing hard. "Who are you?" he repeated, his voice a tenor, full of anger and what I could only describe as power. He sounded powerful.

Which meant there was no way I was giving him my name—I remembered that much from Gran. "I'm with the Hollows."

"Meddling idiots…" he growled, and slowly stood. Very tall, very slim, his face was hooded with a cloak, so he was definitely the bad guy here. Or at least he looked the part.

I didn't lower the blades, but instead lifted them to eye level and pointed the tips at him. "Who are you?"

"I am one of the council, here to check on this… criminal." He spat the word at me. "What are you doing here?"

"I'm friends with Feish."

"Fish? You're friends with a fish?" The hood concealed his eyes and face, but I could hear the condescension as clearly as if he'd tried to spell the word and failed.

"Her name is Fe-ish," I said, "And she works for Crash."

"That is not his name," the man said, then snorted. "And he is a criminal, so anyone working with him is criminal by association, including any and all fish." His tone made it clear that he felt that included me as well.

I arched a brow as best I could, my arms shaking from holding them up so long, but I didn't feel he'd warranted me lowering them. "Fine, he's a criminal. What are you doing here?"

"You dare to question me?" he snapped. "I am one of the Thirteen."

I shrugged. "Means nothing to me." Which wasn't entirely true. In fact, even as I spoke, the memories of Gran explaining the Thirteen blinked on inside my head like a string of Christmas lights. Well, a string of Christmas lights with several bulbs still blinking off and on, and a few more completely dark.

But this, I recalled some of this. The Thirteen were the heads of the Savannah Council of Shadows. Thirteen to keep the rest of the supernaturals in line. Thirteen to represent all the factions. Witch. Shifter. Fae. Necromancers…those were the ones I remembered. I did lower the blades then. "You're not doing a very good job of keeping your people safe."

"Excuse me?" His tone was dark, and I suppose it might have sounded terribly frightening to some people. I, on the other hand, was tired, hot, sweaty, and old enough to not give two figs about his hurt feelings.

"Don't you use that tone with me, *boy*," I snapped, assuming he was younger than me by the way he was acting. "I am old enough to not take your garbage, and I won't apologize for pointing out the obvious. If you *are* part of a council that is supposed to care for those in the shadows, then you *are* doing a piss-poor job of it!" I turned not completely away from him, but away enough that I could search the area behind Crash's workstation.

"We do a fine job—"

"Really? Is that why you have a bigfoot that's been kidnapped and is probably going to be put on a chopping block if I don't find him?" I put one knife back in its sheath and pulled my flashlight out. "Is that why you've lost control of this *criminal*?" I swept the area, saw a few spots of blood. Still keeping the council member somewhat within sight, I continued looking for Feish. She wasn't here that I could see. "This is why you have demons running around in daylight?" He sucked in a sharp breath and I ran over him with my words. "What is your name?"

"Darvin," he said. "And yours?"

"Ms. Noneofyourdamnbusiness," I said. "And don't think for a second that I believe your name is Darvin. That's a made-up name from a man who thinks he's dealing with an idiot." The more I looked around, the more my blood boiled. Because not only was Feish not here, it looked like she'd been taken by force.

How did I know?

Because Gran had trained me for this, or at least, she'd hired someone to train me. Officer Jonathan's training was distant, but the more I was in this world, the more it came back to me, bit by bit. She'd been dragged out by her heels with the way the marks were on the ground and the scales that had been pulled off her skin.

"Then we are at an impasse," he crooned. "I am here for *Crash*, as you call him. And any who would conspire with him. Demons are not my issue."

"Not worried about the bigfoot at all, are you? A rare and endangered species that someone is trying to kill?" I did a slow turn and faced him, satisfied that I would not find anything else here.

"Again, that is not my area," he said. "Another of the council will be in charge of—"

"That's stupid," I said. I waved the tip of my knife at him. "Stupid not to know what the other arms of the council are doing, or at least be aware of it. How the hell can you keep track of everything? It's no wonder you lost a criminal!"

His silence said it all. They didn't keep track of everything—they didn't talk. Power structures were a real pig whatever world you lived in, especially if some of those people were trying to climb to the top of the heap. I sighed. "I don't have time for this. My friend is hurt, I'm trying to save a bigfoot—crazy as that may seem—and you are *in my way*."

I deliberately strode past him, to show I wasn't afraid. And I wasn't. Which was a nice change from all the screeching and jumping away from things that went bump in the night.

He was the one to step back. "You have one of his knives. How could you possibly afford it?"

"I made a deal," I said.

"I'm sure you did," he murmured. "I suppose flat on your back is one way to make a deal."

My feet froze, and before I thought better of it, I spun and drove the point of the knife to the edge of the hood of his cloak, right where his throat would be, could I have seen it.

"You had better learn to show some respect, boy. I am not like the others." I said those words and they flowed off my tongue like water. Like I meant it, even if I didn't understand exactly what I was saying. How the hell was I not like the others?

Talk about bluffing my way out of something.

"Understood," he said quietly, and the condescension was gone. "Clearly understood."

I stepped back and strode away from him, pushing my way out of the door as I jammed my knives into their sheaths. The wood panel banged behind me, a loud boom that broke the still air on the other side. Irritation, fear, and confusion fought for dominance inside of me and I was shaking hard. "Jinx, let's find us a bigfoot."

She snuffled and opened her eyes, rolled to her feet and started walking. "Who were you talking to in there?"

"A council member," I said.

Her rounded ears flicked back to me. "Really? Which one? They're all kind of dicks."

I dropped a hand to the thick fur on her back and she tensed. I sighed. "You are right about that. But I'm starting to think anything with a dick, can be a dick."

She relaxed and we started out again on foot. I didn't take my hand off her back. "You okay with me touching you?"

"Yes." She rolled her shoulders, which caused a ripple down her spine. "I actually don't mind you much. You scream a lot and that makes me laugh."

My lips twitched. "Glad to be so amusing to you."

We only got a few looks as we made our way through town. "Do they see you?" I asked after a group of tourists with cameras walked by us with barely a glance.

"They see what they want to see. Probably a dog. Maybe a pony."

At that I laughed. "A pony would make them stop and want a ride." A small child glanced our way, her big blue eyes going exceptionally wide. Not unlike the little boy who had seen Feish pulling me back toward the metal shop after Jinx had stuck me with her hairy legs. Some of the children saw just fine, apparently.

I gave her a wave, and she gave me a tentative wave back.

Jinx didn't move as fast as I would have liked. The sun was shifting, sliding downward by the time we reached the edge of town. "How far?" I asked.

"Out toward the shadow graves," Jinx said.

That did not ring a bell. "Where?"

"You know it as Bonaventure Cemetery." Jinx yawned. "I'm tired. Give me the book. The path goes all the way to the shadow graves, I am sure of it."

I slid the book out of my purse and handed it to her. Or put it in her mouth. She shook her head, crunched down on the book and swallowed it whole. A lick of her chops and she turned her back on me. "I hope it didn't cost you too much."

The smugness in her voice made me smile. "A thousand dollars."

"Excellent. Tasted like at least that much." Her body shimmered and then she was a small house cat bounding away from me, back toward Factors Row.

Bonaventure wasn't too far, about a twenty-minute drive, three times that or more for a bike ride.

The sun was going down. I didn't have a lot of extra time, but I needed my grandmother and her knowledge, and her house was mostly on the way. So, I headed there first. In four days, it would be on the open market. Someone would get it in an auction. Himself would get a handsome payday. Gran would be stuck with people she didn't know. And probably wouldn't like. Maybe when I died, I would haunt the place with her.

I hopped onto my bike, took a couple of pedals and realized that my luck had taken another turn for the worse. Both tires were flat. I got off the bike with a few muttered curses. Dropping the bike where I was, I broke into a limping, foot-aching jog that took me to Gran's house in more time than the bike would have, and produced plenty of sweat. Feeling like I was too old for this was a constant refrain I kept pushing back. Positive thinking, that was what I needed. I was not old; I was midlife at best.

Forty was the new twenty or something like that, right?

I let myself in the back door—seeing as it was broken anyway, no point in using the front door. "Gran?"

She hurried (if floating quickly just above the ground could be considered hurrying) toward me, moving through the barren kitchen. "Did you find him?"

"I think so." I leaned against the closed door. I dug into my bag and pulled out the Advil, downing three of them. I needed all the help I could get at this point. "Gran, what the hell am I doing? I know that you taught me a lot of this, to help you, to protect you and the secrets of the shadow world. But that was a long time ago!" I rubbed both sides of my head. "And...I..." I didn't know how to tell her the worst of it.

She drew closer to me, her eyes as real and solid as if she were still alive. "What is it?"

Even now, with her dead, I didn't want to stress her out. I sighed and slid down the door. "I'm old, Gran! I know you don't see it that way because here you are dead as a doornail but still floating around!" I waved an impatient hand at her. "How the hell can I do this? How can I save Eric and Feish when I hurt everywhere. I'm exhausted. I don't remember all the stuff you taught me...and I don't know who to trust! I can't do this! I need to do this, and I just don't know if I can!" I was yelling by that last bit, and all the energy slid out of me. "I'm sorry."

She crouched, settling herself as a ghost would, halfway into the wooden floorboards. "You aren't old. That's the world talking to you, telling you that you have no value because of your age. Darling girl, stop trying to be young and stupid. Own yourself, my girl. Own your wisdom and the things you've learned that brought you here, back to me. Back to where you've always belonged. Those twenty-something...they don't know the power of a woman who owns every part of herself. The good, the bad, the ugly.

"Take it from someone who made it to a hundred and two. A woman of age has far more power and strength than anyone else. Far more than anyone will give you credit for, and that makes you dangerous. Because no matter how amazing you are, they will always underestimate you."

Gran brushed a ghostly hand across my face, and a chill whispered across the tracks of my tears. Her words strummed chords of truth up and down my spine, reminding me who I was, all I'd survived.

I drew a breath and brushed my own hands over the now semi-frozen tears, knocking them from my skin. I pulled her red leather-bound book out of my bag. "Do we have time to find what we're looking for in here?"

She smiled and nodded, her face crinkling up. "I think we do."

The next half hour, I scoured the book, turning the pages as she scanned them, looking for the notes she knew to find better than me.

"Here," she pointed at the page and I brushed my fingers over it, the "recipe" scribbled into the top corner in tiny print. "This is what I think they are trying to do, to open a doorway." The spell wasn't particularly complicated, but did require the death of a ghost with the knife made from demon steel. Two items that were so particular, there really couldn't be anything else.

A doorway? "To what?"

"If you already have demons, then they are looking for more power, a bigger demon, I think," Gran said softly. "That's all I can think. Now that you know what they are doing, it will help you stop them. Take any one of the items out of play, and you will stop them."

"Thanks, Gran." I paused and stuffed the book back into my bag. "I still don't know who to trust."

"What does your womanly intuition say?" She rose from her spot in the floor until she was floating once more, closer to my height than her true five foot nothing.

"Eammon," I said his name and knew it was true. Of all the mentors, I trusted him. He didn't know Sarge had attacked Luke. Even if he was pissy about Crash. Even if he thought I was trouble, he was honest. That was worth trusting.

"Then find him. Take him with you. I think whoever took your bigfoot will be far more difficult to deal with than you can handle on your own."

I raised a brow at her. "You just told me I should own myself."

"I also told you not to be a fool." Her eye crinkled nearly shut as she grinned at me. "Go on."

"I'm going to get this house," I said with as much conviction as I could muster. "I'm not losing you now. Not again."

She shook her head. "One thing at a time, honey child. One thing at a time."

And that first thing was getting to Eammon and forcing him to help me.

22

Eammon was not as easy to reach as I would have hoped. My phone was dead again, the power had been turned off in Gran's house, and the closest little restaurant café was packed with people. They apparently thought that the fried chicken here was legit, but I'd heard rumors of it being made out of house.

"Damn tourists," I muttered. But maybe this could work in my favor.

I got in line behind the other tourists. I tapped the shoulder of the man in front of me. He and his wife were holding hands, and they turned around as a unit.

"Would you mind if I borrowed your phone? The call is local, and my phone died." I put my hands together, literally begging. The woman sighed and nodded.

"Of course. These phones don't last anymore, do they?"

I agreed as she handed me her very slick phone that was twice the size of mine. I stared at it. "How do I turn it on?"

"Oh, just like this." She turned the phone toward her, and it beeped. "Facial recognition."

"Wow, cool." Truthfully, it seemed like more of a pain in the ass to me, but what did I know? I tapped in Eammon's number and thanks be to the stars above he answered.

"Who is this?" he growled.

The couple's faces dimmed in their willingness to help. Apparently, the volume was louder than I realized. "Hey, Eammon. It's me. I'm at the Chicken Shack on Bull Street. The one near the CVS," I looked over at the pharmacy as I spoke, "I need a ride. I'll even get you some chicken if you can get here in like ten minutes."

"I'm not coming to—"

"Eric is not going to make it past tonight…" Their eyes widened and I cleared my throat. "If he doesn't study for his exams. We have to help him, darling."

He coughed. "Fine. I'll be there in ten. I'll bring Sarge."

I cringed. "Don't. Bother, I mean. Don't bother him."

His breathing changed, and then he hung up. I handed the borrowed phone back to the couple.

267

"Thanks, we've been having real problems with our teenager. Especially since the divorce."

They nodded knowingly and I backed out of the line, made my way to the corner of the intersection that the Chicken Shack sat on, and waited impatiently for Eammon to show up. He didn't. And that was a problem.

Sarge did, and a spill of anxiety spiked through me as he rolled up. I stared at him, knowing that he'd been the one to hurt Luke, but not sure anyone would believe me. "Where is Eammon?"

"He's an old man, too lazy to come get you himself," he muttered. "Come on, he's back at the Hollows."

I didn't want to get on with him. But I needed a ride.

Old age and treachery, here I come.

I cleared my throat. "Look, I promised him some chicken, and I'm just waiting for my number to be called. Let me go get it." I turned my back on him and hurried toward the Chicken Shack, limping in a way that required no acting skills. I stopped and rubbed at my lower back. "Sarge, I'm so sore. Will you go in and get it? It's under my name." I dug in my purse and found an old receipt for something I'd purchased a week ago.

He sighed. "Yeah, sure, but only if I can get a bite of the chicken too." He grinned at me, and I winked up at him. Damn, I still wanted to like him, to believe that he was a good guy.

"You can have all the chicken you want," I said.

Whistling, he strode toward the line and then pushed his way into the door.

Now came the fun part. I'd ridden a few bikes in my life, so I knew the logistics of getting one going. But this was a big bike, meant for a big man.

And I was about to steal it.

I straddled the bike, pushed my bag over my hip, and started the engine. It let out a satisfying rumble, and I carefully released the clutch and turned the throttle.

The bike shot forward and I squeaked as I got my balance—barely—and shot down the street. I had no doubt that Sarge would be running after me in a matter of seconds. Which was why I ran three stop signs—telling myself it wasn't because I couldn't stop, but because I was in a hurry and didn't want Sarge to catch up to me. I drove as fast as I dared, not worrying about anything but getting to the Hollows as quickly as possible.

Eammon, I had to get to Eammon. I had to believe he would help me once I explained everything.

Twenty of the most harrowing minutes of my life later, I pulled into the graveyard, shooting down the path that I'd left not all that long ago.

I didn't know how to stop the bike, so I let the throttle off and it coasted until I couldn't hold it up anymore. Rolling off to avoid being crushed, I went spinning across the grass and landed against a large tombstone with a thump.

"Sorry," I mumbled as I pushed to my feet, groaning, cursing my aching body. The Advil wasn't keeping up with me. I was only a short distance from the Hollows tomb and the weeping angel when a howl cut through the air.

I spun to see Sarge running toward me in wolf form, teeth bared, ears pinned back.

My gran told me to trust myself, to trust the power in me as a woman who had seen a few sunrises. I breathed through the sudden fear and reached for one of my knives.

"Bad dog!" I yelled as I pulled the turquoise-handled knife from its sheath, flipped it in the air, caught it tip-side up, and threw it at the oncoming werewolf. I wanted to stop him, but not kill him.

The blade sunk into his left pectoral, and he let out a moan, stumbled, and fell to his side. I didn't go to him. I should have maybe to make sure he was breathing, but I heard yelling from inside the Hollows.

I hurried down the steps. "Hurry up!" Corb yelled. "Sarge, I can't hold them!"

The last few steps flew as I leapt down them— forgetting my age for just a second. I landed in a crouch that made me clench my teeth and bones scream at me that I was being an idiot. What the hell had I been thinking to jump even three steps? The reverberation of my landing kept me in that crouch for long enough to see Corb on his feet—barely. Eammon, Tom, Louis, and Luke had been tied with their hands and feet behind their backs, faces on the floor, blindfolds on and gags in their mouths.

Corb faced off against Darvin.

The one who'd been trying to pin something on Crash.

"Corb!" I yelled his name.

"Help me out here, Bree!" he grunted out as he took a blow from Darvin. Only it wasn't a blow, it was like a push of power erupted from Darvin's fingers as he flexed them at Corb.

Corb stumbled back a few steps and shook it off and pulled a gun. His finger tightened on the trigger, but the gun exploded in his hands.

I pulled my knife and thought about throwing it.

But I wasn't that stupid.

I ran—okay, hobbled—to Eammon and yanked his blindfold off and cut his gag.

"Stop him!" Eammon breathed out.

"Which one?" Because I suspected I already knew, no matter that it was about to kill some of my favorite shower fantasies. If Corb and Sarge were friends, and Sarge was trying to stop me, and Corb was leaving the fellow mentors tied up, it could only mean one thing.

He'd been fooling more than me all along.

"Corb. Stop him!" Eammon yelled.

That's what I'd feared. I spun on my knees before I could change my mind and threw my knife. End over end it flashed, burrowing itself into the back of his right shoulder. He bellowed and went down, and Darvin was on him in a flash, taking the last of his weapons from him.

I didn't watch as Corb went to the ground, bound with what looked like glowing rope. I scooped up a fallen knife and cut Tom, Louis, and Luke free. Luke whimpered but didn't open his eyes.

"Stay away from him." Louis pulled me back. "He is going through the change."

"Because Sarge attacked him and hurt the others, didn't he?" I said. My suspicion was that Sarge didn't really want to hurt anyone badly, but he needed us all out of his way.

Eammon hobbled up next to me. "How did you figure it out?"

I shrugged. "It was a good guess. The bites on Luke were pretty obvious if you'd really been looking."

Eammon flushed and I went on. "But when you said you would bring Sarge to pick me up, I...I knew something was wrong. You were too angry with me to have an audience when you saw me next."

Eammon looked up at me, slowly shaking his head. "You saved us, lass. We owe you."

Darvin sniffed inside his hooded cloak. "I could have taken him down on my own had I needed to."

I looked at him and sniffed right back. "Doubtful, little boy. I, a novice, nearly took your head earlier today, if you'll recall."

Eammon slid an arm around my waist, and I dropped an answering arm across his shoulders. "Go easy on Darv, he's new to the council. Eager, but young."

And stupid. Though I didn't say that out loud. Look at me, showing restraint.

"Here's the thing. I need that favor cashed in tonight," I said.

Corb growled. "You won't find them. And you won't be able to stop them. Why couldn't you have just stayed out of this, Bree? This isn't your job. It isn't your life."

"Already found them, thank you very much," I quipped as I took my blade out of his shoulder. He gave a low grunt, as I wiped my blade on his shirt. Staring down at him, I didn't like the hurt rumbling through me that he'd ended up being so like Himself. I just hadn't wanted to see it. Or maybe I really did have a thing for assholes. "Corb, you can just shut your mouth. Also, I have to say, who needs enemies when I have family like you?"

I turned to face Tom and Louis as they raised their eyebrows at me, ignoring Corb. "Look, some very bad people took Eric, and they're going to kill him tonight in order to open a gateway so they can bring in a big, bad demon. We have to save him."

Tom didn't close off his expression quickly enough, and I saw the horror there before he could keep it from me. "That's bad."

"How bad?" Eammon asked. "Opening a gateway is never good."

"Tonight, the stars align with Venus and Mercury. It's the first…well, it's the start of a lot of things. If a sacrifice is done tonight, especially of something like a bigfoot, it will set us up for any number of potential problems. Zombies. A new plague of yellow fever. Power shifting from one person to another. That gateway could mean a great deal of darkness." Tom's eyes closed as he spoke.

273

All of that sounded bad, but I felt in my gut he was holding something back. Not that it mattered, did it? If we saved Eric, then we were good to go. No zombies. No gateways. "Then we need to go now."

"I will stay with the boy," Louis said. "He will need someone here when he wakes."

That made sense. Luke had always been nervous around Sarge—how was he going to handle being just like him? Sarge. Shoot, was he still waiting for us up top? I turned toward the stairs and made my feet move.

"Where are they doing the ceremony, do you know?" Tom said.

"Bonaventure." I led the way up the stairs, adrenaline fading until I reached the top and saw the human form of a very naked, unmoving Sarge, flat on his face.

Eammon pushed me from behind. "Why did you stop? Lass…oh. Did you do this?" He made his way around me to Sarge's body. "He's still alive, but barely. You need to pull your weapon out. It's draining him."

I forced my feet over to Sarge and pulled my knife. It came out with a sucking pop that made my stomach roll. I wiped the blade on the grass and tucked it away in my other thigh sheath. The blades had saved me more than once now.

Darv came up the stairs, Corb fighting to walk ahead of him, with his still-bound hands and feet. It made for a rather awkward bunny hop move that he had to do up eighteen steps. I couldn't have bunny hopped up two of them. Darv made a motion at Sarge's body, as if he were massaging the air, and a coil of what could only be magic, blue and red lines, whipped out from his fingers and then spooled out and around the werewolf's body, lifting him just above the grass, still face down. "I'll take them both. They'll be at the fort. You won't have to worry about them any longer."

Corb struggled, his eyes suddenly wide with what could only be fear. "No! Not the fort! Darv, not the fort!"

Darv dragged the two men toward a large black van I hadn't noticed. He shoved them in the back while Corb continued to freak out (I could hear him yelling even after the doors were shut), then reversed over several graves and drove away.

Tom and Eammon stood on either side of me. "Sarge put the others out with a spell that wasn't one of Tom's, so he'd bought it from someone else," Eammon said. "Smelled heavily like fish, so I assumed again it was Crash and his pet. Sarge no doubt did it so the trainees wouldn't tell us it was him and Corb that knocked them out."

"Not Crash then after all?" I asked. I wanted to quip about what you get when you make assumptions, but I managed to keep it to myself. I'd save that one for later.

"Oh, he'd come by too, earlier," Eammon grumbled. "But he did nothing but just throw a fit, and then he left. I thought it was him when the fighting started. Assumed."

"Why would they set me up like that? To make you angry with me?" That made little sense, at least to me. "And then there's Joe."

"He's missing too," Tom said, and I shook my head.

"Joe was working with Corb," Eammon said. "He'd be here if he weren't dead."

I glanced at Eammon, thinking it through. "Joe was out watching Eric when I got there, and then he shot at Eric as I was trying to get him away from the demon who'd appeared. The demon took exception and I think it ate Joe." That was my gut instinct anyway. My guess.

Eammon's mouth dropped open and he spluttered. "You survived a demon?"

"Why is that so hard to believe?" I said, irritation flowing through me and out my mouth along with the words.

Eammon held up both hands in mock surrender. "Not because of what you're thinking. One of us, fully trained and comfortable in the shadows, would struggle with a demon. Joe getting eaten is less surprising than you surviving."

I wasn't sure I wanted to tell them it was the second demon I'd dealt with. Nope, I was going to hold that close and let them underestimate me.

"Joe was trained by Corb," Tom said. "Easy to believe he'd been working with them. Helping them keep track of Eric. Damn it, I can't believe we didn't see it coming!"

Eammon rubbed a hand over his face. "All of this—the fight at the Hollows, tying us up after, chasing you off, it was done to keep us busy, and not looking at what was happening," Eammon growled. I looked down at him.

I shook my head. "I don't understand why Sarge and Corb would want me out of the way, or at the worst, try to make it look like it was my fault that the others got hurt by Crash?"

"Corb liked you," Tom said. "He was worried you'd be hurt. If you were kicked out…then you would be safe, wouldn't you? Maybe this was how he figured he'd make you leave and keep the rest of us busy all in one fell swoop."

I didn't like the way my guts twisted with that statement. It meant I couldn't just call Corb the bad guy and let it go at that. He'd been trying to protect me in his own twisted way. Was that possible?

"What about Crash then?" I said. "He made the knife they are going to need to kill Eric with. Which they can't do because," I fished the knife out of my bag and held it up carefully by the unfinished tang.

Eammon let out a low whistle. "Good that you have it, but they could use another knife. It just won't be as effective. If Crash got caught up in something even he isn't strong enough to deal with, then they'll be too strong for us to deal with on our own." He looked at me. "You're sure it's Bonaventure and not somewhere else? There are a lot of places that can work for grave magic. That seems almost…brassy to head out there."

"Yes, I'm sure," I said.

Only I didn't know for sure because I hadn't checked the place out. I was going on what Jinx had told me. A trickster who'd given me the information in exchange for a signed book that she'd promptly eaten. Shoot, I hoped I was right.

I hoped that Jinx wasn't playing with me, because it could cost Eric his life.

23

Tom drove the three of us to Bonaventure in his low-slung sedan that had a skeleton etched into the side. "Not real subtle," I said as I ran a hand over the stitched leather interior. The stitches themselves were all bones and swirls that my brain tried to tell me were magical symbols.

"Around here, it's no big deal," Tom said. "Tourists just think I'm one of the guides."

"He does it to impress the ladies," Eammon shot at him and they laughed like there was nothing wrong, but I could feel the energy pouring off the two of them.

I looked from one to the other. "You two are nervous, huh?"

Tom let out a slow breath. "Louis didn't just stay behind to watch over Luke. This a night for the dead. That is Louis's magic. The problem is there is a bit of madness there too. Old vampire blood runs through the necromancers and if the gateway being opened needs a lot of blood, it could literally set him off."

I nodded as if yes, of course, that made total logical sense. I mean, it did in a very weird way, but there was still part of me that was like *whoa, nelly, this was not what I was expecting.*

Bonaventure sprawled out in front of us, the large wrought iron gate soundly locked, the tall trees weeping with Spanish moss blowing in the night air.

"Keys, anyone?" I asked my companions.

"We can climb over," Tom said with more than a little hesitation.

I shook my head. "I'll pick it." I grabbed my purse and rummaged around until I found the picks. I settled them into the lock, feeling the tumblers quickly. "They keep it well-greased, makes it easy."

A satisfying click, and I slid through the now-open gate. "It's a big cemetery," I said. "You want to split up?"

I turned to see Eammon smiling. "See, Tom? I told you she was a natural."

"I wasn't sure she'd remember her gran's training," Tom said. "Her gran's spell that she put on Breena was something else. Celia told me what she'd done up there in Seattle all those years ago, and I wasn't sure anything could break that spell."

Ignoring them both, I started off to the left of the gate, working my way around that edge of the cemetery. Night had fallen, but it wasn't fully dark, so I didn't bother with the flashlight. It would also be a terrible idea to alert the demons or whoever of our presence.

"Damn," I muttered.

A mumbled yell spun me to the right. I hurried, using the tombstones and weeping angels as cover as the yelling grew louder.

No other voices, just the sound of a gagged person attempting to speak. Eric would be gagged; I had no doubt about that. Gagged and trussed up like a turkey for Thanksgiving.

"Shut up, you!" A man's voice cut through the air, sharp, like the crack of a whip. I shivered and crouched lower against the gravestone to my right. I peeked around it.

A perfect shaft shot high into the air, like the steeple of a church but with no church attached to it, the spire high above our heads. Feish lay against the stone base, lightly illuminated by a lantern on the ground, her yellow-green skin looking even more yellow than normal.

Next to her was a second figure, this one trussed up differently, and far more securely than her simple ropes. Bound in metal, he didn't move, but there was no doubt in my mind it was Crash.

What the hell was this? I wasn't expecting to have to rescue him.

One person watched them. One person?

281

Where was Eric?

Those two questions banged around inside my head, telling me they were important. Why only one person if Crash was so dangerous?

I pushed it away, getting myself ready to do something. Feish needed to be saved. And apparently Crash too.

I had no idea where Eammon or Tom were. But the knife-throwing thing that Officer Jonathan had taught me all those years ago would do just fine if I could get the guard to turn away from me and give me his back. I scooped up a couple of rocks in my left hand and threw them to the other side of the spire thing, away from me. There was a muted thud. The rock had hit something other than stone or the hard ground, but it didn't matter—it had worked.

The guy watching Feish and Crash turned his back to me.

"You there!" he roared, pointing into the darkness, and then Eammon yelped as he was dragged out from his hiding place.

Whoops.

No way was I going to try and throw a knife when this guy had Eammon in hand.

What else did I have?

I swung my bag around the front of me, stood, and walked toward the spire as if I belonged here. "Excuse me, can you help me? They seem to have locked the gates and I can't get out."

The guy spun around to face me, still holding Eammon with his feet hanging high above the ground, his face slowly going purple.

I frowned. "You should put him down. He doesn't look well."

"Listen, *Karen,*" the guy drawled, dropping Eammon and walking toward me. "You need to leave before you see things you can't unsee."

Call me Karen, would he? I put my hands on my hips. "I want to speak to your manager. Immediately. Is this how you treat tourists?"

He looked over his shoulder at Eammon as if they were suddenly friends. "Tourists, am I right?"

He turned back to me as I swung a right hook I'd been just waiting to use. I caught him in the side of the head, right in the temple.

"Get him!" Eammon yelled.

"What do you think I'm doing?" I yelled back as the guy went to his knees. I completely forgot about the knives, because let's be honest, I'd done enough damage.

I used my bag that was full of all sorts of stuff, including Gran's book.

I swung it like a golf club, in a good uppercut that clapped his teeth shut and made his eyes roll in his head as he fell backward. He lay flat on the ground as Tom arrived, no doubt attracted by all the commotion.

He shook his head and scratched the top of his head. "How are you doing this?"

"Lucky? I do have a leprechaun with me." I pointed at Eammon. "Even if he is half strangled."

I hurried over to Feish's side and cut her loose of the bonds around her wrists and ankles. She threw herself at me and I hugged her back, hard. "I'm so sorry!" I said, "Are you okay?"

"No," she said. "Not your fault. Bad men came back, and Boss was sleeping."

"It was my fault they came, looking for the knife I took." I touched my hand to the purse at my side. Did a quick check and indeed it was still there, I could feel its shape through the leather. I looked over, assuming that Eammon and Tom would have set Crash free.

Nope. They stood a few feet back while he glared at them. I grabbed the lantern the guard had and dragged it over to where I could see the chains around his feet. I pointed to Eammon and then the guy I'd knocked out. "Eammon, see if boy-o over there has some keys."

A moment later, a set of keys was pressed into my hands. I unlatched the ankle wraps first and dragged them away from Crash. I looked up to see him watching me. "You don't have a gag on. Did you bite them?" A flash of something I would have called fire whipped through his eyes, enough to give me a shiver. "I'd be pissed too if I was dragged out of bed and wrapped in chains. Especially after someone stole your knife." I grimaced. "I was going to bring it back. Honest. At least until I realized it was going to be used to kill my friend."

He didn't say a word. That was not good.

When I moved to Crash's wrists, Eammon grabbed my shoulder. "Be careful, lass."

"Back up then, if you're so scared," I said as I slid the key into the lock. I really should have listened to him. I should have remembered how easily Crash had knocked me across the room. And I'd just reminded him that I'd basically stolen from him, which was kind of what had put him in this position.

He lunged forward, grabbed me by the elbows, and stood as smoothly as if I weighed nothing. "Where. Is. The. Knife?"

"Put me down," I said.

"WHERE IS IT?" He roared the words and a feeling washed over me that had no place in our present situation. Calm. I was totally calm.

"When you're done with your little tantrum, we can discuss it." I kept my eyes on his, so I caught the flicker there. Just the slightest crack in his armor. "Seriously, I know you're strong, we all do, but I still have to find Eric, and you're slowing me down. I won't allow it. And you aren't getting the knife back. Just so that we're clear on that point."

His fingers tightened to the point that I knew I was going to have bruises, but I didn't flinch. If anything, I channeled a little of my gran and tipped my chin upward so I could look down my nose at him. "Grow. Up."

Eammon let out a strangled noise that might have been a laugh, or maybe a groan. I wasn't sure which. "You made a knife for some bad people. I took it. Get over it."

Crash lowered me to the ground. "You are a thief."

"Why, because I stole your heart?" I said it with all the flippancy I could muster. "The truth is, you're the criminal here, not me. Right?"

His eyes narrowed. "I am not a criminal."

"Tell that to the council." I turned and he grabbed the bag from my shoulder, slick as could be. "HEY!"

He reached into it and pulled out the knife, spun it once and then it just kind of disappeared. "That's mine."

"Son of a bitch! If Eric dies on that blade, I will never forgive you!" I glared at him as if my glare would mean anything to him. He tossed my bag back to me which I caught in mid-air, still as light as if there were nothing in it.

His eyes were hard. "You cost me a sale."

Was that how it was going to go then? "You are about to cost me a bounty if Eric dies. Which is rather beneficial to you, if you recall?"

He put both hands on his hips, mimicking me. "Is that so? The few hundred dollars that you were going to hand me over because of this cheap ass?" He pointed at Eammon who bristled but couldn't deny that Crash was wrong. That was exactly what Eammon had planned.

I didn't think my spine could stiffen any more, but apparently, I was wrong. "I would never have shortchanged you." A thought struck me then, a guess. "Seeing as Jinx directed me here, to you, in essence saving you, I suppose she is working for you? Is she like your guard spider? Damn it, never mind," I waved a hand between us before he could say anything. "Eammon, we have to go. Eric isn't here."

I didn't wait for them. I hugged Feish again and whispered, "Tea, later this week."

She squeezed me back. "Tea it is."

"You are not having tea with Feish!" Crash snapped.

I raised a brow at him. Knowing it wasn't smart to challenge him, I did it anyway. "You think you can control her?"

Eammon cleared his throat. "He owns her. That's how it works."

My jaw dropped and a spew of profanities flowed from my mouth like a lava spray, burning every ear in its path. Eammon and Tom stepped back from me at the words, and even Crash's eyebrows shot up. "Basically," I said once I'd run out of some steam, "if you didn't catch it, that's a *no* from me. Feish, we need new people at the Hollows. Come with us."

"She isn't free to go," Crash said, and I would have sworn there was a bit of sadness in the way he said it.

I wanted to argue, I wanted to tell him he was wrong, that slavery was nothing short of barbaric, no matter how you looked it. Only it wasn't the human world, it was the world of shadows, and I was now as much a part of this world as he was. Slavery? Really? Some of my gran's teachings bubbled up, reminding me that slavery was still pretty active here, especially for those with underrated powers.

Feish blew me a kiss.

Or I think it was a kiss, hard to say really with those big lips of hers. Maybe she was blowing me a bubble, the equivalent of a fish kiss. "Go, save the bigfoot."

I wanted to do more for her, but it would have to wait. I walked as fast as I could back to Tom's parked sedan, Eammon and Tom beside me. I slid into the backseat and closed my eyes. I was going to sleep for a week once this was over, waking only to down an Advil and maybe get a hot water bottle for my lower back. "What the hell now? How do I find Eric?"

A glance at my slowly dying phone made me wish we'd just untied Feish and Crash and hurried away. The numbers blinked dully up at me. Eleven thirty. Thirty minutes before midnight. Thirty minutes, and Eric's life would be taken from him, and whatever magic was needed from him would be woven into a spell that was no doubt dark. Who would know where Eric was?

"Corb!" I shot forward in my seat. "Is there any way we can get smarmy Darv to let us talk to him?"

Eammon handed me his phone. "You can try. I may be a leprechaun, but luck doesn't seem to be on my side lately."

I opened his phone and found Darv's number, then dialed it into mine.

It rang twice before he picked up. "Eammon, do you have news?"

"Not Eammon, Bree," I said. "I need you to put Corb on the line. Now."

"You aren't the boss of me," he snapped. Like a freaking child!

I gripped the phone. "If we don't find the bigfoot, and this spell happens, any number of terrible things could come of it. Do you want to explain to your other council members that you got pissy and that's why zombies are now roaming the streets of Savannah? Or that there's some monstrous gate that is allowing demons to wander through on vacation? That's going to take tourism to a whole new level."

He was quiet for just a moment. "Zombies. Can't your necromancer handle that?"

"I'm using it as an example," I bit the words out, trying not to sound snarky because I needed him to help. Even though I wanted to reach through the phone and strangle him.

"No, I won't help you," he said finally, and the little turd hung up on me!

"What?" I yelled at the phone and then snapped it shut. I put my hand on my purse, resting it there, thinking that I needed someone who knew the graveyards, someone who could…

"Oh my God! Pull over!" I had someone who'd help. I just had to get him out of my purse.

24

Tom yanked the car to the side of the road, and I scrambled out and onto the grassy side median. I dug through my purse until I found the single bone that was Robert. I put it on the grass. I didn't really know if there was a magic word, or some other less obvious way to make him appear, so I went with simple. "Robert, I need your help."

His body grew from that single bone until he was just *there*, swaying next to me, his long hair covering a face I still hadn't fully seen. "Friend," he whispered.

"You are my friend, and I think you can help me. Can you find…" Hell, I didn't know if he would understand what a bigfoot was. And I doubted he could smell, so there would be no tracking that way.

But he knew graveyards, and I was hoping he had some sort of connection to the burial places of the other dead.

"Ask him if he can find a powerful ceremony happening in a cemetery." I looked past him to see Crash and Feish walking toward us on the side of the road. How in the world had they caught up to us? Crash's hair was disheveled, and he looked irritated as a bear woken from hibernation, but his words made sense. I still glared at him as I spoke to Robert.

"Robert, can you find a ceremony happening in a cemetery? A powerful one." Please, please, please.

Robert slowly turned and faced back toward Bonaventure, then started moving at a far quicker pace than I had thought possible for him with his swaying walk.

I followed, because not only was it the only lead I had, I trusted him. Yeah, I trusted a freaking skeleton.

My life was about as weird as you could get lately.

A hand on my shoulder stopped me, and Eammon turned me around. "Corb lives near Centennial Park. There a lot of ceremonies out here." He let me go and pointed toward Bonaventure. "Most of them in Bonaventure are benign. The ones in Centennial, not so much. He was supposed to be watching the park for anything that shouldn't be happening. It makes more sense that it would be there, that he was distracting us all by acting like nothing was wrong."

Eammon was probably right, but Robert was in point mode, like a dead golden retriever. I felt it again, the sense that I could trust him, and I was going to stick with my gut, just like my gran had said.

This was not a time for indecision. "You and Tom go to Centennial. I'll stay here with Robert."

Eammon and Tom both leaned to one side. Tom shook his head. "Who is Robert?"

I looked at them, and then looked at Crash. "You can see him, right?"

Crash nodded. "But not everyone can." He didn't explain why that was, and I didn't have time to ask. Eric didn't have time.

I pushed Eammon in the direction of the car. "Go, we don't have a lot of time, and this is the best we can do for Eric."

Just like that, I split up from them again, only this time Crash stood in my way. Well, not quite in my way.

More like to one side, watching me. "I'll come with you. Seeing as I owe you. For releasing me from bonds that Eammon would have left me in."

I shrugged and hurried after Robert, who hadn't slowed his swaying walk down the road. He slid through the iron slats of the gate and kept on walking. We'd left the gates open, and I slipped back through.

Feish stopped at the gate. "I wait here."

There was no time to argue. "Robert, can we go faster?"

Ten minutes gone. Twenty left.

Robert's swaying sped up and I jogged to keep up as he wove his way through the massive graveyard, beelining it for the edge that led along the water. The unnamed graveyard that was the Hollows hideout was directly across from us—across the water, that is.

As quickly as he'd started this trek through Bonaventure, he slowed and came to a stop. Crash put a hand on my hip and tugged me to one side. I grabbed at him to keep from falling, which was my excuse for finding myself pressed up against him, hands on his chest. Just a flash of touch, but it was enough to remind me that while he might be a bad guy, a damn criminal, my stupid hormones didn't care.

All they wanted was to have me mount up and ride that pony off into the sunset.

I tried to push away from him. One of his hands tightened on my hip, the other lifted to his lips.

Only when I stopped struggling did I hear the low chanting. How the hell had we not noticed before?

"Did you know they were here?" I whispered.

He shook his head. "They're cloaked."

Like freaking *Star Wars*. Or maybe that's *Star Trek*? I got them mixed up.

I held still and listened to the words roll over me. Not Latin, they were…tribal was the only word I could come up with.

"Hoodoo," Crash whispered. "Grave magic."

I turned so my back was against him and I could look across the graveyard sprawled out in front of me. There was a tiny speck of light, so small that I wouldn't have seen it if I hadn't been looking for it.

Then again, I might have, seeing as Robert was now going straight for it.

"Robert," I whispered as loud as I dared, and he paused in his forward movement. Crash tried to hold me still, but I elbowed him and dropped down to my hands and knees, crawling across the graveyard, using the tombs as cover. A slapping sound made me look over my shoulder.

Crash was on his hands and knees, following suit. Most undignified, and it stupidly made me like him more.

Undignified, he looked more real.

Idiot hormones.

I looked toward the light, to where Robert waited, silhouetted. Three figures stood with their hands above their heads, raised to the sky. In a simultaneous sweeping motion, they brought their fingers down and brushed them across the ground. The air crackled all around us and it was the strangest sensation.

Like the power they were calling called to me too. I wanted to stand and go to them, to lie down in the middle of their circle and let that magic wash over my naked skin, let it burn through me in a cleansing I wanted like nothing else. I ached for it.

A hand clamped on my ankle, and I shook Crash off, dragging myself forward as the chanting grew louder. And with the chanting came waves of that power that made me catch my breath as though I were being dunked in a not-unpleasant bath of hot and cold water. My skin prickled and danced with the strength of it.

I was right at the edge of their circle, tucked in behind the single gravestone big enough to hide me. Robert stood beside me, and I was fairly certain they lacked the ghost-seeing ability. That or they were so focused, they just hadn't noticed him. I closed my eyes for a quick second and then leaned out around the stone to get a good look at things.

Eric was trussed up in the middle, and the big-foot was staring in my direction. Which meant he saw me. His eyes immediately flushed with tears.

The three around him were not what I'd expected.

The first was a man with the palest of skins, so white that his hair and eyes were white too. An albino.

The second was also a man, but his skin was as dark as the night around him.

It was the third figure who shocked the crap out of me. Seriously, I had to clamp my legs together, so I didn't let out a stomach-clenching toot.

Hattie—Gran's best friend, sweet old lady, won-derful person my whole life—led the chanting in a long, flowing dress, her hands covered in rings and bracelets, the gray poof of her hair bobbing with her moves. Her body moved stiffly, but there was no hes-itation as she chanted through the litany that would bring the spell to fruition.

My gran's best friend was at the center of this? She wanted to kill Eric? Suddenly the smell of dead fish at Crash's made sense. It wasn't from Feish being hurt; it was from the stink of Hattie's canning.

Someone brushed past me and in my shock, I didn't move.

More accurately, Crash brushed past me.

The chanting slowed and I froze in place as he stepped out into the circle. What the hell was he doing? No, scratch that, I knew exactly what he was doing.

"Hattie," Crash said with a soft venom that did nothing to make him less scary. "You had your men attack me."

"Oh, lovely boy," she crooned. "I need that knife you were making. I thought you were hiding it from me."

Mind blown, I sat there in a bit of a daze. He was going to give it to her.

"I have it," he said.

He was going to give it to her.

He was just going to hand over the knife that would be used on Eric.

Nope. That was a big fat nope from me.

I edged out around the other side of the gravestone. The two men, mirror opposites of each other, had stepped toward Crash and Hattie. Belly to the ground, I crept along the side of the circle.

I made it to Eric without anyone but Crash seeing me.

He could have made a noise. He could have given me away. But instead he pulled the knife out and held it in his hands, balancing it on one fingertip. "Demon steel is valuable, Hattie. How did you get the demons to help you?"

I wasn't waiting for her explanation. Time would be of the essence here. I pulled the turquoise-handled knife from my leg sheath and cut through the ropes holding Eric in a quick slash, which was when all hell broke loose.

"Eric, run!" I yelled, and the bigfoot was up and moving, like the sort-of-ghost that he was. Which was what I'd been banking on.

Ten minutes was all they had to catch him a second time. The albino came at me first, and I stumbled backward, my heel catching the edge of a grave marker set low in the ground. "Robert!"

The skeleton lunged forward, slashing at the albino, who screeched as Robert's clawed fingers raked across his face.

I rolled to my belly, not feeling anything but pure adrenaline. I just had to keep Eric clear of them for ten minutes. We could do that.

I bolted into the dark, barely dodging the first couple of markers. We needed more protection than a single skeleton and me.

"Eric!" I tried to call quietly, but it was hard to hear over the fire raging in my lungs and the adrenaline that made my heart pump hard enough to concern me. Like, this would be a terrible time for it to stutter and stop.

A furry hand wrapped around my wrist and yanked me to the side. I yelped, and then I was smothered in long, musky-smelling hair. "They can't see us if we hold still," he whispered into my ear.

I wasn't so sure about that. Call it one of my good guesses, but if Crash could see Robert like I could, then I suspected he'd also be able to see Eric when he was playing ghostie. "Crash can."

"Turd toast," Eric whispered, his arms tightening around me as footsteps ran by us.

"Find them," Hattie called out. "They won't go far. A scared bigfoot and an even more terrified little girl. Breena, come out, you don't understand. Without his death, I will die soon. You don't want that, do you?"

I didn't answer her, because she was not the Hattie I remembered. If it had been Missy out there, I would have believed it far easier.

I looked up at Eric, getting my first glimpse of him in his other shape. He looked a little like the Wookie from *Star Wars*. Only his fur was a bit longer, and his face was more human, less animal. He blinked down at me and his glasses drooped. His bowtie was still on too, nearly buried in all that fur.

Neither of us dared to say anything, but I knew what I had to do. "Stay," I mouthed the word as I peeled his arms off me. I could draw them away from him. I could still keep him safe. Because Hattie was wrong.

I wasn't afraid.

I was fed up and tired, but I wasn't afraid, and I most certainly wasn't a little girl to be patronized.

I crouched even though my legs protested. I pushed myself through the pain, knowing I had to for Eric. And maybe a little for me too.

I slipped away from him, circled around and back toward Hattie. She was still shouting at her helpers. I didn't see Crash there with her, but she held the knife he'd made from demon steel.

I stood and walked toward her, pulling my own knives. "You crossed the wrong person this time, Hattie. My gran told me once that you were a bit crazy, but I would never have thought you'd stoop to killing."

Her pale gray eyes swept over me. She put one hand on her hip, and the other pointed the demon-steel knife at me. "You think that you can stop me? You have no idea what you've walked into. When I told you to leave Savannah, that it wasn't safe, I gave you the chance to be safe. I can take your memories away for good. I can let you go back to the normal world."

I stared her down. "My gran watched over Savannah until she died." A sense of understanding flowed over me. "She loved the shadow world and devoted her life to protecting everyone in it. And I'm taking her place."

The air around us sighed, as if the graves and those in them understood what I'd just declared. That I would protect those who could not protect themselves, so they wouldn't end up dying early.

Hattie's lip curled. "The shadow world was what killed her, Breena. She didn't die a quiet death—she was a long time from dying, and yet she was taken. Early. That was no cancer that ate her away, but a poison."

Some people would beg to differ. Gran had lived to a hundred and two. And I knew exactly what Hattie was trying to do.

Footsteps came up on either side of me. I didn't run, didn't turn to look at her two henchmen. "Then I'll find them, whoever hurt my gran," I said, "*after* I stop you."

"You can't stop us." She smiled and tucked the knife away. "You and the Hollows, such fools to only see what is in front of you. To see what I *let you see*."

She turned her back on me and snapped her fingers. "Come, boys, the time has passed."

I breathed out as the two figures brushed by either side of me. The albino bumped me, but I'd already set my stance to hold steady. I barely moved.

Time, it had all come down to holding them off just long enough.

Eric was safe.

No one had died, which in and of itself was a miracle in my books, given all the weapons, magic, and bad guys floating around.

So why did it feel like we'd lost?

25

I found Eric still huddled up to a small child's statue in the back of Bonaventure Cemetery, clinging to the stone as if the girl would protect him. Maybe she had, because he'd survived a night that I wasn't sure any of us would make it through.

His dark fur helped him blend into the night, but I still found him.

"Hey, they're gone." I held a hand to him. He stood, took a step, and put his hand in mine. The furry mitt completely covered my own hand. "They ran out of time?"

I couldn't tell if he was happy, sad, or what. Between the dark and the fur covering his face, I couldn't even guess. "I guess they did. You okay?"

"Maybe. It seems strange that they would just give up. They didn't fight you?"

I shook my head. "No." I didn't like that his own feelings echoed my instinct. "But the timing is off now. Midnight is past, and this"—I waved a hand at the sky to encompass whatever was going on that made tonight special— "won't happen again for a long time."

I tugged him forward, tucking my arm in the crook of his elbow as if on a stroll through the cemetery, just checking in on the old ancestors.

Of course, it didn't occur to me that we'd walked right into a trap.

As we approached the circle where the ceremony had been set up, we both slowed. "That would have been bad," Eric said.

I nodded, the skin along the back of my neck prickling, and I yanked him to the ground without really understanding why.

There was a whistle, and something flew through the air, landing with a thunk into a tombstone. The knife quivered where it *stuck into the marble.* My first thought was *holy crap, that was a sharp knife,* followed quickly by the realization that Eric and I were in serious trouble.

Hattie and her henchmen circled around us. Eric stayed on the ground.

"What the hell?" I yelled at Hattie. "Just because he got away?"

"You need to learn to read the stars, little girl," Hattie cackled at me. "And think twice the next time you trust what you see on your phone. A little spell that spread to all your devices, and you thought it was earlier than it was. You can thank the smith for that."

The only person who'd been near my phone besides me…was Crash. When he'd held me tight, he'd have been able to put a spell on the phone before I got into the car. I swallowed hard. Feish's sadness when I'd said we'd have tea rolled back to me. Because she thought I'd be dead.

And it would be because she'd not been able to warn me about what was going to happen with Hattie. She couldn't warn me what her master was going to do. But why would Crash put the spell on me? What did he gain?

There was no time for me to wonder too much. I still had a job to do. I just didn't know how much time we had.

"Eric, any idea how long we have to hold them off?"

Hattie circled, and I moved with her while I waited for his answer.

"Thirty minutes by the line of the moon." He let out a whimper.

So be it.

Maybe everything hurt, maybe I was older and slower than the others in the Hollows, but they weren't here, and I was. "I'm not going to hold back, Hattie."

Her eyes narrowed. "You'd hurt an old lady?"

I barked a laugh at her. "You'd hurt a child you used to babysit?"

303

"Take the bigfoot," she said to her men. "Do your best not to kill her."

That was when I said a line I'd waited my whole life to say. I crouched into a fighting stance and pulled out my knives.

"You'll have to go through me first."

The two men came at me so fast that all I could do was stumble back out of their way. As long as I kept them busy, they couldn't complete their ceremony. All I had to do was stop one of them.

"Eric, go!" I yelled as I took a swipe at the henchman with the midnight dark skin. A slash of red opened across his cheek and he let out a low hiss and bared his teeth at me. Teeth that were not human, but narrow like needles, as if his teeth had been filed down.

I took another swipe and another, and I realized they were just toying with me. Hattie laughed as she watched us play this game of cat and mouse. At least until my back was pushed up against a wrought iron fence surrounding one of the tombs. It dug into my waist, and I went over backward, the points of the tops of the fence dragging along my flesh and opening me up.

I couldn't help but grunt as I hit the ground, the wind knocked out of me, fire along my spine. The two henchmen followed me over, crawling up and over the fence like spiders.

I needed help. I needed a friend.

"Robert, now's a good time!"

The albino lunged for me and I sidestepped, right into the arms of the midnight-skinned man. Well, maybe man was a bit of a push with those teeth of his.

Teeth that were awfully close to my own flesh now. I snapped my head back, cracking the back of it into his nose. He bellowed and the smell of his breath about suffocated me.

Sulfur and rot filled my lungs and I gagged on the stench, but I stuck my butt out and leaned forward and took him with me, flipping him over my body onto the ground.

Stunned, he stared up at me and I saw the same power in him that the demon at Crash's place had possessed. My knife was in my hand and I drove it into his left eye.

An explosion of wings swept up around me, his body breaking apart into a thousand flying bugs that swept up through my hair, biting my face, my neck, any bare skin they could find. I batted them away, trying to catch a glimpse of the albino through them.

When they finally did clear, all I saw was Robert swaying, a single bone held in his hand, a thigh bone. "Help. Friend."

"He's gone? You killed him?"

"Dispersed," Robert said.

I turned and limped around the edge of the fence to see Hattie bent over Eric, that blade in her hand.

I couldn't get to them in time.

I had to throw a knife and hope I could do it again. Third time's the charm, right?

One flick of the wrist upward, I caught the knife on the way down and threw it with all I had.

End over end it flew on what was left of my strength and a prayer that I threw true, to save Eric.

Hattie stiffened with the sound of a thick thunk, her arms raising over her head, the demon-steel knife clutched between both hands. Slowly, she turned to the side, my knife sticking out of the middle of her back.

"Just like your gran, always messing up my plans," she whispered as she slowly went to her knees, then forward onto her face.

"Best compliment ever," I said. I watched her body from where I stood, because a) I was too tired to move and b) I didn't think I could survive another bluffing. "Eric, are you okay?"

"I think so." His voice was shaky, with the hint of tears in it.

I made my way around to the opening in the fence and limped my way over to him. I pulled my phone from my bag and flipped it open. Still no juice.

I looked around for Crash, but he was nowhere to be found. Good thing too. I'd have thrown my other knife at him.

I did a quick frisk of Hattie and found a phone. I flicked it on and dialed Darv's number.

"Bonaventure," I said when he picked up, and then I dropped the phone back into Hattie's still body. I pulled my knife out of her back, wiped it on her shirt and tucked it away.

I probably should feel worse about the whole killing another person thing, but remember what I said?

Behold, my field of ducks, and see that it is barren. Absolutely not one duck in sight as far as I could see.

Eric trembled so hard the tips of his fur shook in the limited light of the moon, stars, and the bare coals under the brazier. There was no doubt shock was settling in. I needed to fix this. I'd just rescued him—the last thing I wanted was for him to fall over dead from shock.

"Is that a bottle of whiskey?" I pointed at a sealed bottle of amber liquid that Hattie had set up across from the brazier.

"I think so?" Eric mumbled through chattering teeth.

I stumbled across to the bottle, picked it up, cracked the seal, and tipped it up to my lips. Three big glugs later, I handed it to Eric as the fire burned its way down my throat and into my very empty belly. "Drink."

By the time Darv arrived, Eric and I were singing the sea shanty from *Jaws* and the bottle was more than half empty.

"I'm tired and I wanna go hooooooome!" I bellowed as Darv shoved me into the back of the van.

"You saved him, but it would have been nice to find out who she was working with," Darv snapped as Eric and I fell into a fit of giggles in the back of the van. "We had insiders that were trying to find out who she was with, you little idiot! If the bigfoot had died, it would have sealed the deal!"

I looked up from the floor up the nose of a rather familiar face. "Oh, hey, Corb! You need to shave those long hairs still." I blinked a few times. "Wait, aren't you supposed to be in jail?"

His jaw ticked. "Out on good behavior."

"Oh, I doubt that!" I laughed. "What did you give them? Wait, are you the insider?" I lowered my voice to a whisper.

"There was another ceremony at Centennial Park," Darv sneered. "There were two sacrifices being made. We don't know which one was the more important one. Maybe they both were."

"Oh." I blinked a couple times and then reached for the bottle. Eric handed it off to me with a burping giggle that he tried and failed to cover up with a big mitt of his.

"I love you, Bree. You are like the best. You are amazing. They were going to let me die, and you saved me," he slurred out as he lay on the floor and went promptly to sleep.

I patted his head and tried to take another swig, but Corb snatched it from me. I pointed at him. "It's good."

He sighed and took a quick drink, then made a face. "Never liked whiskey much."

I kept looking at the ceiling of the vehicle, and then my eyes must have closed because we were picking up Tom and Eammon, both of whom took drinks from the whiskey bottle.

They all seemed a bit cozy to me, but I didn't care. Of course, maybe they'd known Corb was the insider all along? Possible. Would have been nice if they'd filled me in on it.

Someone picked me up and carried me at one point, and then I had my face buried in my own blankets and pillows. I think a large furry animal might have curled up across my feet, but for the first time in days, I slept like the dead.

Funnier when you didn't think about what had just happened.

Of course, nothing was funny the next morning when I woke up with a pounding headache, fuzz all over my tongue, and not one but two large animals on top of me.

26

Amber eyes and dog breath filled my vision and my nose as I tried to pull myself out of a funk that was undeniably self-induced. I might love me some whiskey, but it didn't always love me back. To be fair, I didn't mind all that much. After all, what was a celebration without at least one person hung over?

"Sarge, get out of here," I mumbled, pushing the dog breath away.

Sarge.

I jerked backward and would have fallen out of my bed on the far side if not for the bigfoot sleeping across my legs.

Eric muttered something and rolled over so his back was to me, grabbing a blanket and tearing it off me so he could wrap it around himself. Still all furry, he hardly needed the blanket. Then again, he'd been living in a house that he'd had cranked up as hot as he could have it for months.

I just stared at Sarge from the far side of the bed as he stood there, filling the doorway, staring right back at me. "You can't be here. You hurt all the trainees! You bit Luke!" I was shouting. The shouting hurt my head, but this was so not okay.

He was one of the bad guys.

He shook his head, turned and walked out of the room.

Voices filled the air. A whole bunch of angry male voices. I stood up abruptly, immediately regretted that movement, and sat down. Screw it. Sounded like there were enough people around to handle the situation. I didn't need to solve every problem.

It took me ten long, pain-filled minutes to find clean clothes, not so easy through squinted eyes, and a few more minutes to get to the shower across the hall.

The hot water was heavenly, but it barely muted what was now shouting in the other room. "Idiots," I muttered as I scrubbed my hair.

The shouting escalated further, what sounded like a plate hitting the floor reverberated.

"Fools," I said a little louder as I rinsed out the conditioner.

Something in the other room crashed. Maybe a chair?

Enough of that. I didn't know what was going on, but I wasn't about to rush in on their behalf.

I wrapped myself in a towel, left my hair hanging down loose and sloppy wet, which meant I trailed water all the way across Corb's hardwood floors to the kitchen and living area.

Corb, Sarge (on two legs), and Darv were on one side of the room, and Eammon, Tom, and Louis were on the other.

And every single one of the "hurt" trainees sat on the floor between them. Very much unhurt.

I gave them a nod and they all gave me weak waves, even grumpy Chad.

Onto the yelling. "Hey!" I snapped the word and every head swiveled my way. I glared at them. "If you are going to behave like children, you can all go sit in a corner and wait until the *one adult in this house is done showering!*"

I turned on my heel and slipped and slid my way back to the bathroom. I took my time drying off, braided my hair and put on clean clothes. My jeans were looser than the last time I'd tried them on.

Looked like almost getting killed, not having time to eat, and stressing about keeping a bigfoot alive was the diet for me. I snorted as I padded back out to the kitchen. Maybe I wouldn't need to keep on that keto diet after all.

By the time I reached the kitchen, I felt a little better, less nauseous, less like smacking heads together.

It was quiet.

In fact, no one was talking now.

I sighed and pointed at Corb. "Talk. And don't make me put you in the same bracket as Himself."

Corb's mouth twisted to the side. "I'm nothing like my cousin. He's an ass."

I agreed that Himself was an ass. I wasn't sure yet about Corb.

"You mean you don't lie and manipulate people?" I asked with as much innocence as I could muster that early in the morning.

He had the grace to flush. "Not to take advantage of them."

"Oh, that makes all the difference," I drawled, and Eammon gave a rather obvious coughing guffaw.

Corb cleared his throat. "Sarge and I were working under cover. We were supposed to get close to Hattie. Darv was the one who set us on to her."

Eammon folded his thick arms across his chest. "Why didn't you tell us? We could have helped."

Darv stepped forward. "Information is at a premium, and it is not for the weak. And we weren't sure that she," he tipped his head at me, "wouldn't side with Hattie. They were close when she was younger, and there was a chance that she'd get sucked into the witch's web."

My jaw tightened. I could see the concern, and if they'd accused Hattie in front of me, I probably would have defended her before last night.

Louis, Tom, and Eammon started shouting all at once, and I knew then that there would be no reconciling these men anytime soon.

I sat on one of the thickly cushioned chairs, sinking into the pillows and wishing I could sink back into my bed, pull the covers up, and then just ignore the world for a good long while. I noticed the other trainees were saying nothing. "And the group of you?"

"We had no idea," Suzy said. "Sarge came in with donuts, we all had one and then we passed out."

"And the attack on Luke?" Again, I could feel my head spinning as I put the pieces together. "You were going to do it anyway, weren't you? That was why he was so afraid of you, Sarge."

Sarge shrugged. "Wanting to be a werewolf is a whole lot different than actually getting there. At least he was drugged so he didn't feel the wounds as much. By the way, you haven't apologized for sticking me with your knife."

I glared at him, annoyed by his audacity. "And I won't. You're lucky I don't stick you again." I paused. "Darv, you just took Corb and Sarge out of there. Why didn't you tell us they were undercover then?"

"Because we still weren't sure who was helping Hattie. We knew Joe was, but we also knew you were close to Hattie when you were a child. There was a chance that we could still flush you out."

My jaw dropped. "You thought I was one of the bad guys?" Then it hit me. Of course they did. I'd been friendly with Crash and Hattie.

I did a slow turn to look at Eammon and the other mentors. "Did you all think I was in on this? Was this entire thing a setup?"

Every single face was a careful blank, a mask of their thoughts. My guts clenched. So much for thinking I belonged. This whole thing had been a sting to flush out those working with Hattie. Even if Eammon, Louis and Tom hadn't known what was going on, they hadn't trusted me because of Crash which had worked into Corb's plans. Joe had been the only true one working with her, Sarge and Corb had been trying to flush out others. And one of those others they thought it could be, was little old me.

Darv held up his hand. "The council thanks you, the Hollows Group, for your help in this matter. We will be in touch." He turned and strode out of the loft, his booted feet clicking on the stairs as he went.

I pulled myself out of the chair, my body hurting and, worse than that, my heart hurting more than a little too. I was no fool. I knew when I was being used as fodder. Himself had done it for so many years, it was easy for me to see now that my eyes were wide open.

The remaining men argued, and I headed down the stairs and out the front door. I was surprised to find Darv standing on the front step, looking at the cemetery across from us.

"Your gran, Celia, was of great service to the council. We hope that you will follow in her footsteps." Darv handed me a card.

I flipped it over. Just his name and a number, different than the one I already had. "I'll discuss it with my gran, see how it was working with a council that didn't know their arse from their head. When they throw innocents under the bus." I smiled and his smile faded.

315

"You do not want to make enemies of us," he said as he stepped off the sidewalk and crossed to the other side. A truck passed between us, and he was gone. Poof.

Like magic. "Nor do you want to make an enemy of me, you little idiot."

I walked across the road, barefoot but not really caring. The road was cool on the soles of my feet, and then the grass of the cemetery was soft and inviting. I wove my way through, avoiding stepping on any obvious graves, until I found a stack of tombstones that didn't belong to anyone. The names had worn off to the point that the etchings were barely there, unreadable, but at some point had belonged to someone. Now, they just leaned up against the fence as if waiting for something to happen. Or maybe for someone to help them get home. For some reason they called to me, and I just stood there, trying to decipher their names that I knew had been scoured by far better professionals than me.

A swaying body stepped up to my right. "Hi, Robert," I said. "They all thought I was one of the bad guys. And you know what, it sucks. All along they thought I was a mole, and I was just trying to do right by my gran, by everything I'd been taught all those years ago."

"Friend."

I sighed. "Friend is tired. Friend is…confused." I paused. "Thanks again, for your help last night. I'll get you something to eat. What do you want?"

"Whiskey," he grumbled and I laughed.

"You're my kind of skeleton. I'll get you some whiskey."

He didn't say anything more, didn't respond to my thanks. I glanced at him and he was pointing back the way I'd come. I turned to see someone approaching who I really, really didn't want to see.

Not then, not ever.

Himself strode across the grass, stepping on graves as if they meant nothing, as if no one was in them. "Robert. Don't kill him."

Robert let out a low grumble.

"Breena, what the hell are you doing here?" Himself snapped. "I came here to talk to my cousin about the new business he's starting, and I see you *leaving* his apartment?" His face was flushed, bright spots of color racing across his cheeks and forehead, right up to where his hair receded. Badly receded, I amended.

Here's the thing. You shouldn't argue with a woman who knows all your secrets. Certainly not in public. "I got tired of waiting for you to get it up, Alan. Corb knows how to treat a woman right. He's very, very good at it."

His eyes about bugged out. "You're *sleeping* with my cousin? Are you serious? You can't be."

I smiled, didn't deny or agree. Just smiled. "What are you doing here, Alan?" I almost called him Himself.

"I'm selling *my* house." He put his hands on his hips and began to pace in front of me. "I want to know what you're really doing here. There is no way that Corb would ever date a woman like you. And you won't stop me from selling the house. No judge will rescind the divorce papers, I made sure of it."

My eyes narrowed. "You got my text?"

He gave me a smarmy grin. "You aren't the only one with connections."

Oh…that son of a….

Corb strolled toward us across the grass. Here was the moment I needed Corb to follow my lead more than any other. "Corb, would you tell your pansy-ass cuz here that you are thoroughly satisfied with me as your current sexual partner?" He owed me, so he'd better pay up in spades.

Himself turned his back to me and I lifted both hands, palms up, and shrugged at Corb. His face was tight as he strode past Himself, his eyes locked on mine as he headed straight for me. "I'm sorry, I can't do that."

Crap, so much for irritating Himself. Corb slid an arm around my waist. "I've been trying to get her into bed since she got here, but she's been so busy at her new job, she's barely looked my way."

I blinked up at him as he lowered his face and kissed me.

Corb kissing me was not something that I had on my list for the day, though I wasn't complaining. Certainly not the kind of kiss that leaves your tongue tangled and sends your heart rate soaring, forcing you to grip his shirt so you don't stumble. He broke it off but kept his face close. "Sorry. Got carried away. I'm sorry, for everything." Those last four words were spoken quietly, just for my ears.

Himself stormed off, and I do mean stormed. He even pushed through a couple walking hand in hand. They shouted after him and I laughed as I untangled myself from Corb's arms. "Thanks. That will put a bee in his bonnet that he won't be able to get out for at least a week." Maybe two if I were lucky.

Corb didn't take his arm from around my waist, and I was suddenly very aware of just how close we still were. "Corb. You can let go of me."

He did, but his hand slid down my arm to my hand. "I always thought you were much too good for him, Bree."

I pulled away, not because I wasn't intrigued, but because he'd lied to me. "One kiss isn't going to make it all better, Corb. You lied to me, and you put us all in danger because of your lies. That's not how friendships work."

He gave a slow nod. "Fair enough. Then I'll just keep on proving that I really do care. I never wanted you to get hurt, Bree. And I never for one second thought you were in on it."

I nodded slowly, feeling the truth in his words. "That I believe." I paused and shook my head. "I need to check on one more person, today," I said. "Two actually."

Corb looked away from me, toward the river, toward Factors Row. "I don't know if either of them will be there. He said something about leaving. Getting out of town for awhile."

I walked with Corb back to his loft and he handed me the keys to his baby, the bright red Mustang he loved so very much. "Just don't dent it."

"I can drive, Corb. I'm not that old," I muttered. I slid on shoes, grabbed a towel and wrapped up what I needed to return, and then slid into the sleek muscle car.

Not exactly inconspicuous with the way the engine revved and the flashy racing stripe down the center of the hood.

It smelled like Corb, like spice and a little bit of honey, maybe. Something sweet for sure to offset that sharp man smell. Damn it, that kiss had shaken me. But it had been play acting. I knew that. Right?

I shook it off and drove downtown, parking as close as I could get to Factors Row.

Tucking the keys into my front pocket, I pulled out the bundled-up towel, cradling it under one arm.

The sound of people, cars, and the river rattled along as if nothing had happened last night. Strange how they could just keep going when we'd all barely averted disaster.

I saw Jinx long before she saw me. "Jinx, are they still here? Should I even bother knocking?"

The spider spun around and dropped to the cobblestones, scuttling across to me a little faster than I would have liked. She stopped about ten feet out from me. "Yes, for now. I think they are leaving tonight."

I nodded. "Thanks. And thanks for the help too. You were spot on."

"Of course I was." She sniffed at me and flexed her fangs.

I made myself walk past her to the boarded-up door of 66 Factors Row. I rapped my knuckles on the wood. "Hello. Returning merchandise. I don't know if I can get a full refund, or if I have to take store credit? I would prefer a refund seeing as store credit wouldn't work since you're a bad guy and all."

The door pulled open to reveal Feish as pale as I'd ever seen her. I locked eyes with her, and she slowly lowered her face. "He is sleeping."

A slow smile slid over my lips. "Good."

As I walked by her, she lifted a hand and, at a look from me, dropped it. "I didn't want you to get hurt."

That stopped my feet. "What?"

"You're the first friend I've had in a long time, and those that the Boss was dealing with…they are bad news." Feish lifted her eyes to mine. "I thought you would leave if he changed the time, and you almost did."

A sigh slid out of me. "We almost got killed because of him."

She covered her face with her webbed hands and a gurgling flowed from her that I realized was tears. I mean, it was beyond pitiful, and I do not have a heart of stone. I reached over and hugged her, and she all but collapsed into my arms.

"I get it, Feish. I screw up all the time. It seems to be a gift of mine. But this was not your fault." I patted her back.

Slowly, she stood under her own power again, her yellow-green skin mottled now with little blue flecks. "You…are we still friends?"

I thought about it for a moment. "Feish, his mistake is not yours. Okay?"

"You are sure? I am belonging to him," she whispered.

Gawd in heaven, I hated that. "Look, I will do my best not to get you into trouble with your boss." I smiled.

Her head swiveled and she looked toward his chamber. "You're still going to wake him up, aren't you?"

I nodded. "Maybe you just stepped out for a bit? Didn't see me come in?"

Her eyes lit up. "Good idea. I will be at Death Row if you need me."

In a flash, she was gone, and I walked toward Crash's bedroom. The door was heavy, and it took me pushing with all the strength I had left—which wasn't much after the previous night—to get it open enough to slip through.

I stood on the far side of his bed, so he couldn't grab me like he had the last time and fling me against the wall. The bedroom was once more lit up with candles, and the sheet was again pooled around his waist which showed off a portion of tattoos. Damn him for looking yummy even when he'd turned out to be the bad guy. I tried not to think too much about how he'd kept Hattie's attention, so I could get Eric away. I didn't want to give him credit where it might have just been him being him. "Crash."

Nothing.

The bundled-up towel in my hands felt heavy. I lowered it to the bed. "There's a note in with the knives and the belt. But I'll say it now because I need to." I took a slow breath and let it out even slower. "I refuse your deal. You have my four hundred dollars, which we will call a rental for this last ten days for the weapons and the belt that holds them. I've cleaned the knives and the leather, and there is no damage to them."

Still nothing from the body on the bed. In the shadows, I could see that his head was partially covered by a pillow, and the sheet had pulled down to his waist, showing off that broad back of his that practically rippled with muscle that drew my hands like a bee to pollen. I sighed.

I really had to get these hormones under control.

I took a step back, and he moved.

"I do not allow returns," he mumbled from under the pillow.

"Piss off. I don't want them," I snapped. He didn't move anything but one hand. Palm up, he crooked a finger at me.

I laughed at him. "Um. Much as I *would* rock your world, if you were so lucky, Crash, I think that's a terrible idea. Terrible. Awful. Worst one in a long time. You're on one side of the shadows, and I'm on the other." That last bit? Yeah, that last bit was something I'd heard my Gran say more than once.

There are two sides to the shadow world. The side that lay in true darkness, and the side that protects the darkness from the light. I now had a better understanding of what she'd meant.

He finally lifted his head, sleep still trying to keep its grip on him. "You cannot return them."

I let myself sit on the edge of the bed. "Crash, I wanted to like you. I even thought we might be friends. But you made a knife—knowingly—out of demon steel. You had to know that it wasn't for any good purpose. And then you gave the knife to Hattie, when I'd told you she wanted to kill Eric!"

God in heaven, how could he not see that was a problem?

"That is what I do," he said. "I am the blacksmith."

I twisted where I sat. He had propped himself up on one elbow. Damn it, he really was luscious. I should not be lusting after the guy who was on the wrong side of the shadows. I made a face for myself as much as at him. "Look, nothing I can do about your moral compass, okay? But I can keep mine working. Which means you keep the knives."

He shook his head. "No."

"Damn it, Crash!" I yelled.

"It is far more complicated than that," he said. "You drew blood with them both, you've killed with them. They are marked to you now and would not cut for many other people. Which makes them useless for me to take back. Hence, no returns."

He was more and more awake; I could see it in his eyes. "You're a jerk."

"I am honest. Occasionally that makes me the bad guy." He reached out and took hold of my wrist so fast, I didn't see him even move.

With a swift yank, he drew me to him until we were nose to nose. One fingertip traced the side of my face. "You are very interesting, Breena O'Rylee. It's been a long time since I've been so intrigued." The heat of his fingertip was doing really wild things to my insides, cranking up the heat as though I were the forge and he knew exactly how to light my fire. In fact, I was sure he did. And that was the thing. Men like him were dangerous. In all the wrong ways.

I couldn't breathe, couldn't move if I'd wanted. So, I did the next best thing. I used my mouth. Not that way, get your head out of the gutter. "My gran warned me about men like you."

His lips quirked up. "What did she say?"

"She told me to kick them in the balls and run for the hills."

He burst out laughing, his smile like the sun coming out from behind a cloud. I didn't know if it was whatever magic he had, or just him. I was betting on a combo of the two. But I tried to pull away from him anyway.

I thought he'd try to hold me, but he let me go. I scrambled back across the bed, the remembered sensation of his body pressed against mine still very much felt on every inch of my skin, hot and wanting.

Damn it.

"Take the knives." He lay back. "Or I'll just throw them in the forge and melt them down to nothing. And you still owe me for them on that last bounty."

My jaw flapped. "You really are an ass."

But I scooped up the knives, unable to believe they could just be melted into nothing, and strode out of his room, followed by his low chuckle that continued to tug on parts of me that I hadn't noticed for the last ten years with Himself.

A few weeks in Savannah, and I was like a raging hussy.

I would have slammed the bedroom door shut if it had been possible, both out of annoyance toward him, and myself for my reaction to him. But it was too heavy, and I had to settle for the satisfying screech it made as I slowly shut it.

And that was how I ended up with two knives, two men who were maybe somewhat interested in me, and a job I actually loved in a town I loved even more.

Forty-one suddenly wasn't looking so bad.

AFTERWORD

Thanks so much for coming along with me on this new trip down a rather paranormal lane. I hope you are as excited as me to see what happens next in Breena's over forty journey! There will be more action, serious amounts of Advil, and some more overheated hormones.

Check out the second book in "The Forty Proof Series"
Fairy Crossed Bounty

Need more than that to tide you over? You can check out more of the amazing authors in paranormal women's fiction genre at:

www.paranormalwomensfiction.net

OR you can check out my big list of books at:
www.shannonmayer.com